Treasures of the Fourth Reich

Treasures of the Fourth Reich

by

Patrick Parker

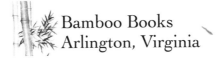
Bamboo Books
Arlington, Virginia

This book is a work of fiction. With the exception of well known historical events, the names used herein and the characters and incidents portrayed are fictitious and any resemblance to the names, character, or history of any person, incident, or artwork is coincidental and unintentional.

Copyright © 2005 Patrick M. Parker. All rights reserved. No part of this publication (including text, artwork, and map pages) may be reproduced or transmitted in any form or by any means, electronic or mechanical, without permission in writing from the publisher, except by a reviewer who wishes to quote brief passages for inclusion in a review.

Second Printing January, 2006

Cover design by Carolina Cid
Map by Kiry Yin
Typography & interior design by Books AtoZ (Seattle, Washington)

ISBN-13: 978-0-9722610-4-4
ISBN-10: 0-9722610-4-4

Published in English by:
Bamboo Books, Inc.
2111 Wilson Boulevard, Suite 700
Arlington, Virginia 22201
www.bamboobooks.com

Manufactured in the United States of America

Acknowledgments

I want to thank my wife and best friend, Carole, for her confidence and support. You have been my best critic and provided invaluable input. To my two daughters, Dionne and Brandi, thank you for your input and suggestions. You have been my best cheering section.

The Café Writers Group of Tulsa, Oklahoma is a special group that encouraged me to write and helped bring my story to life. Through the many writings, critiques, edits and rewrites, thank you. You are all so special to me. Each of you contributed a great deal and gave me the enthusiasm to write. Tawna Wheeler, Steve Chalmers, Terry Collins, Bob Meixner, Liz Whiting, Jason Mical, Elizabeth Griffin, Nancy Payne, John Affleck, Jamie Naifeh and Jean Kelley, I appreciate your candor, support and confidence.

Bob Sabasteanski, a big thank you for your critique, suggestions and attention to detail. And enduring gratitude to Elaine Serafina Cassara, a friend and supporter.

Anita Vreeland for your research and assistance, thank you. Your help with the medical and makeup scenes allowed me to get it right.

To Patricia Peters, a superb editor, who is terrific! You very quickly understood what the story was about and took it to the next level. Your attention to detail kept me straight. You are a wonderful person to work with.

Finally, I would like to thank David E. Meadows, author of the "Sixth Fleet" series, for his encouragement to continue.

Foreword

This story is based on true events that occurred during the end of World War II. As the Allied Forces closed in on Germany, they discovered tremendous amounts of treasures—sculptures, jewels, paintings, and other objects of art as well as gold and silver—looted by the Nazis in the territories they occupied. The Nazis had secretly stored these treasures to fund operations in the post-war period, the so-called Fourth Reich.

Realizing the treasures required expert care, in 1943 the U.S. Army created the Monuments, Fine Arts and Archives unit (MFA&A) to protect cultural treasures in the European war zone. The staff was hastily hired from art colleges and museums across America. While some commanders resented them, others such as Patton never went anywhere without their "Monument Men."

When it became evident that the Germans planned to proceed with subversive actions after hostilities ended, another more secretive unit was created in November 1944. Code named "Project Orion," this unit resided within the Counterintelligence Branch of the Office of Strategic Services (OSS)—the predecessor of the CIA. Officially known as the Art Looting Investigation Unit (ALIU), it had the mission "to collect and disseminate information bearing on the looting, confiscation and transfer by the enemy of art properties in Europe, and on individuals or organizations involved in such operations or transactions, as will be of direct aid to the United States agencies empowered to effect restitution of such properties and prosecution of war criminals."

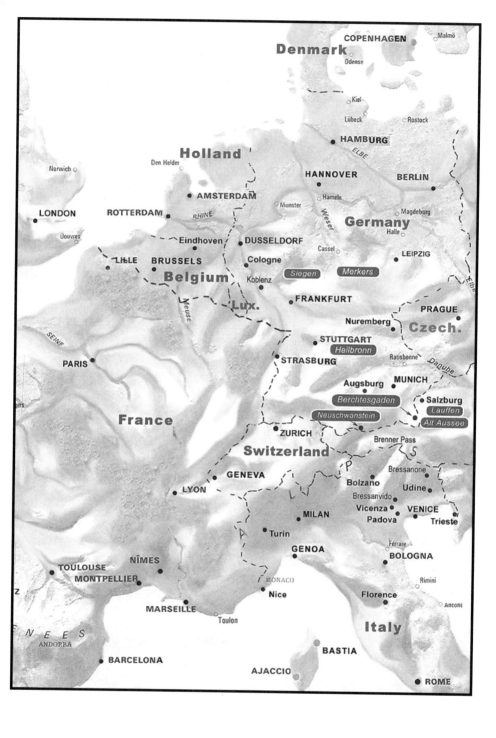

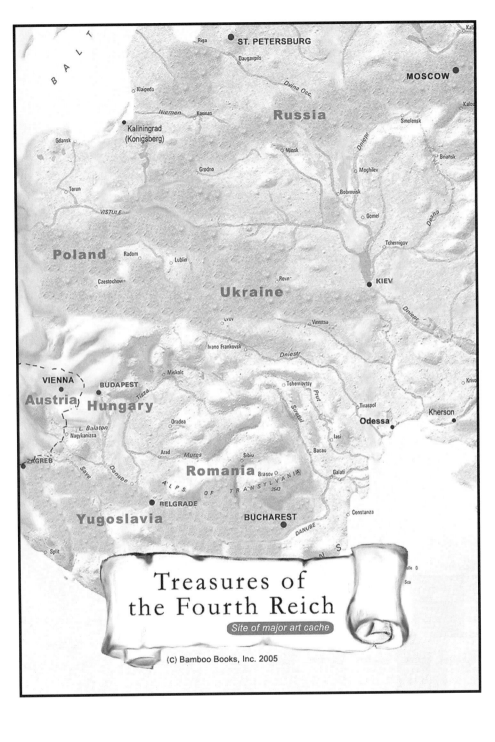

PART ONE

1

Alt Aussee, Austria
September 12, 1944

He is a bad one, the waitress thought as she placed the cup and saucer in front of him, the same as she had done many times over the past few months. The aroma of strong coffee wafted through the morning air. Unlike the other officers, this one was charming and always had time for a kind word—but she sensed evil.

From his vantage point the staunch and attractive SS major watched the posting of guards to the mine of Alt Aussee. He observed more than the formation of the troops. He studied Dr. Pochmuller, director of the mines, as he checked the train, made notes in his journal and wiped his brow. He surveyed the small train, laden with crates of gold, jewels, paintings, tapestries and other treasures, as it disappeared into the entrance of the salt mine. The train was en route to one of the main chambers that lay more than a mile inside the mountain.

He raised the cup to his lips and scrutinized the soldiers and workers that moved about, treating the cargo as if it were mere chunks of salt.

The magnificent pines swayed in the gentle breeze that found its way through Bavarian Alps. The air was fresh and clean in the high mountains southeast of Salzburg. It was a tranquil place isolated from the fighting and horrors of war. It was easy to see why this area in the Salzkammergut was a fashionable summer resort.

Mein Führer, you're mad! You've cost us the war and our country, the major thought as he lit a cigarette. *It is amazing how the soldiers disregard the magnitude of the treasure that arrives each day and is carried into the mountain by the train. Maybe it's this place—it's safe duty. Maybe they don't want to risk being sent to the front... or maybe they just don't care anymore. Anyway—that's good.*

Major Ulrich V. Fabian of the elite Grossdeutschland Regiment was special assistant to the SS Intelligence Chief, General Ernst Kaltenbrunner, and in charge of security. But his duty went beyond Alt Aussee. He also escorted treasures to the mine and established hideouts for high-ranking Nazis in South Tirol. Realizing the war would end soon, Fabian was already well into the execution of his plan for postwar retirement. He found himself in a unique situation. The once powerful Third Reich was crumbling into disorder and survival of the elite had become its focus. He knew he would probably end up in prison or shot for war crimes once the war was over. Fabian did not plan on being captured by the Allies, nor did he plan on being shot by the failing Third Reich as a traitor. Disappearing in Europe is what he intended to do. At the right time and under the right circumstances, Fabian would make his final move.

Breakfast finished, he set out on his morning rounds. His first stop was his usual visit to Dr. Pochmuller.

"This is insanity, it's a mad house," Pochmuller protested as he wiped his brow and scribbled in his journal. "There is too much for us to handle. We are overwhelmed, Major!"

"You're doing fine, Herr Doktor. Perhaps I can get a few

more soldiers to help you."

"Just tell your general this must slow down."

"I'll pass on your concerns, Herr Doktor," Fabian said as he mechanically returned the salute of a passing soldier. He had no intention of mentioning the Doctor's concerns at his ten o'clock meeting with General Kaltenbrunner.

As the two walked, Fabian positioned himself so he could eye Pochmuller's notes. He memorized more of the detailed diagram of the chambers within the mine on the left side of the journal. Pochmuller had outlined one chamber labeled *König Josef*, indicating the worksite where the treasures were currently being deposited. Each chamber in the vast network of the mine had been named after royalty and famous people from Germanic history. The current worksite honored Franz Josef, the Hapsburg monarch who ruled the Austro-Hungarian Empire for half a century. The 1914 assassination of his nephew, and heir to the throne, led Europe into World War I. Just as Franz Josef's chief ally had been Kaiser Wilhelm II in the so-called Second Reich, twenty years later the rump Austrian state entered into political union with Hitler's Germany at the beginning of the Third Reich.

"Major," Pochmuller said as he checked off an item in his journal, "a load of gold will be ready for delivery this afternoon. Remember, be discreet."

"I know, Herr Doktor. How much gold this time?"

"About four million reichsmarks."

Fabian nodded without speaking as he watched a truck enter the work area and stop beside the tracks to unload its treasures. Two soldiers got out of the truck and entered the small guard house as casually as if they were delivering a load of corn.

"I must be on my way, Herr Doktor."

Doctor Pochmuller raised his right arm to signal a goodbye, without looking up from his journal.

Major Fabian entered the building near the entrance to the mine that contained the offices of General Kaltenbrunner and Doctor Pochmuller. Fabian knew that Pochmuller usually returned from the mine between 11:00 and 11:15. He kept up with the general's schedule through the Second Secretary, Fräulein Griselda von Englehoven.

Griselda was a small Bavarian woman with plain features and short, wavy brown hair. For the past two months, she had dated Major Fabian and was now helplessly in love with him. Through her friendship with General Kaltenbrunner's mistress, Griselda kept well informed and often provided privileged information to the major.

Fabian arrived early for his ten o'clock appointment with the general. He approached Griselda's desk and, with a small flourish, laid a chocolate bar with hazelnuts in front of her.

"Danke schön, Major!" She removed her glasses and struggled to contain her feelings for him. "Would you like some?"

"Nein," he replied, taking a seat near her. "Is it all arranged?"

Her eyes instinctively searched the empty room to ensure no one was present, then she replied softly, "Ja, you leave for Königsberg in three weeks."

"Good. I'm to deliver more gold for the Fourth Reich this afternoon to the Nazi safe houses in the mountains. The director said it would be about four million reichsmarks. Watch for the paperwork."

"Ulrich, I'm worried. Shouldn't we leave as soon as possible? I've heard rumors we're losing in the east and south."

"Nein! It is not time. If we don't follow the plan, we will be shot! We must be patient."

"All right," she whispered, grasping his arm. "I'll take care of the paperwork, but be careful.... I love you."

"I must see the general now."

Major Fabian, with Griselda's help, had gained the complete trust and confidence of General Kaltenbrunner. The chaos brought on by the Allies' advance from Italy and France, along with the Russians' success in pushing the Germans out of Russia occupied most of the general's time. He also struggled with the Führer's orders. Consequently, Major Fabian operated with semi-autonomy.

After greeting Fabian with a cursory salute and summoning for coffee to be brought, the general retrieved from his desk a black leather folder embossed with a black on white swastika. As he stepped from behind his desk, he pulled the ribbon and released the knot. The corporal entered the room with a tray and the general returned to his large, leather chair.

"Put it on the table, Corporal. That will be all."

"Jawohl," the corporal replied. He set two cups on the walnut table that separated the two officers, then left the room, closing the door behind him.

"Major Fabian," the general began, "the Einsatzstab Reichsleiter Rosenberg wants the Amber Room of Tsarskoe Selo brought here to the salt mine for safe keeping. It will be on display at the Prussian Fine Arts Museum in Königsberg until the end of the month. You are to take a detail of men and bring it back here."

"The Amber Room, Herr General?"

"Ja, the Amber Room was a magnificent room in the Summer Palace of Peter the Great, consisting entirely of carved amber panels. After we captured the palace, the room was dismantled and sent to the museum. It's worth at least twenty million reichsmarks."

"I'll pick my best men, Herr General," Fabian replied earnestly, pleased at being entrusted with such a mission. He took a long sip of his coffee and returned it to the table.

"Of course, the shipment has been arranged in utmost secrecy. You will have full authority. Your orders will be signed by the Führer himself and will arrive by courier at the end of the week. You will depart in three weeks."

"I will start making preparations right away, Herr General."

"One more thing. The doktor doesn't know about it yet. I will tell him when he returns this morning. Do you have any questions?"

"Nein, Herr General."

"That will be all, Major."

The two stood. The major clicked the heels of his shiny black boots as he raised his arm to salute. The general returned the salute, then slid the papers back into the leather folder.

2

Königsberg, East Prussia
October 1944

The train pulled away from the Königsberg station promptly at 16:15 on October 7, 1944, laden with a shipment of gold bullion and every type of art imaginable—paintings, engravings, sculpture, tapestries, porcelain, crystal, and furniture. The crowning glory of the shipment, however, was the Amber Room, packed in twenty-seven massive crates.

Major Fabian sat in the cabin of his first-class sleeper car, sipping a fine Bordeaux as the train steadily wound its way to Salzburg. He retrieved a cigarette from the silver case in his shirt pocket and meditatively lit the cigarette, drawing the smoke deep into his lungs. He felt his muscles begin to relax as he slowly released the smoke. Fabian took another sip of wine, opened his leather-bound journal embossed with a gilt Reich Adler—the national eagle clutching a swastika—and began to write.

The scream of the train's whistle punctuated the hypnotic clattering of the train. Satisfied that he had recorded the day's events, Major Fabian returned his journal to his briefcase and placed it by the head of his berth. He tucked his Mauser HSc 7.65mm into the opening of the briefcase, leaving the wooden pistol grip exposed. Fabian thought back two years earlier to when he had been given the sleek Mauser by Reich Marshal Goering to replace his standard issue Walther P38 9mm automatic. He had been assigned to Einsatzgruppe D in the southern Ukraine, whose function was to eliminate "undesirables" such as gypsies, Jews and Jewish sympathizers.

In a rural village outside Kherson, Ukraine, Fabian found a little Jewish girl in a vacant house that his unit had cleared of all Jews the day before. He entered the house of the once affluent family to see what was left behind. The house was quiet and cold. As he cautiously proceeded into the living room, looking over the paintings on the wall and overturned furniture, he heard a noise from the kitchen.

There he discovered, crouched in a corner, a girl of six or eight years old with a dirty face. She had hidden from the soldiers of the Einsatzgruppe when they came to the house and took her parents away. He knew he should have shot her or taken her to the collection point, but the girl's eyes reminded him of his twin sister, who had died when she was about the same age as the frightened girl. The thought of his sister prevented him from either shooting the girl or taking her in.

Instead, he holstered his pistol. Then he retrieved all the money he had in his pockets and laid it on the table. He stepped back into the living room and lifted a painting from the wall before he left the house.

During a subsequent operation he was wounded, and, because he had not been medically cleared to return to combat duty, he was given a special assignment to Reich Marshal Hermann Goering. The temporary assignment was to escort trainloads of treasures back to Germany, much like the current shipment. Impressed with Fabian's performance of his duties, Goering had rewarded Fabian with the Mauser HSc, telling him it was more fitting for an SS officer than the larger issue 9mm. Moreover, it wouldn't hurt his wrist. Fabian reciprocated by giving Goering a painting he had removed from one of the houses in the Ukraine. Not long after he completed his temporary assignment escorting the treasure trains, Goering had had Fabian transferred to his current position at Alt Aussee.

As the train rattled along, Fabian removed his boots and trousers, then emptied the remaining contents of the wine bottle into his glass. He lit another cigarette and leaned back on the bed, mentally rehearsing the next day's sequence of events. When he finished the last of the wine, he extinguished the glowing ember, switched off the light, and returned to the comfort of his bed.

The treasure-laden train jerked to a stop in the Salzburg station where it was greeted by a convoy of military trucks. Major Fabian supervised the transfer of the precious cargo onto the vehicles for the remainder of the trip to Alt Aussee. As usual, he meticulously recorded the entire trip in his journal, detailing the route that led the convoy east through the countryside. Everything proceeded according to plan, except for one unusual stop at a mine near Hallstatt on the west bank of a small lake southwest of Bad Aussee, which Fabian dutifully recorded in his journal later that night. One million reichsmarks of gold bullion was unloaded at this mine in accordance with the written orders of General Kaltenbrunner, orders that Griselda had carefully forged on the general's official stationery just days before. When the gold was in place, Fabian's sergeant signed the orders verifying that they were carried out.

The next morning Major Fabian sat in his usual place for breakfast. The hustle and bustle at the mine was unaffected by the light mist that hung in the morning air. Fabian watched the posting of the guards, then studied Dr. Pochmuller as he walked briskly up and down the length of the small train, dutifully making notes in his journal. Fabian surveyed the procession burdened with another load of treasure as it slowly vanished into the entrance of the salt mine.

Gut! Fabian thought. *Everything is normal. The doktor seems his usual self, the soldiers too—nothing is out of the ordinary.* He finished his breakfast, and started out on his morning rounds with his customary visit to Dr. Pochmuller.

"Morgen, Herr Doktor," Fabian said as he approached the director.

"Morgen, Major. A late night for you, ja?

"Ja, it was quite late."

Fabian positioned himself where he could see the director's notes. He pretended to study the actions of three men working in front of him, but his eyes furtively scrutinized the exposed pages of the director's journal.

Gut! They're still working in the König Josef chamber, Fabian thought to himself.

"How are the soldiers doing that I sent you?"

"They're clumsy! They are costing me time," Pochmuller protested.

"Patience, Herr Doktor. You must teach them."

"Ja, you teach dogs…." Pochmuller grunted, then stopped without finishing.

"I must be on my way, Herr Doktor."

Doctor Pochmuller raised his right arm and briefly looked up from his journal without speaking.

It began to rain as Major Fabian entered Griselda's office. She stood in front of an open window watching the rain drop from the pines, not seeing him. The sedative rhythm of the raindrops on the roof filled the spacious room. Fabian quietly surveyed the room and observed that the general's door was closed and Griselda was alone.

"Morgen, Fräulein von Englehoven."

Startled, Griselda jerked around. "Morgen, Major." She removed her glasses, stepped in his direction, and kissed him, long and passionately. "I'm glad you're back. I missed you."

"I guess you did."

"It was late when you finished last night, ja?"

"Ja, it took longer than I anticipated to finish the shipment. It was already late when I got back to Hallstatt to move the gold and almost four this morning by the time I finished."

"You poor dear." Griselda squeezed his arm. "I'm going to fix you a nice meal tonight, rouladen and knödel."

"Gut, you know me well! Here are the forms for the shipment. Make the change we agreed upon—one million reichsmarks of gold bullion less than the original forms show. Bring the copies home with you tonight and we'll burn them."

"You missed me, ja?"

"Ja. Is the general in?"

"No, General Kaltenbrunner left three days ago to meet General Karl Wolff—he just relocated his headquarters to Verona. The Allies are pushing north of Florence."

"It must be getting pretty bad if the commander of all SS operations in Italy pulls his headquarters back to the north."

"I'm worried. The news from the Eastern Front is very bad, too. Let's go now! We have enough to live comfortably for the rest of our lives."

"Nein! The time is not right. We need more."

"How much do we have now?"

"By my calculations about three, maybe four million reichsmarks in gold, some jewels, and several paintings," he replied.

"That's enough! We need to get out of here."

"Not yet. I want a copy of all the locations of the Fourth Reich caches. Get it for me today. Locate all of the copies but don't remove them yet. We'll destroy them later."

"I...I don't know."

"You must do it!"

"It's very dangerous."

"You can do it, my dear." Fabian kissed her lightly on the lips, then smiled as he looked into her eyes. "I'll see you tonight."

Major Fabian poured more wine into Griselda's glass as she cleared the dinner table, then refilled his own. Griselda placed the dishes in the sink, then stepped to where Fabian sat, his back toward her. She slid her hands slowly down his chest and hugged him as he sat motionless. Slipping free the first three buttons on his shirt, she inserted her right hand, lightly stroked his chest from side to side, and inhaled his masculine scent. Her heart raced.

"Why are you so quiet?" Griselda whispered. "Did you miss me?"

Fabian grasped her arm. "Ja! I'm just a little tired. A good meal, some wine and peaceful surroundings.... I was just relaxing."

Griselda released him and turned toward the cabinet where she took a piece of paper from a large envelope hidden beneath several books. She hesitated, then turned and stepped to the table.

"Here is a copy of all the locations of the Nazi hideouts."

"Gut! You've done well, Griselda." He looked into her eyes and smiled as he took the paper.

Griselda's heart pounded at the sounds of his words followed by his wide smile. She turned and walked into the bedroom.

Unaware that she had left, Fabian memorized the locations. He laid the paper aside and lit a cigarette from the candle that still burned on the table. Lifting his glass again, he caught the light as it sparkled in the wine, and filled his mouth once more. He smiled as his eyes fell on Griselda as she walked from the bedroom in her robe.

Her bare legs parted the robe with each step, exposing her legs to mid-thigh. The robe, tied at the waist, exposed her breasts as she approached him. She leaned over and kissed him softly, tasting the wine on his lips. His lips parted and she received his exploring tongue. As his hand moved gently from her knee to her thigh, her heart pounded and she gasped for air.

Fabian stood and led her by the hand into the bedroom, stopping by the bed to kiss her gently. He slipped her robe free and brought his hand up, lightly touching her breast before guiding her onto the bed. As she watched, Fabian slowly unbuckled his holster and draped it over the bed post, then removed all of his clothes.

Griselda's body surged at the sight of his nude form—illuminated by the moonlight bursting from behind a cloud. Her body tensed with passion and she felt her nipples tighten as his hand found her inner thigh. His touch was teasing and searching; his mouth covered her with sensuous kisses. Her hands explored his firm muscles. She craved him. Her body quivered beneath his touch. He penetrated her, and her body responded with equal force to each of his moves. She felt his body stiffen as he arched his back and she felt his warmth. Her body convulsed and she exploded in ecstasy. The euphoria overpowered her. She hugged him and sank beneath him.

"I love you," she whispered.

Fabian raised his head, kissed her lips, then rolled onto his back.

I do love you, Griselda thought. *I love you so much.*

She turned onto her side and tenderly placed her arm on his chest. Without speaking, Fabian got out of the bed, put on a robe, and walked to the next room. He picked up his journal and sat at the table, taking a cigarette out of the silver case and lighting it. He looked at the paper with the locations of the Fourth Reich treasure caches, then began making notes in his journal.

Griselda pulled the sheet across her body as she lay watching him. She wanted to hear his declaration of love which had not come. She was hurt and fought against her feelings of being used. She tried to convince herself that the man she loved did indeed love her. *He is tired,* she thought. *And the war doesn't allow him to express his feelings.* She lay relaxed but felt somewhat cheated in her long awaited bliss.

3

Alt Aussee, Austria
April 8, 1945

Fabian marched into the office building. He hesitated as Griselda turned and placed a box stuffed with files onto a table next to her desk. Paper littered the floor and overflowed from three boxes set against the wall beneath the window. A private entered the room, picked up an overflowing wastebasket, and carried it out of the room. Fabian and Griselda made eye contact, but did not speak. She signaled to him that the general was in his office. Fabian acknowledged her signal with a nod, then knocked on the general's open door.

"Major Fabian, come in. Close the door," the general said as he remained seated at his desk.

"You wanted to see me, Herr General?" Fabian asked as he approached the desk.

"Ja, Fabian, the Russians are outside Vienna. There isn't much time left. I want you to gather all the trucks you can and load them with art from the mine and distribute it to the Fourth Reich's hideouts around the Tirol."

"Jawohl! Herr General, there are only a few trucks available on short notice. Many are out on detail."

"Get what trucks you can. This may be the last delivery. The Führer will not consider surrender. He has gone mad. In two days, on the tenth, special bombs will arrive and we are to make preparations to blow up the mine."

"Blow up the mine, Herr General?"

"Ja, blow it up. Bormann is sending his assistant, von Hummel, on the thirteenth to meet with Doktor Pochmuller and me to discuss disabling the mine."

This was just the kind of news Major Fabian had hoped for. He could at last set into motion the final stage of the plan he had worked on for months. Fabian knew exactly where the treasures he wanted were located in the mine. With the Allies closing in and the Russians outside of Vienna, he would have to act soon. If he made even the slightest miscalculation, he would become a prisoner of war and never again see the treasure he had amassed for his post-war survival. If he were found out, he would be shot for treason.

"Jawohl, Herr General! I'll do my best."

"Major, keep this information secret. Also, be careful. There are reports that the Austrian Resistance is active in the area."

"Jawohl!" The major clicked the heels of his black boots as he raised his arm to salute. *This is playing right into my hands,* the major thought, struggling to hide his excitement. *I think I'll just add the Amber Room to my collection, too. Why not? I hauled it here from Königsberg. Why should I allow the Russians to take it back?*

The general returned the salute and watched Fabian leave his office.

"Griselda, it is time for the final phase of the plan," Fabian whispered. "I'll start making the preparations."

"I'm frightened. Let's go now! We can easily disappear in all of this chaos. We have plenty to live on."

"Nein! Not yet. I'll tell you when. The final preparations

must be made. When the time is right we'll fake our deaths and disappear. Now is the most critical time."

"But it's getting dangerous. I'm afraid the Russians are going to take us prisoner. The rumors about the Russians are horrible. I'm frightened! I can't—."

"Shut up, Griselda!" Fabian said, grabbing her arm and gritting his teeth. "Calm down. You're going to get us shot, damn it. Do what I told you! We are not going to be taken by the Russians, or Americans either, for that matter."

Griselda's eyes shot to the private who entered the office to pick up more boxes. Fabian released her arm and backed away, trying to restore his impassive facade. The private glanced at the two and walked directly to the boxes.

"Auf wiedersehen, Fräulein von Englehoven," Fabian said, looking at Griselda but intending for the private to hear.

"Auf wiedersehen, Major Fabian," she replied.

By April 27 the phone lines to Berlin were no longer working and chaos reigned at the mine. The miners were angry that their sole source of livelihood was about to be destroyed in order to keep the treasures from falling into the hands of either the Americans or Russians. Fabian's preparations were complete. He waited for the right moment, which came late in the evening of May 1.

A gentle breeze blew into the room that night, carrying with it the fresh scent of the Bavarian forest. Griselda turned over and pulled the sheet across her exposed shoulder. The disorder at the mine and latest war news frightened her, but she felt safe next to Fabian as she snuggled closer to him. The soft light of the moon illuminated his muscular bare chest as he slept. The phone rang, startling her and waking Fabian. He lifted the receiver on the second ring.

"Ja. Major Fabian," he said as he sat up.

"Major Fabian, this is General Kaltenbrunner."

"Jawohl!" Fabian responded, becoming fully awake.

"The Führer is dead!"

"What did you say?"

"The Führer is dead. He killed himself yesterday and things are going to hell! Come to my office first thing in the morning. You are to escort and protect Hermann Stuppack, cultural assistant to Baldur von Schirach, the Nazi governor of Vienna. The Kunsthistorisches Museum in Vienna put their things in the Lauffen mine at Bad Ischl. They don't want their treasures found with Hitler's. They want them scattered around the Tirol."

"Jawohl, Herr General."

The phone went dead with his words and Fabian slowly returned the receiver to its cradle.

"Get dressed," Fabian commanded.

"What is it? What happened?"

"Hitler is dead. We must move quickly. There are some things we must do tonight. I am to meet the general tomorrow for one last job."

Griselda was relieved that they were finally about to leave, yet frightened of the uncertain future. The news meant that the war would surely end soon and she would escape with the man she loved. Her emotions prevented her from responding.

In a little over an hour Fabian led Griselda along the path he had marked, occasionally parting low-hanging branches. The bright moon provided enough light for their journey in the dark woods. They walked along in silence for several minutes, then suddenly he stopped.

"This is it," he said as he turned and released her hand.

"Where are we?"

"This is what we have talked about. Our treasure. It is time I showed it to you."

"I don't see anything," she said as she looked around the darkness.

Fabian removed several large tree limbs from a pile of small boulders, then moved the boulders aside to reveal an opening. He flicked on the flashlight to expose the entrance, then shined the light into the cave.

"Here it is. Watch your head," he said, motioning her to enter.

Fabian gave her the light as she passed in front of him. He hesitated and looked at the sky behind him. Flashes of light burst in the distance. *That will be the Americans,* he thought. *The 3rd Army commanded by General Patton.*

Griselda entered the cave and stopped. The flashlight illuminated a stack of gold bars, which reflected the light in all directions and made the dark cave shimmer with yellow light. After several seconds, she went deeper into the cave. Several boxes and paintings were stacked against the walls. She approached one of the boxes.

"Go ahead, open it," Fabian said from behind her as he lit a lantern.

Griselda was speechless; the sight of the treasures overwhelmed her. She smiled at Fabian, then knelt in front of the box. Gently, she lifted the lid and shined the light inside. A spectrum of colors burst out as the light hit the jewels. She reached in and scooped up the contents, then allowed them to trickle between her fingers. She did this over and over, like a child in a toy box.

"They're beautiful!" she exclaimed, beaming at him. "We're rich! I can't believe it. We can finally get away from here." She turned and plunged both hands into the box again. "I love you," she said.

Griselda was thrilled at what she now had—a handsome man she was in love with and a fortune to live on for the rest of her life. She imagined them walking together, hand in hand. She saw them in bed together, savoring feelings she had never felt before.

Major Fabian stood behind her, coldly observing her joy. He slowly grasped the smooth wooden grip of his Mauser automatic and eased it from under the flap of his holster. He raised his arm and aimed the small pistol. He hesitated, then squeezed the trigger. The gun twitched in his hand with a mild recoil. The flash of the exploding shell momentarily overpowered the beam of the flashlight. The sharp crack echoed throughout the cave, followed by the tinkling sound of the ejected empty cartridge case bouncing off the stone floor. Finally, silence.

As if in slow motion, a small opening appeared behind her right ear. A piece of her skull and a stream of blood parted her hair on the left side of her head between her ear and eye. The red liquid sprayed outward, splattering droplets on the wall beside her. Griselda's body slumped to the ground, a pool of blood forming as her heart struggled with its last spark of life.

The confines of the cave captured the thick, heavy odor of burnt gun powder and blood. The revolting stench and the sight of the body he had made love to just hours before repulsed him.

The last time Fabian was seen was at the Lauffen Mine on May 3, 1945. At gunpoint, he had ordered the trucks to be loaded with several crates of gold bullion, one hundred eighty-four paintings, and forty-nine tapestries. The tapestries were from the renowned collection of the Kunsthistorisches Museum. The paintings included all the great Breugels at the mine, as well as numerous Rembrandts, Velázquezes, Titians, and Dürers. He led the convoy onto the road under constant Allied shelling and disappeared.

On May 8, 1945, Lieutenant General Patton's 3rd Army reached Alt Aussee and soldiers of the 8th U.S. Infantry secured the mine. The entrance had been blasted shut.

At the same time the American forces were pushing deep into Germany from the south, the Russians were advancing on Berlin from the east. Word reached Supreme Headquarters, Allied Expeditionary Force (SHAEF) that the Russians were looting Germany in their march toward Berlin. U.S. Army Captain Robert Hamilton from the Art Looting Investigation Unit (ALIU) of the OSS's Counterintelligence Branch was sent to Berlin to investigate the reports. In Berlin, Captain Hamilton discovered the Soviets were indeed seizing the opportunity to reclaim treasures they felt were rightfully theirs. In addition, the Soviets were helping themselves to other Nazi treasures for their state museum. A steady stream of treasures—under the guise of "repatriated and compensatory restitution"—headed for the top-secret archives in Russia.

When the mine at Alt Aussee was inspected, it contained the greatest concentration of Nazi loot accumulated during the war. No record of Fabian's take or its next destination was found. A week later, a charred body was recovered nearby and identified as that of Major Ulrich Volker Fabian of the elite Grossdeutschland Regiment and special assistant to SS Intelligence Chief, General Ernst Kaltenbrunner.

PART TWO

4

Northeast Italy
May 11, 1993

The spring rain stopped and an early afternoon sun burst through the clouds over the beautiful city of Udine. Backing up against Alpine foothills and surrounded by vineyards, this city of 100,000 people sat on a wide plain northwest of Trieste.

Udine was graced with museums, galleries, and beautiful churches. Art scholars called it the City of Tiepolo, after the famous eighteenth-century painter who had been commissioned to paint frescoes around the city. At the center of this cultural gem was one of the most beautiful "Venetian" squares on the mainland, the Piazza della Libertà.

Overlooking the city was a castle dating back to 983 when Otto II was Emperor of the Holy Roman Empire, the so-called First Reich. The castle now served as headquarters for the Civic Museums and their outstanding art collection. In one of the castle's out-of-the-way offices, Maria Connor sat researching her second coffee-table book. She had previously published two art history books, establishing her reputation in the art world. The royalties from these books paid the bills, but her coffee-table book had been lucrative and she anticipated even higher sales for the next one.

Maria, a native Panamanian, had been a successful art dealer in Panama prior to the American invasion in December 1989. During the problems in Panama prior to Operation Just Cause, she actively led the Free Panamanian Resistance. She had met her husband, then Major Dixon Connor, during his top-secret mission to Panama, which paved the way for Operation Just Cause.

Shortly after Noriega's surrender in January 1990, Maria and Dix married and moved to Italy when Dix was promoted to lieutenant colonel and transferred to a NATO assignment in Vicenza. There, Maria established herself in the European art world. They had both fallen in love with northeastern Italy.

Breathtakingly attractive, Maria could easily have graced the cover of a fashion magazine. In her late thirties, she had a slender body and smooth tan skin. With her looks and position in the art world, one would never suspect that she once led the Panamanian underground. She never talked about this aspect of her past, only her art gallery in Panama.

Folders and files covered Maria's work table where, for the past several hours, she had pored over dozens of dusty records and books. She had decided to devote a major section of her new book to art destroyed or lost during World War II. In school, Maria had studied how the Nazis had robbed Europe of many of its treasures, and as an adult she had seen firsthand how General Noriega separated Panama from many of its treasures. Although there wasn't room to include all the missing art in the book, she wanted to showcase some of the more famous works. Great art deserved to be remembered, she felt, and she wanted to remind the world what magnificence had been lost.

"Maria, my dear, you are working too hard. You have been here all afternoon. You must take a rest," Signore Afferi said as he set a glass of chilled white wine in front of her.

Signore Afferi, a director at the museum, was a small, thin

man with a pot belly; always well-dressed and very much a gentleman. Maria had met him when writing her first art history book. The two hit it off immediately and had remained friends ever since. He was captivated by Maria's charm and knowledge of art. He liked the ladies and was a flirt, but quite harmless. Maria played on his charm, as well, and was as impressed by his stories and knowledge of art as he was of hers.

Signore Afferi was an art expert in his own right, having worked for the Udine Civic Museum before World War II. During the war, as a partisan behind German lines, he had assisted Rodolfo Siviero, the head of the espionage unit, in keeping track of art objects in northern Italy. Siviero later developed the world's first Ministry for Treasure Hunting. This body had been so effective that its techniques were adopted to combat modern art theft, and Signore Afferi had been consulted many times since the war in matters of art security and treasures lost during the war.

He also advised and mentored Maria on her earlier books. His reward was her company and artistic insights.

"Thank you, Signore Afferi," she replied, brushing her shoulder-length dark hair back from her face. "The time got away from me. It's time to stop. I must get back to Vicenza."

"Must you go home so soon? We could take a little stroll and look at the frescoes."

"I'm sorry but I can't today. We're going to dinner with friends."

"You tell your husband he is a lucky man to have you."

Maria smiled then finished her wine. She kissed Signore Afferi on the cheek and stroked his bald head. She stopped to call Dix before she left the museum.

"Dix, I'm catching the train back to Vicenza."

"OK, see you later," came the reply.

"Did you rewrite that section I told you about?"

"No, I got side-tracked. I'll have it done by the time you get here."

"Dix, you know I need to send it out tomorrow. Are you sure you can finish it by the time I get home?"

"Yes! Don't worry."

"And don't forget we're going to dinner tonight with Mariano and Julia."

"Oh, man! I did forget."

"Dix, one more thing."

"What is it?"

"There is a letter on the top of the desk. Would you reply to the lady for me? I was going to write it on the train but I forgot it. I need to get it in the mail."

"Okay, what do you want me to say?"

"The letter has an Antwerp address. The lady's name is Sonja Abramovych and she is searching for a painting that was stolen from her family during the war. Write the same letter you wrote for me before. I don't remember the man's name or his address but it basically said I would watch for it and let him know if I found out anything."

The letter described the painting as an oil on canvas of a castle. It was a general query letter asking for help or information about the painting. The woman added that it had sentimental value and it was taken from the family home after her parents were killed. The woman's letter impacted Maria but there was little she could do to help her.

Maria had received similar letters from people seeking lost art objects from World War II since her first book was published. In the woman's short letter, she stated that her parents were killed when she was seven years old. She wanted the painting as a remembrance of her father.

"I remember it. Anything else?" Dix replied unenthusiastically.

"Thank you. See you soon," Maria replied, slightly miffed.

"Ciao!" Dix replied, mentally noting to expect Maria in about three hours.

Seated at his desk in their house, the forty-one-year-old former lieutenant colonel hung up the phone. Dix Connor was a ruggedly handsome man with short light-brown hair. A barely noticeable one-inch scar crossed his left cheek—a souvenir from Vietnam.

After six months into his new career as a freelance journalist, only a few of his articles had been published and the mound of rejection letters continued to grow. Believing that his writing skills equaled Maria's, he was frustrated that his writing had not met with her same success. On the outside, he appeared happy for her but inside he was miserable and somewhat resentful. He was puzzled that his articles on foreign affairs and political intrigue went ignored, while the dull-as-dishwater stuff he researched and edited for her did quite well. Sitting back in his chair, he surveyed the awards, certificates, plaques and artifacts that adorned his office and told the story of his illustrious military career. He felt alone. The fast-paced life of camaraderie and adventure ended with his retirement six months ago. Believing he was failing was uncharacteristic of him, but he couldn't figure out how to change. He poured another glass of wine and pondered the current events around him.

The fall of the Berlin Wall signaled the collapse of communism in Eastern Europe and the break-up of the Soviet Union. Democracy and freedom, once only dreams, were fast becoming realities for those who had survived the oppression of the Soviet Union. These events were especially significant to Dix because he had spent much of his life fighting for democracy during the Cold War. Now, NATO was faced with new challenges, and Dix—like the rest of the world—was unsure what would follow. But one thing was certain: the former Soviet Union was in chaos.

For the first time in his life, the successful former Army officer was questioning his skills. He knew he had passion for his subject, and he had an impressive background. But did he have the writing skills necessary to achieve the journalistic laurels that he believed to be within his reach?

His thoughts drifted to the many friends he had throughout Europe and the United States, many of whom were civil servants or still in the Army.

One of those friends, Colonel Mariano Simione, accompanied by his wife, Julia, would be dining with Dix and Maria that evening. Mariano and Dix first met more than ten years ago in Vicenza when Dix was on a temporary assignment to the Southern European Task Force Headquarters (SETAF) and Mariano was in the Intelligence Section of SETAF. They had become good friends, and it was Mariano who had been responsible for getting Dix assigned to SETAF three and a half years ago.

The pea gravel crunched beneath the tires of the Volvo 960 as it eased into the parking lot in front of La Farina, Dix and Maria's favorite restaurant in Vicenza. At seven in the evening, the only other cars in the parking lot were a Fiat and a Saab.

"Even after living here for over three years, I can't get used to eating as late as the Italians," Dix said as he opened the car door.

"Me neither. Nine o'clock is too late," Maria agreed.

Dix, wearing a blue blazer, yellow shirt, and beige slacks, opened the door to the restaurant, allowing Maria to enter first. He caught her light and subtle fragrance as she entered. They were instantly greeted by a tall, handsome Italian man in his mid-twenties, the oldest of the owner's three sons.

"Buona sera, Signore Connor, Signora Connor!" he welcomed them with a warm grin. He had watched the beautiful woman in her long beige linen dress and delicate gold necklace walk with Dix to the entrance. "Your table isn't quite ready. May I get you a drink while you wait?"

"Buona sera!" Dix replied. "Yes, a drink would be nice. Maria?"

"Mineral water, please," Maria said, smiling as she stepped to the side.

"And I'll have a Campari," Dix said.

"Your table will be ready in just a few minutes. I'll be right back with your drinks," he said.

A few moments later, the young man returned. Just as he was handing drinks to the Connors, the door opened.

"Buona sera, Colonnello Simione, Signora Simione," the young man said, as the Chief Intelligence Officer for NATO's Land South Headquarters in Verona entered with his wife.

In unison, Dix and Maria turned around and exchanged cordial greetings and customary kisses on the cheek with their old friends.

Mariano was a medium-build Italian man with a large mustache and black hair a little too long for a soldier. He spoke almost perfect English and had been assigned to NATO his entire career except for one short assignment in the Abruzzi in southern Italy. He was well-educated and had attended several military schools in the United States. Smoking was his only vice, and he was never without his 9mm Beretta automatic. Always well dressed, tonight he wore a lightweight, tan double-breasted suit over a white shirt. His tie shimmered with tan and yellow diagonal stripes.

"Have you been waiting long?" Mariano asked.

"Only a few minutes," Dix replied.

Julia Simione, a trim and beautiful Italian woman, immediately engaged Maria in conversation. She was a professor of political science and international affairs at the local university. She smoked as much as Mariano, which Dix thought detracted from her beauty. Childless, she had had two miscarriages but still hoped for a full-term pregnancy. She was as gracious as she was beautiful.

Her hair, bleached golden blond, pooled on the shoulders of her teal silk pant suit that clung to her feminine form. Three gold necklaces gave way to a fourth, which supported a large pearl pendant between her partially exposed breasts. All this was topped off by her commanding fragrance.

"Colonnello, Signore Connor, your table is ready—on the patio off the main room," the young man said, looking at both men. "This way, please."

The grapevines had grown together, weaving a natural cover above the patio. The late spring sun was setting like a giant orange ball aglow in the sky and the air was warm and calm. Their table was square with a white linen table cloth, set with only a red salt-and-pepper cellar, and a few cut flowers and an ashtray. This was a perfect place for an evening dinner with good friends.

The owner's daughter, an attractive Italian girl of not more than eighteen who pleasantly filled out her tight dress, set the table.

"To drink? Red or white wine?"

"White and two bottles of mineral water, please," Dix replied.

A second son approached the table and greeted the two couples. He began to recite the menu for the evening, smiling as he gave them the last choice—their favorite on the menu.

He knew exactly what they would order.

Both couples smiled and agreed immediately when he said, "Bigoli with duck sauce, roasted guinea, vegetables and mixed salad." They always enjoyed this specialty of the Veneto region, a fat spaghetti with a hole running through the middle of the strand—more challenging to eat than regular spaghetti, but well worth the trouble once the art had been mastered.

With the orders placed, both couples fell into conversation, occasionally interrupted by friends and acquaintances who greeted them on the way to their seats. As usual, Dix and Mariano's talk soon turned to what was happening in NATO.

"With the newfound freedom in the former Soviet Union comes the basic need for survival," Mariano said. "No one is in control and no one knows what to do. As you know, this had already started before Gorbachev resigned."

"President Yeltsin has faced almost insurmountable problems ever since he took over," Dix added. "There are no jobs, their currency is virtually worthless. The huge East German military is disbanding and only a select few are being taken into the West German military."

"The Soviets are cutting back their military forces too, Dix. The changes are happening faster than the soldiers can be absorbed back into the Soviet Union. Most aren't even getting paid. There was a story on the news of Soviet troops rummaging around dumps for food. I hear the desertion rate is incredible. All this makes for a very dangerous situation."

"Oh! I almost forgot," Julia interrupted, as she pulled a folded piece of paper from her purse. Her gold bangle bracelets jingled on her left wrist. "Dix, this is for you. I thought you might want to go to this."

Dix took the paper and unfolded it. The paper was an invitation to attend a symposium—"The Emerging Democracies in Europe"—to be held in Budapest in two weeks.

"Sounds interesting. Thanks, Julia," Dix said. "We haven't been to Budapest in a long time, Maria. Shall we go?"

Dix thought the symposium would provide material for a new article—this might give him the break he desperately needed. He also knew that he would probably bump into several old friends.

"Will we have time to go to Gergo Zámbori's art gallery?" Maria paused, then looked at Julia. "Why don't you and Mariano go too? We could have a lot of fun in Budapest!"

Before either Dix or Julia could respond, the young man who had greeted them at the door told Mariano that he had a phone call.

"Please, excuse me," Mariano said as he stood.

The three others continued their meal and the topic of Budapest changed as abruptly as it had begun. Within five minutes Mariano returned to the table and sat down, his mood noticeably changed. He took a long drag on his cigarette.

"Business," he said somberly through the smoke he exhaled.

Not another word was spoken about his phone call or what the business was about.

They finished their meal with traditional after-dinner drinks—espresso for the ladies and caffè with Sambuca, a clear, licorice flavored liqueur, for the men. They made casual plans for their next get-together.

"It's late and I have to go to Germany tomorrow," Mariano said as they stood.

"What's going on there?" Dix asked, suspecting this was related to the earlier phone call.

"Yugoslavia is embroiled in civil war and NATO is watching in fear," Mariano uncharacteristically snapped. "Remember your history, Dix—it was in Sarajevo in 1914 that the secret Serbian society Black Hand assassinated Archduke

Ferdinand and sparked World War I. NATO is afraid the neighboring countries will get dragged into this conflict and start another war in Europe. Russia no longer has any influence over the Balkans and can't provide the stability to defuse the conflict. Hell, they're struggling for their own damn survival." Mariano paused, realizing he was lecturing his friend. He had made it clear he didn't want to talk about it. "I must attend a meeting on NATO security matters in Berlin," he continued, after regaining his composure. "I'll be back in a few days and will call you then."

Why is he so uptight? Dix thought. *That must have been some phone call!*

5

Dix and Maria lived in the small village of Bressanvido, twelve kilometers northeast of Vicenza. Their spacious villetta was a Mediterranean-style house of peach-colored stucco with a wraparound portico and clay tile roof. Red geraniums cascaded from the window boxes and terra cotta planters along the walkway.

Dix had been in the garden all morning and was just about ready to take a break from weeding when he heard Maria call out to him.

"Dix, I made some fresh iced tea! Want some?"

"Be right there," he replied. "I'll get the mail."

Dix laid the mail on the table as he walked through the house to wash his hands. When he returned, Maria was reading a small article in the paper.

"What's in the paper?" he asked as he sat at the table and wiped his brow.

"Edgar Kohne." Maria paused and looked into his eyes. "He was killed in a car wreck."

"What? Edgar? What happened?" Dix was stunned to hear the news of his long time friends.

"It only says the accident occurred in the outskirts of Berlin. Apparently it was late at night, the streets were wet and he lost control of his car. It crashed into a ditch filled with water." Dix took the paper from her and read the headlines:

AMERICAN CULTURAL LIAISON TO
GERMANY KILLED IN CRASH.

"I can't believe it! We went back a long time." Dix stared at the newspaper, then forced the words, "I'll find out about the funeral."

The phone rang and Maria answered it on the second ring. Dix looked up as Maria stood, then continued to read while she talked on the phone.

"That was Julia. She's coming to pick me up to go shopping. She said Mariano will be back from Berlin tonight. We're going to stop by the Marstons' house on the way home; Lydia said the Colonel bought a new painting and wants me to see it."

Maria's books on art history made her a favorite of the Allied officers stationed in the area and their wives. She was active in the community events. Occasionally, she traded art and advised her clients on new pieces. In addition to consulting on the authenticity and price, she was able to verify that the art work they were interested in was not stolen. In this particular case the Marstons purchased the painting without consulting Maria in advance.

"I'll tell Mariano about Edgar when he gets home. Ask Julia to have him call me."

"Do you want to go to the funeral or just send flowers?" Maria asked.

"I don't know yet; let me find out about it and we'll talk. I should know by the time you get back this afternoon. The symposium in Budapest is next week."

"We could make a long trip of it; take the train to Berlin for the funeral then go to Budapest. Need anything from town?"

"No, I don't think so," he said absently. "Have fun."
"I love you, Dix," Maria said, then kissed him.
"I love you, too."

It was a dreary, rainy day in Berlin. The funeral service for Edgar Kohne was held in the Kaiser Wilhelm Memorial Church, on the east end of Kurfürstendamm in the American sector. With its tower reduced to a bombed-out shell, the church preached a grim warning about the horrors of war. Like Dix, Edgar had spent his career fighting for peace and democracy. *This is an appropriate place for Edgar's funeral. I know Edgar would have wanted it held here*, Dix thought as he entered the church.

Approximately one hundred people attended, and Dix recognized a number of them, even though he had not seen them in several years. After the service Dix and Maria filed out of the church and made their way to Ida, Edgar's widow.

"Ida," Dix said, taking her hand and hugging her, "if there is anything I can do, please let me know."

"Thank you for coming, Dix." Ida wiped her eyes with the embroidered handkerchief she clutched in her right hand, then led Dix several steps away from her escort for privacy. "Dix," she whispered urgently, "I don't think it was an accident."

"Why do you say that, Ida? The newspaper said the Berlin police concluded it was just an accident."

"I *must* talk to you, Dix. You are coming to the house, aren't you?"

"Yes, we'll be there."

"Good. We'll talk then."

The Kohne residence was a two-story townhouse not far from the church. It was a typical modest house of the middle class. Colorful area rugs accented the ceramic tile floors of the foyer, living room, and kitchen. In the dining room was a worn brown carpet with a close-woven nap. A carved walnut grandfather clock stood like a sentry in the hallway outside the dining room. Paintings and sketches decorated the walls. A brick fireplace was centered on one wall of the living room and a three-section cupboard with beveled-glass doors lined the adjoining wall.

Guests congregated in the living room. When Dix left to refill his and Maria's glasses, Ida took Dix's arm and led him into the kitchen. When they were out of sight, Maria studied the furnishings as she mingled. *All tasteful but a little dated,* she thought as she made her way into the dining room. She glanced at the first painting, a colorful landscape by a local artist. Continuing her exploration, Maria was caught off guard by a painting that was totally out of character with the furnishings. *A Titian! A nice reproduction*, she thought. *Reproductions aren't usually this good. This is the nicest thing in the house.* The subject was a fleshy nude Venus relaxing with two cupids, which Maria assumed was a reproduction of a work by Tiziano Vecellio, better known as Titian, the famous sixteenth-century Venetian painter.

Just at that moment two people walked into the room. Maria quickly turned to the table and picked up a finger sandwich. Although the light was poor in the room, Maria had seen enough to be intrigued. Another person entered the room, followed by another. *I need a better look at that painting*, Maria thought, *but too many people right now.*

Maria made her way back to the living room but maintained a spot where she could observe the dining room, which she planned to revisit as soon as it emptied.

"I really do appreciate your coming, Dix," Ida said as soon as they were alone in the kitchen, beyond hearing range of the others. "As I said earlier, Edgar's death was no accident!"

"But what makes you think it wasn't?" Dix spoke softly and held her hand.

"Edgar had been uptight and edgy for the last month or so. Two days before his accident, he told me he thought he was being followed."

"He was followed many times. He was probably just working on something."

"No, I think it was more than that. He went to a funeral in Trieste back in the winter, and shortly after that he wanted to retire. The only thing he ever said about it was…'they've gone too far. It's too cold.' Then, two days before his accident, I knew something was wrong. I think he knew someone was after him."

"He never indicated who he meant? He never said anything else?"

"No, but he had something he wanted me to give you if anything happened to him. Wait here just a minute," she said, then went upstairs to the bedroom. She immediately returned and took his hand, placing seven gold coins into his upturned palm.

"Why would he want me to have these? What do they mean?" he asked as he studied the coins.

"I don't know, Dix. Edgar just wanted you to have them. He said it would provide the answers you're looking for. I don't know what he meant."

She gently closed his hand around the coins, nodded and wiped her eyes. Dix hugged her then kissed her cheek and deposited the coins in his pocket.

"Please see if you can find out anything," she sniffled. "Oh yes, one more thing. Edgar said you should be careful who you trust."

"Okay, Ida, I'll see what I can find out." Although he was puzzled by the coins and Edgar's message, Dix thought Edgar's death was merely unfortunate, and not the result of some sinister plot. He assumed Ida would think so too as soon as she recovered from the shock of Edgar's death.

"Thank you again for coming, Dix, Maria," Ida said, hugging them as they departed. "You'll call as soon as you've found out anything?"

"I will," Dix replied as he held up his hand to signal goodbye.

"What was that all about, Dix?" Maria spoke softly as she took his arm on their walk toward the car.

"She doesn't believe it was a simple car accident," he replied in a low voice. "I'll tell you later."

Once in the car, Dix told her what Ida had said. He quickly added that he thought Ida was merely upset, that it was just an accident.

"How much money did Edgar make?" Maria asked, surprising Dix.

"I don't know. He was a civil servant, GS-15, I think. He didn't make all that much but they were comfortable. Why do you ask?"

"He couldn't afford a painting by Titian, could he?" She was still trying to make sense out of the painting she had seen.

"A Titian? You mean a copy?"

"No, an original."

"No, I don't think so. Not by a long shot."

"You didn't go into the dining room, did you?"

"No, why?"

"There was a Titian hanging on the wall. I got a good look. It was an original!"

"Maria, you *must* be mistaken."

"Dix! Any freshman art student would recognize a Titian by his bold, sweeping brush strokes and vivid use of color that is soft and glowing—they look alive. If it wasn't an original, it was the best damn copy I've ever seen."

"It must have been an inheritance because I know he didn't make that kind of money."

"I guess it could have been," she admitted, "but you'd have expected it to be better protected. I didn't see any sign of a security system for the house, nothing on the windows or sensors on the painting. I looked. Nothing. Something doesn't make sense—the way it was hanging so casually in the house.

"They probably thought it was just an old painting and didn't know what they had."

"Possibly." Maria sat quietly as she pondered the painting.

Dix's thoughts returned to his strange conversation with Ida. In spite of what she'd said, he was convinced that Edgar's death was an accident, and he had no intention of looking further into the matter.

6

After leaving Ida Kohne's house, Dix and Maria took the train as planned to Budapest for the symposium he wanted to attend. Their route took them back to Frankfurt, then to Salzburg and on to Budapest in order to avoid the turmoil in Yugoslavia. "I wish Julia and Mariano could have come along," Maria said. "Too bad Mariano has to attend that meeting in Udine tomorrow on the Yugoslavian refugee problem."

"This is becoming a common occurrence for the Italians," Dix said. "They always seem to have urgent meetings on what appear to be simple problems. All the show and production!"

Yugoslavia was hardly a simple problem though. The country has fallen apart along ethnic lines and the resulting civil war was escalating.

"It's terrible there," Maria said. "The people are frightened. They are just trying to escape the fighting."

"And Italy is the logical place for them to go," Dix replied. "I can understand their tasking Mariano all the time—the Italians have little experience with this kind of crisis. But they can see it's inevitable and they're making preparations to handle the refugees. Italy is a strong member of NATO and is just trying to defuse the situation and keep it from spreading."

The evening before the symposium on "The Emerging Democracies in Europe," a reception was held in the grand ballroom of the Hotel InterContinental. The magnificent five-star hotel was located on the east bank of the Danube between the Elizabeth and Chain bridges, overlooking a splendid stretch of the river. It was especially enchanting after dark when the lights on the bridges sparkled. It also offered the perfect vantage point for a breathtaking view of Castle Hill on the opposite side of the Danube.

Above the din in the ballroom, a woman's voice called out, "Dix! Dix Connor!" The voice belonged to Francesca Martin, an American-educated Italian who had married an American Army colonel. After he retired, Francesca continued her career as a political affairs journalist and was an accomplished writer on European politics. In her late forties, she was by no means past her prime and radiated energy.

"Dix! Dix Connor!" Francesca waved and shouted again, her black hair shining.

"Francesca! Good to see you. You look terrific!"

"It's good to see you too," she said as they embraced and exchanged the traditional kisses to both cheeks. "I'm so glad you could make it."

"Francesca, this is my wife, Maria."

"We finally meet," she said as she shook her hand. "You are a lucky girl to get him."

"Thank you, I know," Maria replied as she threw a look at Dix.

"I'm the lucky one," Dix said.

"Dix, this is going to be a great symposium. I think everyone is here. You'll meet a lot of people."

"Good, I hope so."

"Have you been to Budapest before, Maria?" she asked.

"Dix and I were here once before, about a year or so ago."

"How long are you going to stay?" Francesca asked.

"We'll be here for a couple of days after the symposium."

"Great! You'll have a wonderful time. Did you take the Danube cruise when you were here before?"

"No. How is it?"

"It's fabulous! Dix must take you before you leave," Francesca said. "The evening one is the best—very romantic." Then turning to Dix, she said, "Dix, take Maria on the cruise."

"Okay, okay, I know when I'm outnumbered." Dix grinned and winked at Maria.

"All the G-7 representatives are here, the NATO guys, a UN representative is here, representatives from the former eastern bloc countries and I don't know who else," Francesca said as she scanned the crowd.

Francesca continued leading the conversation for several more minutes which turned to European politics, then steered Dix and Maria around to other groups and introduced them to as many people as she could. Waiters circulated, offering champagne and a variety of hot and cold hors d'oeuvres ranging from stuffed mushrooms to canapés with red and black caviar to various meat and seafood. A steady stream of fresh trays kept flowing into the ballroom, replacing those that had been emptied. Francesca, with Dix and Maria in tow, continued her tempo of greetings, introductions and small talk at the same pace as the waiters. Francesca seemed to know everyone. When a lull appeared in the gripping and grinning, Dix volunteered, "Ladies, would you like some more champagne?"

"Sure, thanks," they replied in unison.

Dix looked around for a waiter and spotted one nearby with a tray of champagne glasses. He started toward him and had taken only three steps when he noticed a man with blond hair out of the corner of his eye. He slowed to a stop and nonchalantly observed the man.

"What is it?" Maria said, stepping to his side.

"Oh, it's nothing. That blond-haired guy caught my eye." Dix nodded toward the man.

"What about him?" Maria asked as she briefly shifted her attention to the man.

"There's something about him. He doesn't seem to fit."

"Dix, you're imagining things."

"I guess," Dix agreed.

The waiter he had been approaching now came toward Dix, and he reached for a glass of champagne. Handing it to Maria, he then picked up two more, one for himself and one for Francesca, then he turned and walked the short distance to where Francesca was waiting.

"Here you go, Francesca," he said as he handed the drink to her.

"Thank you," she said.

After taking a sip, Francesca picked up her routine of introductions and small talk as they meandered through the crowd. The room had filled to capacity and the piano was drowned out by the hubbub of conversations. As Dix turned, he saw the blond man again and casually studied him.

He had close-cropped blond hair, was in his mid-thirties and physically fit. His stance was guarded, more out of conditioning than by chance. He was not drinking or eating. Dix watched him take a stick of gum from his pocket. The man gently slid off the yellow wrapper, unfolded the foil, and placed the gum into his mouth. He then refolded the foil as though it were around a stick of gum and inserted it back into the yellow wrapper. Finally, he folded the empty wrapper in half and placed it into his pocket.

"Francesca, who's that blond guy over there?" Dix nodded his head slightly to the left.

"The one with the gum? I don't know. I've never seen

him before," she replied. "The man he's talking to is the American desk officer for the G-7. Why do you ask?"

"No reason. He caught my attention and that little thing he did with the gum wrapper was unusual."

"There are a lot of unusual people here, Dix. But chewing gum is definitely out of place."

The social continued for another hour, the hors d'oeuvres dwindled and the champagne slowed. The noise of the crowd subsided as the guests departed.

"See you two tomorrow," Francesca said.

"Good night."

The next morning the symposium on Emerging Democracies was held on the second floor of the hotel. Dix and Francesca arrived thirty minutes early. As others arrived and congregated by the tables filled with pastries and refreshments near the staircase, Francesca began introducing Dix. The two mingled and talked, and everyone shared their expectations for the symposium.

As Dix was hoping, the keynote speaker presented an in-depth account of the civil war in Yugoslavia. Other experts debated the future of each of the Balkan states and the peril they all faced. One of the most engaging speakers was a NATO representative who offered NATO's perspective on the civil war and the growing threats to the neighboring Balkan states. The last half hour was devoted to questions and answers. The symposium gave Dix what he had anticipated: the makings of a compelling article.

Maria was more interested in shopping and visiting Gergo Zámbori's art gallery than in attending the symposium. His gallery was in the fashionable shopping district on Váci utca. She spent the hour before his shop opened window shopping.

When it was time for the art gallery to open, she walked with determination the last two blocks to his shop.

She was almost half a block from the entrance when she saw a man enter the gallery carrying a large leather case, which she guessed contained a painting. *That's odd,* she thought. *It's the same blond man that Dix pointed out to me at the reception last night. I guess art lovers come in all types.* Maria was usually good at picking out people interested in art and was even better at targeting those ripe for a sale. For whatever reason, she would not have guessed that this particular man was interested in art, especially the finer pieces in Gergo Zámbori's gallery.

Curious about who he was and why he was there, she stopped at the front window and pretended to look at the painting on display. Her sunglasses reduced the glare, allowing her to see the two men inside. Although she couldn't hear their conversation, it appeared to be a normal business discussion. After a few minutes the man nodded, then walked out the door without his leather case.

Maria entered the gallery after he passed by and was greeted by Gergo. "Maria, a pleasant surprise to see you again!"

Gergo Zámbori, in his early forties, had unruly gray-streaked hair and a dingy mustache that drew attention to his crooked and stained teeth.

"A pleasure to see you too. You are doing well I see," Maria said as she motioned at the number of paintings on the wall and stacked along the floor.

"Business is picking up. There seems to be a lot coming on the market now. What can I interest you in today?"

Maria soon lost track of time and spent the entire morning in the gallery studying the paintings and various works in gold and porcelain. She selected two gold chalices and a porcelain vase to purchase. Gergo took great care in handling the items and set each on the counter.

"I have something else to show you," he said, holding up his index finger, then disappearing into a back room of his gallery.

When he returned he was chattering as usual, making a production about the painting he was carrying. Maria was not really paying attention until he said, "It came from a recently discovered cache of the Third Reich."

Gergo held up an oil on canvas of Mercury and Argus. It was a stunning piece by Gerbrand van den Eeckhout showing Mercury putting Argus to sleep with music. The two discussed the painting and he told her how lucky he was to get it, that it would go fast. His price was right. The temptation for Maria to buy it was powerful, but eventually she decided to pass. She paid Gergo for the chalices and vase. As he wrapped the items, he told her about two art shows in the city over the next two days. He assured her that all the exhibitors were reputable and encouraged her to visit them if she could.

When he finished putting her purchases in a shopping bag, he smiled and shook her hand. Maria thanked him and told him she would think about the painting he had showed her. She spent the remainder of the afternoon perusing other shops on Váci utca.

That evening Dix and Maria took the Danube river cruise Francesca had raved about. It left at dusk and featured a three-course dinner. During the meal a gypsy band played while folk dancers performed traditional Hungarian dances. The dining room's large glass windows allowed diners to enjoy the sights the guide pointed out. In addition, large monitors around the dining room projected a magnificent 360-degree view of the river boat's surroundings. Several passengers opted to go on deck, but most, like Dix and Maria, remained enchanted at their tables.

Maria found the cruise to be just as good as Francesca said

it would be, but Gergo's disclosure that afternoon about the painting he had shown her plagued her thoughts throughout the evening.

7

The morning sky was clear and a light Adriatic breeze carried the scent of blooming flowers across the village of Bressanvido. Church bells punctuated the tranquility of the new Italian day. Dix and Maria sat at their patio table drinking coffee, nibbling on blood oranges and cherries, and enjoying the fresh air and early morning sun. They had returned from Budapest late the night before. Maria, barefoot and clad only in her robe, had slept in and wasn't feeling her usually bubbly self.

"Are you tired this morning?" Dix asked as he looked up.

"A little. It was just a long trip back from Budapest. The cool shower felt nice."

"Are you ready for breakfast?" Dix leaned over to kiss her cheek.

"In a minute."

Dix studied her for a while. He knew something was on her mind. They had stayed in Budapest two days after the symposium so Maria could visit the two art shows and talk to an art dealer she had met the year before.

"Dix, the painting I told you about, the one that Gergo Zámbori recently acquired—I haven't been able to get it out of my mind. He said there seems to be a lot of art coming on the market now, most of it from the former eastern block countries and Yugoslavia. It was a beautiful piece."

"What's bugging you about it? Because he said it came from a recently discovered cache of the Third Reich?"

The numerous stories and legends of the Third Reich's pillaging of art the world over, especially in Europe, fascinated Maria. Ever since coming to Italy, she had pored over historical records about the confiscation, concealment, and perilous transportation of treasures through the war zones. Newspapers and magazines worldwide often reported on searches for an unknown number of missing works of fine art, gold, silver, jewelry, porcelain, bronzes, ceramics, coins, books, and tapestries. There had even been reports of caches discovered through the years, some real and some false. She disbelieved most of these—except on occasions when a photo or eyewitness account proved that a lost piece of art had actually surfaced.

"Gergo said the man he had gotten it from was now dead, and he was kind of vague about it. He was just a little too mysterious. Maybe it did come from a Nazi cache."

"I doubt it. I think he was just trying to get you all excited about it to get a higher price, especially since you bought those two chalices and vase. He would've come down more. Besides, he even told you that a lot of fakes are popping up, not to mention phony maps to caches."

"I don't know. There was something about it, and the way he acted. And yes, I *do* know the Hungarians are becoming entrepreneurs."

"If it had come from one of the Nazi caches, it would have been in the papers and on the news," Dix said. "Have you heard anything about a recent discovery?"

"No, but still, he was careful about it and he didn't have it displayed out front. It was locked up in the back."

"Well, don't get too excited about it. I still think he was just putting on a show," Dix said as he stepped to the cabinet for the jar of Nutella.

Maria didn't hear his remarks as she was deep in thought about the painting. She nibbled on another orange section, while he slathered his toast with the hazelnut spread.

"I'm going to get started on my article while the symposium is still fresh in my head." Dix stood and picked up his cup and napkin.

"Don't forget to get the mail from next door," Maria said.

"I'll go now if you'll fix us some more coffee," Dix whispered as he bent over to kiss her cheek.

"Okay," she said softly, putting her arms around his neck. "Oh—you may as well go by the electrician's house and tell him we're having trouble with the gate again."

Without looking back, Dix held up his hand to indicate that he understood. Notifying the electrician was the easy part—he lived only four houses down—but getting him to fix it was a different matter. The security gate was a heavy tubular steel device that slid back and forth across the driveway. It had failed to open on several occasions, including the night before. Each time the electrician came, he studied the problem, removed his cap and wiped his brow. It was always "a problem... very strange." The problem really was that the control switch needed to be replaced. But the electrician always insisted—waving his screwdriver—that it just needed a little adjustment. Dix and Maria laughed at what they saw as lovable *commedia dell'arte* performances the workers came. It seemed like they never really solved the problems, just postponed them. "Domani, domani" seemed to be the national motto.

After Dix left, Maria continued to puzzle over the painting in Gergo's art gallery. Her thoughts then drifted to the painting she had seen in Ida Kohne's house. Not wanting to suffer Dix's sarcasm or pressure about her suspicions, she decided she would not tell him—at least for the time being—that she was going to follow her hunch. She was in an important phase of her coffee-table book and needed the next three weeks to finish the work before she could do any research on the paintings. Hearing Dix, she realized she had lost track of the time and hadn't even started the coffee.

"Mailman!" Dix said as he sprang through the door. "Is the coffee ready?"

"You sure are chipper and full of energy. What happened? Did Signora Fiorenza kiss you?" she said teasing him about the neighbor.

"Klaus Müller sent me a note. He wants me to join him in Brussels in three weeks for a conference on NATO security matters. I should be able to get some good information for that other article I've been working on."

The conference at NATO Headquarters was by invitation only and not open to the general public. Noted scholars, representatives of the member countries and several bordering countries, as well as selected journalists were invited. Klaus, as a noted academic, had used his influence to get Dix an invitation.

"Who is Klaus Müller?" Maria asked.

"You remember. He's the East German who was traded in a spy swap a few years ago. I helped get him settled Germany and a teaching position with the University of Maryland-Europe. Now he's a professor for Boston University in their overseas program in Germany."

"Oh, yeah, I remember! He's the guy who had me dancing the polka until the wee hours of the morning that night in Longare."

"That's him. You have another letter from the woman in Belgium." Dix replied.

"Thank you." She took the letter and stood. "I'm going to

get dressed now. Then I'll make more coffee," she said as she headed toward the bedroom.

Maria's letter was the second one from Sonja Abramovych. In the letter, she thanked Maria for the kind reply to her letter, then went on again how important it was for her to locate her family's missing painting. Maria remembered her previous letter and how she was touched by it. The idea occurred to Maria that she would accompany Dix to Brussels and meet Sonja Abramovych to find out more about her painting. She thought the story behind the woman's painting might be useful information in her book.

Dix picked up the newspaper Maria had left on the table. He turned to the Nazionale section, anticipating an article about NATO or the civil war in Yugoslavia. Not finding anything, he picked up his legal pad on the counter and jotted down ideas about the articles he was working on. Hearing a car honk its horn in front of the house, he looked up to see Mariano and Julia getting out of their car.

"Good morning, Dix!" Mariano shouted, seeing Dix through the window.

Dix immediately laid the paper on the table, then turned and pressed the button on the wall to release the electrical lock on the personnel gate. He called out to Maria that company had arrived.

Julia, her gold necklaces and bracelets glinting in the morning sun, was as elegant as ever. She was dressed fashionably, in a becoming shade of fuchsia. Mariano, wearing a blue blazer with a red-silk ascot, was the perfect escort.

After exchanging greetings, Dix and Maria led Mariano and Julia into the kitchen. While preparing coffee, Maria placed a bowl of cherries on the table. Their conversation eventually turned to the meeting that Mariano had attended in Udine on the Yugoslavian refugee problem.

"The Italians have set up a refugee camp along the Tagliamento River in the Army training area," Mariano said. "I'm not sure how many refugees there will be, but they've planned for fifty thousand. I'm beginning to wonder about the undesirable people who are sure to arrive among the refugees. I'm afraid I'll lose some of my staff to intelligence sections assigned to assist in the refugee operation."

"Yeah, remember what happened with the Cuban refugees in the U.S.? Castro cleaned out his prisons and sent the prisoners to the states as 'refugees.' What a mess that was," Dix added.

The weekend prior to the conference in Brussels, Dix and Maria had planned to have dinner out with Mariano and Julia. They watched each other's houses whenever either couple went away and usually made final arrangements during a social outing. However this weekend was different, because on Friday, Dix learned that Mariano would not be back from his trip to Turkey until Sunday. So Dix and Maria took their house key to Julia.

Mariano and Julia lived in a spacious fourth-floor apartment on Via Curtatone in Vicenza. Julia's flair for decorating was evident in this stylish and modern home. Various Mediterranean plants decorated the rooms, absorbing the sun as it burst in through the large windows. Highly polished black-and-white marble floors reflected the beauty throughout. A number of paintings, lithographs, and sketches of Venice, Florence, and Vicenza, accented each room. They captured the beauty of the balconies, the canal in Venice, Ponte Vecchio in Florence, as well as castles and buildings. A delicately etched gold plate hung by the fireplace.

Julia invited Dix and Maria in and motioned them to sit

on the white couch as she filled three liqueur glasses with Amaretto. She served the drinks on a sterling silver tray, then took her seat in the white overstuffed chair opposite them.

"I am sorry about this weekend," Julia said. "Mariano's trip to Turkey was very sudden."

"That's okay," Dix said. "These things happen."

As Dix sipped the almond-flavored drink, he felt a chill when his eyes fell on a stack of gold coins on the fireplace mantel. *One, two, three…seven,* he thought. *That's curious. They have seven gold coins just like the ones Ida Kohne gave me. What does it mean? Are they somehow connected with Kohne's death?* He considered asking Julia about the coins but remembered Ida's warning.

"Mariano is traveling a lot now. Some of his trips are short notice," Julia sighed. "The poor man is getting tired and stressed. I wish he would slow down."

"Why is he traveling so much?" Dix asked, hoping she might unknowingly provide a clue about the coins.

"Who knows? All he ever says is 'business.' He gets angry if I persist. I should have called you as soon as we found out he was going to Turkey. I am sorry."

"That's fine, don't worry about it," Maria replied.

"No, I should have called," Julia said. "Things were so crazy. He could have brought you back a rug or maybe some gold to have made into jewelry."

"He buys gold in Turkey?" Maria asked.

"Yes, they have the best. You buy it in bullion and bring it back to Vicenza to one of the gold factories. The best gold jewelry in Italy is made here. We have over a hundred factories here. Surely you know that." Julia paused, then insisted with a stage whisper, "Dix, you must buy Maria some gold."

"Okay, next time." *I wonder if there will be any left,* Dix thought as he glanced at her gold necklaces and bracelets.

"How long will you be gone?" Julia asked.

"About a week," Maria replied. "We'll call as soon as we return. The geraniums on the porch get dry pretty quick. Would you give them some water?"

"Sure."

Their visit lasted about two hours, a quick visit for a country which has no such thing as a short visit. Their conversation was lively—Julia had made sure of that. As usual, it meandered in all directions. Before seeing them out, she took another opportunity to urge Dix to buy Maria some gold jewelry.

As Dix and Maria left the apartment building, Dix thought about the coins he had just seen on the mantel, wondering if there was any connection to Edgar Kohne's death. *Mariano had been in Berlin around that time, and he was taking frequent and unexpected trips out of town.* Suspicious of what Mariano was up to, Dix had hoped to slip questions to Julia during the course of the evening. Unfortunately, he didn't know whether he could trust her. Halfway to the front gate, a dark car turned at the intersection to the left. Its beams swept the darkened area and buildings across the street, partially illuminating the figure of a man standing in the shadow. Dix stopped. He stood rigid and gripped Maria's forearm while his eyes inspected the blackness. She froze immediately and remained silent, her eyes searching for what or who threatened their safety.

"What's the matter?" Maria whispered. "What did you see?"

Another car approached from the opposite direction. As its headlamps splashed light in all directions, the dark neighborhood gave up whatever it harbored. Dix concentrated his full attention on the area in front of them, but there was no one there.

"I saw a man standing over there in the shadows."

"Are you sure? I don't see anyone."

"He's not there now." Not wanting to alarm her he added, "It was probably just the light playing tricks."

"If a man was there, he probably lives around here and was out for a walk," Maria said as she scanned the darkness.

"You're right. Let's go," Dix opened the gate and inspected the neighborhood again. He knew he had seen something.

8

Dix and Maria, the only occupants of the train's first-class cabin, made themselves comfortable for the long trip to Brussels. To pass the time, they read and watched the countryside as the train sped along, whistling as it approached the crossings. Cities and villages turned to countryside then back again. Lush fields were full of the new season's crops and terraced vineyards burst with the promise of an abundance of grapes. Occasionally, a farmer could be seen tending his fields. Windows of homes were filled with flowers in bloom.

Dix unfolded the newspaper he had bought at the station kiosk and began to read.

"Hey, here's an article you'd be interested in," he said, turning the paper toward her.

"What is it?" she asked, peering over his arm.

"It says Italy's Art Theft Investigation team is extremely busy." Dix summarized. "A probe was commissioned in January after the arrest of the deputy commander of the team. The evidence led the authorities to believe that a ring was trafficking in counterfeit art and passing it off as art stolen by the Nazis. Most of the art is proving to be *fake*. There have also been reports of maps which supposedly show Nazi caches are also turning up—these are proving to be bogus, too." He paused and looked at Maria, then continued. "It says they're seeing a lot of art coming in from the former Yugoslavia. They're also investigating the theft of the 'sacred chin' of St. Anthony. 'The relic, containing the saint's jawbone and several teeth, was stolen from a basilica in Padua in October 1991.'"

"Hmm," she mumbled, then took the paper out of his hands to read the article. "I still think the painting of Mercury and Argus I saw in Budapest may have been one that disappeared during World War II. I've studied the records. I'm pretty certain of it."

"Sure," Dix said, backing off the subject. "I just don't want you to get all excited about it if it turns out to be fake."

"Okay, but I still think it's the real thing."

It was late afternoon when Dix and Maria registered at the five-star Hotel Le Plaza on Boulevard Adolphe Max, a short bus ride to NATO Headquarters where the conference would be held. Klaus Müller was not due until that evening. Once inside their room, they unpacked and relaxed from their trip. Dix turned on CNN, slipped off his shoes, and lay back on the bed.

"I'm going to take a shower and freshen up," Maria said as she removed her shoes. "Would you get us a Coke?"

"Okay, I want to shower, too," he replied. "Be right back."

Dix bought the drinks, filled the ice bucket, and was back in the room in less than five minutes. "Here you go," he said as he handed her the drink.

"Thanks." Maria took a long sip, then said, "Umm, I needed that."

She was standing in the bathroom in her natural form. Dix slowly examined her with his eyes and felt an overwhelming compulsion to feel her, to hold her close. *She's like a painting,* he thought. He loved the woman who stood before him with a love that was deep and pure. She was not only a part of his life, she was his life. He placed his arms around her soft, smooth skin and drew her close, pressing her breasts firmly against his chest and kissing her, passionately. "I love you," he said.

"I love you, too. Now, go sit down. Let's hurry and take our showers, and then we can walk to Grand Platz and check out some of the shops. There are some nice ones there and maybe you can buy me some lace. We can eat dinner at one of the restaurants around the square."

"All right," he agreed, although not that inspired.

Klaus Müller—a chemist by training and professor by necessity—met Dix and Maria for breakfast at the hotel before the conference. His brown, curly hair and distinguished grey temples made him look, at forty-nine much older than Dix.

"Klaus, over here," Dix said, holding up his hand. As Müller approached, Dix observed that his inexpensive suit looked ready for the cleaners, and his brown shoes were worn and scuffed.

"Maria!" Müller said, then kissed her cheek. "It is a pleasure to see you again, my dear. And, Dix, how are you my old friend?"

"Fine, fine. What about you?"

"Oh, as usual," he replied, but his slightly sunken eyes with bags underneath suggested a man exhausted and under strain.

"You look a little tired," Dix said.

"Only the trip, but I have been very busy. And your trip, it was good, ja?" He shifted in his chair, then filled his cup with coffee from the pitcher on the table.

"It was a little long, but okay," Maria said, noticing his hand tremble slightly as he held his cup.

"This will be a good conference, ja?" Müller said. "Things are happening fast in Europe now. We are watching history being made."

"Yes, it's very exciting," Dix replied. "What do you think will happen in Yugoslavia?"

"Very bad," he said looking around the room. "NATO must stop it. You will hear the Greeks and Italians today screaming."

"It is affecting them, too," Dix said. "They have the refugees to contend with."

"Ja. Good news," he said as he pulled a folded copy of the *Berliner Morgenpost* from his coat pocket, dropping wrappers, a pen and a match book to the floor. "Here in the paper is good, ja?" He flopped the paper onto the table, flipped it open and tapped an article he had circled.

Dix read the eye-catching title: GERMANY, RUSSIA MAY SWAP SPIES. The newspaper reported that Germany and Russia were ready to make an exchange of jailed spies and would include the United States in the talks. The Germans wanted to trade Russian agents who were in prison or known to be in the West for Western agents who were in Eastern prisons plus certain Stasi files. These files, currently in the possession of the former KGB, shed light on the closing days of World War II.

"It says the spy swap will be discussed when President Yeltsin meets with world leaders at the Group of Seven summit in Munich," Müller said. "About one hundred fifty East European agents have been uncovered in Germany, but not all have been arrested. Yeltsin is going to turn over the files in Munich as a good-faith gesture."

"That is good news," Dix replied as Müller nodded.

"The paper says the files of the secret police contain 'highly sensitive material' about former East German Communist leaders and their intelligence system," Müller continued. "The KGB obtained these files and an undetermined number of other Stasi files, previously thought destroyed, during the days of confusion when East Germany was crumbling. Good news, the files, ja?"

"What about the files on the former East German leaders?" Dix quizzed. "What's in them?"

Müller glanced around the room, then leaned toward Dix and whispered, "The files have a few people worried. They contain some old records of Nazi SS General Kaltenbrunner and information about what happened at the salt mines near Salzburg during the last days of the war. The information in the files was never mentioned in the Project Orion report of the U.S Army's Art Looting Investigation Unit."

"What kind of information?"

"Information that will save some lives—and cost some lives as well. The report was a 'white wash.' These files reveal some Nazi hideouts and caches never mentioned in any report. Let's talk later, not here," Müller whispered. He sat upright, took a folded paper from inside his coat pocket, opened it and slid it in front of Maria. "This is a copy of the conference agenda. You will find interesting the first item after the remarks, ja?"

"European Art: Past and Present," she read with surprise. "I don't understand. Why are they discussing it here?"

"Politics, my dear," he said with raised eyebrows. "They never miss a chance. This is give and take. After World War II much art was never recovered or repatriated and to this day remains a very serious issue." He paused and looked into her eyes, his brow furrowed and eyes solemn. "The West always accuses the East of harboring treasures and delaying the investigations, and repatriation or that the East ignores them. The damn French, Italians, Austrians and now Yugoslavians—they all accuse each other, especially when one wants something from another."

"It sounds like it might get emotional," Maria remarked.

"Ja, very. The concessions or accomplishments, depending on which side you are on, will affect the rest of the conference. Sometimes they get to bickering so much between themselves that nothing gets done. Sometimes the French get hard-headed and nothing gets done. Other times it might be the Italians, Germans or Spanish and so on. A friend of mine told me the issue of the Amber Room will likely come up."

"The Amber Room?" Maria's interest escalated, her dark eyes, wide and inquiring.

"Ja. The Germans say it is theirs and is of German origin. The Russians say it is theirs. It was put in the salt mine at Alt Aussee and some claim that the Austrians have it. None of them really know. It depends on who wants what and what is at stake."

"But the Amber Room," Maria said, intrigued by the elusive and mysterious work of art "I've read the records; everything indicates it was destroyed during the war."

Klaus leaned toward her and whispered, "That is what you were supposed to think. The records are wrong. It exists to this very day like many other treasures. Those files Yeltsin is going to turn over will answer a lot of questions. Many will be embarrassed. Others will go to jail."

"I think we better go," Dix interrupted as he looked at his watch. "The busses should be here to take us to NATO Headquarters."

Chartered buses carried the attendees to and from NATO Headquarters. With traffic heavy, the buses discharged the passengers across the street, just a short walk to the main entrance of the compound. Billowy clouds floated across the deep blue sky. The morning air was cool, making a light jacket advisable. Rush hour traffic was subsiding as Dix, Maria, and Klaus strolled along, greeting people along the way. They arrived with a crowd of commuters at an intersection, paying little attention except to check the crossing light and traffic.

"Müller!" a man in the front of the crowd called out.

"Excuse me, my dear," he said as he dropped Maria's arm and waved at the man. "I shall be right back." He walked away with a guarded stride.

Dix searched for the man who had called out to his friend. He noticed his friend's head moving as if he was searching for someone other than the man who had called out to him. Then Dix saw him talking to a nondescript man in the crowd. The two appeared to be business associates rather than friends. Dix continued to observe them as the light changed and everyone else began to move. Klaus took an envelope from the man, turned and walked back toward Dix and Maria. Dix looked beyond Klaus's shoulder for the man but he had disappeared into the crowd.

As Klaus approached, Dix and Maria stepped into the crosswalk together. Dix immediately sensed that something was wrong. He looked at Maria on his right, then he looked to his left. His eyes focused beyond Klaus and the crosswalk, and locked onto the chrome grille of a Mercedes barreling down upon them. The crowd began to scatter in all directions.

"Get out of the way!"

"Look out!"

"Watch out!"

The car continued to advance, the roar of its powerful engine growing louder and louder.

Commanding his muscles to respond, Dix pushed hard with his feet, drawing back with both arms as he clutched the arms of Maria and Klaus. Suddenly he felt weightless—falling backward, parallel to the pavement. He saw Maria and Klaus falling backwards, too. The edge of the Mercedes connected with the left heel of Klaus's shoe. It flew upward, and spiraled over the car. When it was all over, the trio lay in a heap on the sidewalk.

The crowd converged on them, lifting them to their feet and gathering Maria's purse and folders, which had spilled onto the pavement. Voices, all excited, talking, asking, "Are you all right? Are you hurt? Do we need the ambulance? Did anyone get the license number?"

"Maria!" Dix called out. "Are you okay?"

"I'm okay," she replied as she ran her hand through her hair and straightened her dress.

"Klaus, are you okay?" Dix asked, looking to his left.

"Ja, ja fine." He said, checking his pockets and dusting his clothes.

Someone handed Klaus his shoe; he nodded and slipped it on with a trembling hand.

"That was close," Dix said as he held on to Maria, his own legs wobbling.

"Too close," Maria replied. Her hands trembled.

"We must go!" Klaus said, still shaking from the experience.

"Shouldn't we call the police?" Maria asked.

"Nein! Nein!" Klaus ordered. "The conference. The polizei can do nothing. We will go now, ja?"

Dix sensed a difference in Klaus. It was more than the incident. He seemed afraid, as if trying to escape from something.

"Let's go," Dix said, taking Maria's arm.

"That was no accident," Maria whispered.

"I know. There's something he's not telling us."

Dix knew it would be hard to target someone in a crowd for an assault. He mentally replayed the sequence of events leading up to the Mercedes almost running them down. Then he remembered a man had called out to Klaus and had given him an envelope. *Perhaps he was identifying Klaus to the driver—but why would anyone want to run down Klaus? Or was the envelope the target?*

"They are trying to kill me," Klaus said in a cold, low voice. "There have been other 'accidents.'"

"Kill you?" Dix asked. "Why? Who were you talking to back at the intersection?"

"I know what is in the files Yeltsin is going to turn over in Munich, and they are trying to kill me for what I know. I thought the man I was talking to back there was a friend. But obviously, I can't trust who I thought I could. We will talk later, ja? Not now."

"Hey, come on, tell me what's happening."

"Not now, later!"

The three proceeded to the NATO building where the conference was being held. The incident dominated the chatter as everyone made their way to the security checkpoint. Escorted to the meeting room, the crowd filed into the reception area at the back of a large conference room. Theater-style seating faced a blue lectern with a raised white NATO logo and a long table set for nine panelists. The member countries' flags bracketed a gigantic projection screen. Within twenty minutes, the room had filled with people and a dull roar spilled into the hallway.

"Ladies and gentlemen, please take your seats!" the chairman finally called out. "Mesdames et messieurs, s'il vous plait. Prenez voz places!"

"Dix. Look!" Maria said as they approached their seats. "Isn't that Mariano?"

"Where? I didn't know he was coming, did you?"

"No, Julia never mentioned anything."

"We'll find him at the break."

The chairman began with the introductions, greeting and complimentary remarks. Everyone had packets containing information, copies of the slides, and various other conference materials. The sound of rustling paper erupted as he covered the agenda and the contents of the packets.

"Ladies and gentlemen," he continued, "we are facing new challenges. What is happening in Europe today is something we have never seen before. The world is focusing its attention on events in Europe and the reunification of Germany. The Soviet Union is falling apart. Many countries that made up the union are seizing the opportunity to split away from the dominant control of Moscow. NATO security is why we are here. We must resolve old issues and work together so that our alliance will remain strong.

Our security is affected by events beyond the rim of our umbrella. NATO has been the stabilizing force in the North Atlantic area since the signing of the North Atlantic Treaty in 1949. We must overcome our ideological differences and work for the common goal of achieving peace, freedom, democracy, individual liberty, and the rule of law. The world has become more dangerous today than ever before. It is up to NATO to provide leadership for all of Europe. Let us make this conference productive and not let emotions thwart our progress...."

"The same spiel he gave the last time, always the same," Klaus whispered to Dix.

"He's right though," Dix replied.

"You watch, when we come back from the break, everyone will get loud and emotional over our first topic—the art. There will be much finger pointing, conditions demanded, and we will see what will be agreed to, ja?"

Dix scouted for Mariano in the sea of people during the

break, finally spotting him.

"Simione!" Dix shouted. "Mariano Simione!"

Hearing his name, Mariano turned and smiled when he saw Dix, and the two walked toward each other.

"Where's Maria? The conference is getting off to a good start, isn't it?"

"It is. She is getting some refreshments. When did you get here?"

"Late last night. I'm a little tired this morning."

"We didn't know you were coming. Why didn't you say something?"

"I didn't think I was. There was a change at the last minute and I was able to come."

"Where are you staying?" Dix asked, just as the chairman called for everyone to take their seats.

"The Hotel Le Plaza. I'll talk to you at the next break," Mariano said as the current of people began to carry him across the room.

After the conference had adjourned for the day Klaus, Dix and Maria returned to the Hotel Le Plaza. Klaus and Maria went to their rooms and Dix stopped off at the bar. As he entered the bar-restaurant l'Esterel on the first floor of the hotel, Dix saw Mariano seated talking with a man in a dark suit. Mariano glanced up as Dix approached, said something to the man, then the man in the suit got up and left the bar.

"Hello, Dix. Are you enjoying the conference?"

"Yes, I'm glad I got to come." Dix wanted to ask Mariano about the man he had been talking to but opted to wait to see if Mariano would offer any information.

"Where is Maria? Want a drink?" Without waiting, he motioned for the waitress.

"She went up to the room."

"CC and Seven," Dix said to the waitress.

"That was a close call you had in the intersection this morning."

"Yes, it scared all of us." Dix was surprised that Mariano knew about the incident. "Klaus said it wasn't an accident, that someone was trying to kill him."

"It was just an accident. But I'll look into it."

Mariano then quickly changed the subject. Dix tried, unsuccessfully, to return to the topic of the incident or to find out from Mariano how he happened to show up at the conference. After a while, Mariano excused himself.

"I have a meeting to attend," he said.

"I'll see you tomorrow," Dix replied. As Dix turned to watch him leave, he saw Mariano rejoin the man he had been sitting with earlier. The two men walked out of the hotel.

Maria had arranged to meet Sonja Abramovych at the Hotel Le Plaza at two o'clock on the second day of the conference. The discussions on European art were finished and the remaining topics did not interest her.

The fifty-eight-year-old Sonja Abramovych was not how Maria pictured her. Instead, a petite woman with beautiful silver hair met with Maria. They sat in the bar-restaurant l'Esterel at one of the small tables. The woman told Maria how she had gone to bazaars, art shows, and museums, and contacted all the art dealers she could find in search of her family's art collection. Over the years she had recovered a few of the paintings and one diamond necklace.

"When I was about seven," the woman said, her blue eyes sparkling, "we were a well-to-do family that lived in a rural village outside Kherson, Ukraine. The Germans were taking all the Jews to the concentration camps. Everyone was terrified. The Nazis just marched in and took whatever they wanted."

As they talked, Maria saw many similarities between the woman's story and what Maria herself had seen in Panama during the last years of Noriega's reign. Torture, murder, rape and pillage. People lost their belongings as well as their lives.

"One day the Nazis came to our neighborhood and my mother hid me. I was terrified when they entered our house. I stayed in my hiding place for an hour or two. I was afraid they would come back and get me. The next day a Nazi officer came to our house and found me in the kitchen. He pointed his pistol at me and I thought he was going to shoot, but he didn't. Instead, he put his pistol in his holster and took all the money out of his pockets and laid it on the table. Then he walked into the living room and took a painting off the wall."

"You were lucky. Why didn't he shoot you?"

"I have no idea. Anyway, for the next several days he brought food to the house. Then he suddenly stopped coming. The painting he took is special to me. I used to sit on my father's lap and he would tell me stories about the painting."

The woman described the painting as an oil on canvas of a landscape with a castle. She didn't know the artist. Her description prompted Maria to think of the Marstons' recent purchase—the painting they bought without consulting her.

"By any chance do you have a photograph of the painting?" Maria asked.

"I thought you would ask." She opened a folder, took a picture out, and handed it to Maria. "That picture was made when I was six. It was taken the year before the Nazis came to our house.

It was a photo that showed a young girl sitting on a man's lap with a painting over his shoulder. The detail in the painting was good enough for Maria to identify a possible match. As she examined the photograph, she knew it was the same painting as the one at the Marstons'.

"You have registered with the looted cultural properties registries, haven't you?"

"Yes, every registry I can find. Germany, France, the United States, Poland and so on."

Maria took the woman's photograph and promised to watch out for the painting. She didn't want to tell her what she suspected. Maria first had to establish a trail in order to verify that the painting was actually this woman's.

She had a lot to do when she got home. For the time being, she would not tell Dix that she thought this woman's painting was hanging on the Marstons' wall.

9

On the evening of the third and final day of the conference, Klaus, Dix and Maria, secluded in the restaurant Cave du Roy at Grand Place 14, dined together. After their meals of duck breast with orange sauce and roast rack of lamb with thyme, they sipped coffee and reminisced.

"You both enjoyed the conference, ja?" Klaus asked. "I thought it was very good. Many things are happening in these dangerous times."

"And uncertain times, too," Dix said. "NATO has its hands full. Each one of the member countries is cutting its military. I'm afraid they'll get caught short-handed."

"You must write about it, Dix. You will keep the pressure on the politicians, ja?"

"Does anyone really know about the missing treasures they argued about?" Maria asked. "Wouldn't it be exciting if the Amber Room did turn up, or someone found Bellini's *Madonna and Child* or even a stash of Nazi gold bullion?"

"Indeed it would," Klaus said. "But do not count on it, my dear. It would open many old wounds that are best left as scars. Some things are best remembered and never recovered. A cloud of death hangs over those treasures."

"But they should be shared with the world," Maria said, emphasizing with her hands.

Klaus leaned forward and replied, "It is more than that. Many people have died because of these treasures. But the treasures have bonded us together with a common goal—their return. Still it is politics," he paused to take another sip of wine. "They will never be found or returned. Most of them probably no longer exist. Nevertheless, it is better this way. It all happened a long time ago and no one can change what happened. Everyone has accepted that the treasures will never be recovered."

"Even the Amber Room?" Maria pressured.

"Ja, even the Amber Room."

Maria stared into his eyes, puzzled. *He just contradicted what he said the day before yesterday. Then, he was so certain that the Amber room existed, but now he says that it—and many other treasures—will never be found. What made him changed his position all of a sudden?*

"Klaus, the other day you said someone was trying to kill you and that car tried to run us down. I want to know why." Dix said.

"Nein, nein! Forget about it. It is nothing. It was just a warning. Nein! Do not get mixed up in this."

"Damn it, we're your friends. Let us help you. We were almost run over, too. What is it?"

"Nein, nein. You go back to Italy. You have a beautiful wife; take care of her. I'm getting old and I am alone now."

"Klaus, let us help you. Who wants to kill you? And why? What are you involved in?"

"Too many questions. I must think."

"Why don't you come back to Italy with us?" Maria asked.

"Yes, come home with us, Klaus. You'll be safe there and maybe we can help," Dix insisted, refusing any alternative. "We'll leave early tomorrow on the train."

"Ja, ja… okay. No more talk of it."

"It's time we got back to the hotel anyway. We've got to get up early."

"Ja, it is late. I need to make a phone call." Klaus helped Maria with her coat, then took her arm as they departed.

At the breakfast, in the hotel dining room, the next morning, Dix and Maria were becoming impatient as they waited for Klaus, who was already thirty minutes late. "Klaus is moving slowly this morning," Maria said. "He'd better hurry up or he'll miss breakfast."

"I'm going to call Klaus's room to see what's keeping him," Dix said. "We need to get a move on. I'll be right back."

Using the phone at the desk, Dix counted twelve rings before he replaced the receiver. He looked at the clock, then at the elevator. *Surely he's on his way down now,* Dix thought. *He must have really overslept. He'll just have to get something to eat at the train station.* Dix picked up the paper and returned to the dining room.

"There's no answer in his room," Dix said, returning to the table. "I'm sure he'll be busting out of the elevator any minute."

"I'm going on up to the room," Maria said.

"As soon as Klaus gets down here, I'll be right up." Dix watched her walk out of the dining room and into the foyer. The early morning sunlight entering through the front windows caught her dark hair as if she were in a spotlight.

After ten minutes and still no sign of Klaus, Dix went up to Klaus's room on the third floor and knocked on the door. To his surprise, it opened. Dix entered cautiously.

Two steps inside he saw clothes strewn across the floor,

drawers opened, and a chair overturned. Klaus was still in bed.

"Klaus! Klaus, get up. What's happened here? We've got to go!"

No response. Dix tensed and his heart raced as he approached the bed. Klaus was not moving. He felt for a pulse, but there was none. Klaus was dead—murdered, Dix suspected—and his room appeared to have been searched. Careful not to touch anything or disturb any potential evidence, he looked for a wound or method of attack. *Nothing,* he thought. *No blood—professional.* He studied the room again, but there was no clue as to how or why Klaus had been killed. Dix turned and placed the DO NOT DISTURB sign on the door handle as he left. Then he stopped by to tell Maria about Klaus and to call Mariano before going to inform the hotel manager. The last call he dreaded was the one to the police. Dix and Maria apparently wouldn't be leaving Brussels as early as they'd planned.

On the morning after their return from Brussels, Dix and Maria sat at the patio table trying to make sense of what had happened in Brussels. The bright morning sun and Adriatic breeze consoled their somber mood. A butterfly danced over the red geraniums. Maria was cradling her cappuccino and watched Dix flip through the paper, then read an article.

"What are you reading?"

"An article about two U.S. soldiers that are being held in connection with an art smuggling ring."

"Really, where?"

"They're stationed in Italy. The paper quotes a Colonel Pasquali of Italy's Art Theft Investigation team. It says their investigation is ongoing, that they are working with the Austrian, American, German, and French authorities. Must have been a pretty big ring."

"That goes along with that other article we read in the paper on our way to Brussels," Maria said. "I bet this case is the same or is at least related to that one. That article was about counterfeit art and this one is smuggling. Let me read it when you finish. I wonder if that's some of the art Gergo Zámbori said was coming on the market?"

"Who?" Dix was not paying much attention to Maria as he read the paper until she mentioned the Hungarian's name.

"Gergo Zámbori, the art dealer in Budapest. Remember?"

"Oh, yeah." Dix looked up at her. "You never know. Maybe these soldiers found the lost Nazi art cache he told you about. Then they got caught smuggling the stuff." Dix teased her, knowing she liked stories about the lost riches of the Third Reich.

"I'm going to ask Mariano about it. He'll know."

"I was just thinking about going over to his house. I want to talk to him about something. Do you want to go?"

"Sure." Maria sipped her mineral water. "What do you need to talk to him about?"

"At the police station in Brussels, he said he would find out all he could. I want to know if he found out anything about Klaus's death. I think he also might know something about Edgar Kohne's death."

"When do you want to go?"

"As soon as I get through with the paper."

"I'm going to go get ready." Maria stood then picked up the plastic watering can and poured water into the two rectangular pots of geraniums. When finished, she kissed his cheek and left him to his paper.

Julia Simione placed four small cups on a silver tray and

filled each half full with the strong black caffè that gurgled in the mocha pot. The aroma of the fresh-brewed drink filled the air as she carried in the tray to the others. Their friendly conversation wandered for about thirty minutes before Dix attempted more serious dialogue.

"Did you find out anything about Klaus's death?" Dix asked.

"Nothing. No clues so far. The room was clean."

"Any ideas?"

"None." Mariano offered no more than was asked.

"What about the car that almost ran us down?"

"The Brussels police ruled that it was an accident. I don't know anything else. Did you enjoy the conference?" Mariano sipped his caffè and avoided eye contact.

"We had a good time," Maria said. "Julia, we missed you. Brussels is very beautiful this time of the year."

"I just had too much to do at the university."

Frustrated with tangential talk, Dix stared at Mariano and asked directly, "Is there any connection between Klaus Müller's and Edgar Kohne's deaths?"

"Their deaths were accidents, Dix. I don't know of any connection. Why do you think there is one? I've told you all I know," Mariano insisted. "Anyway, my time is devoted to the Yugoslavian issue and the threats they are causing to NATO." He reached over to a gold box on the table, took out a cigarette, and lit it.

"Mariano," Maria asked, sensing tension in the conversation, "do you know anything about the two U.S. soldiers in the paper who were arrested for being involved in art smuggling?"

"They were stupid. My old friend Colonel Pasquali told me he thought those two soldiers were just small potatoes. He is hoping they will lead him to the key players, the 'big fish' as the American police would say."

"Do you know if the art was from a Nazi cache?" Maria asked, hoping he would say yes.

"Who told you that?" Mariano stared, talking through the smoke as he exhaled.

"No one. I just guessed after I saw it in the paper."

"Stories like that always circulate when someone is involved in dubious art dealings," Julia commented as she reached to get a cigarette. Her bracelets clinked on the table as she lifted the lid.

"An art dealer in Budapest told me about a recently discovered cache of treasures that was from the Third Reich. I just wondered if the two were connected."

"Pasquali told me there was a rumor going around like that. Let me know if you should hear about any questionable art transactions."

"Sure," Maria said, thinking about the painting in Ida Kohne's dining room and the Marstons' painting. She wasn't ready to talk about either of these just now.

"Did Edgar Kohne have anything to do with it?" Dix asked, thinking about the gold coins.

"No! Stop worrying about this. I told you I'd let you know if I find out anything." Mariano's tone was cold and forbidding.

"Look, Mariano, I know you're holding something back," Dix pressed.

"Stay away from this. It's very dangerous." His dark eyes shot deep into Dix's.

Dix knew he had struck a chord, but Mariano had turned cold and wasn't going to budge. So he pulled back and allowed the conversation to change course and lighten up. When the couples finally parted, they seemed on friendly terms again. Still, Mariano's reticence bothered Dix and made him more suspicious than ever.

Later that afternoon at home, Dix put his curiosity aside for the time being, Dix turned on his laptop to write about the NATO meeting. Maria was absorbing the afternoon sun as she read the Italian magazine *Abitare*. Dix leaned back and admired her while his machine booted. When its familiar beep signaled that it was ready, he accessed the Internet first, and saw that he had mail. He opened the message and read it twice before it sunk in. It read, "Klaus Müller said I could trust you and to contact you if I need help. Beware, you could be in trouble. Someone is after me. I can trust you, but be careful who you trust. The others were murdered and I will probably be next. I must do some things. Can you help me? Ingel."

"What the hell?" Dix murmured to himself. "Is this for real?" A chill went through him. Dix studied the cryptic message for a moment, then typed a reply. "Ingel, can you tell me more? Yes, I will do what I can. Who was killed and by whom? Tell me where you are and what you want me to do. Dix."

All Dix could do now was wait. His mind raced. Some one he knew was in trouble and asked for his help, and Dix needed information. A cold shroud of uneasiness enveloped him. *Why would I be in trouble?* Dix wondered. *I'm retired for Christ's sake. I haven't been involved in anything in a long time. I haven't written anything that someone would want to kill me over. Hell, only a couple of things have been published. What is it? Maria....*

Dix stood and stepped into the hall to look at Maria. She was still on the patio, absorbed in her magazine. He approached the stairs that led to the basement and listened. It was dark and quiet. The upstairs was dead quiet. He walked through the house and peered out of the windows—everything was normal. The last check was from the kitchen window where he could get the best view of the neighborhood. Several kids played soccer in the vacant lot across the street and a neighbor picked tomatoes in her garden. Satisfied there was no danger, he returned to his computer. Still no reply.

Dix picked up the telephone receiver and dialed a number, then hung up the phone before it could ring. His instinct had been to call Mariano but then his thoughts went back to Ingel's warning. *Is it possible Mariano is involved in this somehow?* Dix wondered. *Can't be. Maybe someone in his office? I'll just wait to hear from Ingel.* His anxiety building, Dix couldn't sit still. He walked through the house again, returned to the kitchen window and satisfied himself that the neighborhood was as tranquil as ever. Walking outside, he observed the area then forced himself to settle down as he approached Maria. "Are you about ready to come in?"

"In a while. It's so nice out."

"Come here. I want to show you something," Dix insisted, trying not to alarm her.

"I'll be there, in a minute."

"Maria, please."

"All right! What is it?"

He turned and led her into the house to his computer. "Here, read this," he said as he pointed to the screen.

She read it, then looked at him. "Not funny, Dix!"

"I didn't write it. It's a message *to* me."

Maria read it again. "Who's Ingel?"

"He works at the U.S. Embassy in Bonn, Germany on the G-7 committee. I've met him a few times but don't know him all that well."

"What are you going to do?"

"I don't know yet. I just sent him an email. I'm waiting for his answer."

"Why would *you* be in trouble? And for what?"

"I don't know. I'm hoping Ingel can tell me. I want you to stay inside."

"Help me get the rest of my stuff in."

Every few hours Dix checked his computer for a response from Ingel, but there was none. Dix decided to call Mariano. He didn't tell Mariano much, but convinced him to come to his house.

Mariano arrived at approximately 8:45. His demeanor was more serious and businesslike than usual. Dix prepared two glasses of Sambuca, with three coffee beans in each glass, and handed one to his friend. The two sipped in unison, then set their drinks on the table.

"Do you remember Ingel?"

"Ingel? Yes, why do you ask?"

"I got a strange message from him today."

"What did he have to say?"

"He just said I could be in trouble and that someone was after him."

"What's that German gotten into? What else did he say?" His eyes remained fixed on Dix's eyes, his interest clearly piqued.

"Not much—just that I should be careful who I trusted. He asked for my help."

"He must go to the German polizei. There's nothing I can do."

Surprised at his response, Dix pushed. "But he asked for help."

Mariano remained cold and guarded. He picked up his drink and took a small amount of the liqueur along with a coffee bean into his mouth. He lowered the glass and studied it for several seconds. Then he chewed the bean and swallowed. "I'll look into it. But I'm warning you—stay clear."

"What gives? I'm *already* involved. Besides, Ingel said I may be in trouble and I don't know why or with whom."

"Maybe you should take Maria on a vacation for a while."

"No! Ingel needs help and I plan to help him. Damn it, Mariano, I've got to find out why I'm in trouble!"

"Shit! Okay, but you stay put and let me know as soon as Ingel contacts you again."

"Thanks, Mariano." He paused. "I need to borrow a gun." Dix looked into his eyes and didn't blink or move.

"I'll see what I can do. I must go now."

"Thanks, my friend."

A message from Ingel greeted Dix when he checked the computer at 7:10 the next morning. Dix anxiously read the note. "I am in Budapest. Can you come? I will tell you what I know when you get here. Do not tell anyone. Be careful!! Ingel."

Dix replied that he would be in Budapest that evening, and would book a room at the Hotel InterContinental.

"Maria, grab a few things. We're going to Budapest. I just got a reply from Ingel. He wants me to meet him in Budapest. We've got to hurry."

"But, I can't. I've got too much to do. I have another deadline to meet and I am meeting Signore Afferi tomorrow. Besides, you can move faster without me. Are you going to call Mariano?"

"Calling him now." Dix lifted the receiver, paused, then dialed the number. He left a message for Mariano saying he was going after Ingel, but not where. He also didn't tell him that Maria would not be going.

10

Dix entered the hotel room on the eighth floor of the Hotel InterContinental and dropped his overnight bag next to the dresser. His room overlooked the Danube River and the Chain Bridge below with a picturesque view of Castle Hill on the far side of the river. He threw open the drapes and paused briefly to take in the spectacular panorama. The sun was low in the sky and reflected off the water as two sightseeing boats passed. The phone rang, startling him.

"Hello," he said.

"Dix? Ingel," came the man's reply.

"Ingel! Are you all right?"

"Ja, ja, fine. Meet me on Castle Hill across from your hotel at 6:30 this evening. Go up to the Fisherman's Bastion. Wait for me in the upper court by the statue of Saint Stephan."

"I know it. I'll be there," he replied, then hung up the phone. Forty minutes later, he was on his way.

Crossing the famous Chain Bridge was of particular interest to Dix. He had studied the battles of World War II and was at that moment walking and contemplating where history had been made. *The Nazis were all over the place then,* Dix thought as he paused in the middle of the bridge to survey both sides of the river. He pictured how the Nazis had made a stand against the Soviet Army. In January 1945 they dropped the bridge into the river in an attempt to prevent the Soviet Army from liberating the Castle District. It had taken the Red Army two months to rout the Nazis, and the Soviets practically destroyed the District in the process.

It was hard to imagine that such a beautiful place had such a troubled past. It was finally at peace. The Soviet occupation ended three years ago and the country was well on its way to democracy.

At the base of Castle Hill, Dix opted to take the funicular to the top. The ride up offered a breathtaking view of the Danube and the city below. It also allowed the perfect vantage point to observe if anyone followed. Dix was the only one in the car as it began its slow ascent. Once on top, Dix made his way to the rendezvous point. He stopped at the railing with the statue behind him and waited for Ingel. The offices and museums in the former palace were closed and only a few visitors lingered to enjoy another view from the hill before they departed. A hot air balloon drifted in the evening sky to the northeast and a tour boat to the south cruised north toward Chain Bridge.

"It's beautiful, ja? a man said as he walked up beside Dix and waved his hand toward the former palace.

"Ingel, how are you? Are you all right?" Dix wasn't prepared for the man's disheveled appearance. His cotton pants and shirt were wrinkled, and he hadn't shaved for several days.

"Still alive." The jittery man replied softly, then continued as though he was giving a college lecture. "The Turks captured it in 1541 and burned all the houses. In 1686 the Christian Army recaptured it. The castle was besieged again in 1849. Then the Soviets destroyed it getting the Nazis out. Such a magnificent place. They always rebuild it. It is no stranger to trouble. There is some irony as well for this former royal residence."

"What do you mean?"

"The palace is now home to the Hungarian National Gallery and the Budapest History Museum. Fit for any king. The ironic part is that the castle houses the Museum of the Hungarian Working-Class Movement. I bet the Hapsburgs and every other king that graced its halls are turning over in their graves."

"Ingel, what the hell is going on? You said you were in trouble. What kind of trouble are you in?" he asked, observing the bags under Ingel's bloodshot eyes.

"It is a long story. My life is in danger and I have got to get out of here." Ingel fidgeted and couldn't sand still. The two walked closer to the statue of Saint Stephan.

"I'll take you back to Italy. You'll be safe there."

"No, it is too dangerous. I just need your help to get me out of Hungary and take me to Munich. I have put you at risk just by asking you to come here."

"Nonsense, you're coming home with me. What's this all about?"

"I have worked for the G-7 for the last ten years. It has always been smooth and clean—until about a year or so ago." Ingel's voice trembled as he spoke. "This past winter—January I think, or was it February? I have lost track—they killed Ruggero Baldassare, who was working as a maritime liaison for the Italian government. They made it look like an accident. He was buried in Trieste. Then they killed the American in Turkey, I do not remember his name—Sherard, Eric Sherard I think. I met him only once. We began to watch out for one another. No one suspected a thing, not even our friend Colonel Simione." He paused and glanced around.

At that moment a loud, popping noise burst out nearby. Ingel flinched and ducked. Dix recoiled as a result of Ingel's movements. Both men looked around and saw two boys pushing a motorcycle. The noise popped again as the motorcycle backfired again. The two boys climbed on and drove down the backside of the hill.

"Calm down, Ingel. It was just a motorcycle. Go on."

"Edgar Kohne was killed in the car crash. Still no one suspected a thing. I talked to Klaus Müller and he was being as stubborn as ever. He wanted out…so they killed him, too." He jerked to a stop as a couple strolled by, then continued, "They were all killed in order to protect the organization."

"Klaus Müller was a professor. I don't get it," Dix said. "The Berlin Wall has fallen, Germany is reuniting, the Soviet Union is busting up, Stasi is dismantled, and the KGB reorganized. You worked for the G-7. So why would someone want you and the others dead?"

"For what we know."

"For Christ's sakes, you work for the Group of Seven Industrial Nations, the G-7. They're not the damn KGB or Stasi!"

"Ja, the G-7," Ingel replied. "We were originally supposed to keep track and verify things. You know, simple things like crop production, exports and import compliance. Things like that. It was nice and tidy. It really helped verify that everyone did what they said and it kept everybody honest. That is why the G-7 is so strong. No one was cheating or reneging."

"I don't get it! What does that have to do with someone wanting to kill you? People don't get killed over stuff like that," Dix shot back.

"It is more than that," Ingel said, wrenching his palms together. "All of us got sucked in—Klaus, Edgar, Ruggero, Eric—all of us. At first, they asked us to do little things and told us it was classified. We thought what we were doing was odd but it was quick, easy money at first. By the time we found out what we had gotten into it was too late. Each time someone wanted out they had a fatal accident. Klaus was a part of the organization, and wanted to get out and retire. They would not let him. But he thought he held the key and they would let him go. He had documented the entire operation and had obtained copies of documents dating back to World War II. He was our manager and had more access than any of us. He threatened to release the information if they didn't let him out. He called their bluff and they killed him."

"Who? Damn it!" Dix demanded.

"Our department."

"You're not making sense," Dix said. "What do you mean 'our department'?"

"Klaus told me that if anything happened to him to trust you. But he also said that you could be in trouble just for being seen with us. We just didn't know who all was involved."

"What about this department you were in?"

"We were formed into a special department. It did not really exist."

"Okay, it was classified." Dix had hit a roadblock. "You said you wanted to go to Munich. Why Munich?"

"Well, the department wasn't classified. It just didn't exist. The G-7 is having a meeting in Munich next month," Ingel replied as he looked down and rolled a pebble beneath the sole of his foot. "I should say the G-7 Plus One. The Russians are invited."

"The Russians? Does it have anything to do with the files Yeltsin is going to turn over?" Dix thought back to his conversation with Klaus about the Stasi files.

Ingel paused to scan the area before he replied. "Yes. Klaus told me you and he talked. When those files are turned over, they will expose our department and what it has been doing since the end of the war. Our department doesn't want the files to be transferred because they will go to jail. This bunch is cold-blooded. With a little luck, I can save my life and a few others. I have all of Klaus's information in a safe place. I need to get it and take it to Munich. I can expose them. Munich is the perfect place for me to do what I need to do because it is big enough to hide in."

"What's in the files?"

"Project Orion's report was a cover up—" Ingel started to speak, then with a fixed glaze slumped to the ground.

As Dix grabbed for him, he saw a gaping bullet wound on the left side of Ingel's head. Suddenly, a piece of marble exploded by Dix's head. He dropped to the ground, then crawled behind the statue for cover. He crouched and surveyed the area, searching windows, the corners of the buildings, other statues—any place a sniper might choose as his firing point. The entire area appeared to be deserted. Dix realized he had not heard a shot. *A suppressor. He could be anywhere. Shit! The terrain, with all of its obstacles, prevents a long shot, so the shooter has to be nearby. But where?*

Dix had no gun and no way to call for help. All he could do was wait. Wait until the shooter moved to a new location and took another shot, a shot which could prove fatal to Dix. He studied his options. None of them were good if the shooter was still in the area.

"Help! Over here!" he called out when he saw the same couple that had strolled passed him earlier. "Help me! A man has been shot!" He saw the couple stop, then the man sprinted toward Dix. "Call the police! Tell them a man has been shot!"

The man turned and sprinted back to the woman. The two disappeared behind the building. Dix could only hope they would call the police. It wasn't long before he heard sirens. Knowing the shooter wouldn't stick around, he breathed a little easier as he waited for help to arrive.

11

Dix left Budapest early the next morning after a long night of answering questions and making his statement to police. He arrived back home in the late afternoon. Exhausted from the past twenty-four hours, he collapsed in a chair.

As Dix began to tell Maria about the incident with Ingel, he soon began to feel uneasy. He excused himself and left Maria in order to peer out of the windows and to check the neighborhood. Had he been followed? Did the shooter know his address? He was on the defensive. It was up to the killer to make the next move if Dix was a target. It was quiet. Uncomfortable about what had happened in Budapest and the warnings to him, he sat down for a moment, then took the stack of mail and flipped through it. *That's odd,* he thought, stopping on a padded envelope with a Budapest postmark. He tore it open. *It's from Ingel. He must have mailed it the same day he contacted me.* Inside was a short letter and another piece of paper. He studied the paper and flipped it over to look at both sides, then decided to show Maria.

He found her in the bedroom, her face in her hands, sitting on the edge of the bed. His heart sank. Dix knelt down next to her and put one arm around her. "What's wrong?"

"Just tired I guess. All this mess made me think about Panama. I started feeling like I was back there with people dying all around and danger lurking at every corner. I thought it was over."

Maria's mother had been killed when she was a child and her father died in a freak accident while she was attending college in Costa Rica. It took her a year to get over the shock of her father's death before she could return to college. A year and a half after she returned to Costa Rica, she graduated, and three months later opened a successful art gallery. Her marriage to Dix was her second. Her first husband had been brutally killed by one of General Noriega's death squads in Panama in 1988, the year before she met Dix. The goons beat her husband and forced Maria to watch as they tortured him to death. Then they raped her. That was a part of her life she had left behind in Panama.

"We're fine. No one is going to hurt you."

"Ingel told you it was dangerous and now he's dead. Klaus warned us and he's dead too." Her voice was cold and angry. "I'm afraid I will lose you."

"Not a chance. I'm fine and I will take care of you. We'll both be fine." Dix tried to reassure her, but he knew her fears were justified.

"In Panama, we thought we were safe. My husband said he would take care of us. They killed him."

Maria had talked to Dix only once, just before they were married, about the horrible night when Noriega's thugs killed her husband. He had never brought it up again.

Dix took her in his arms and felt her pounding heart. He held her tight without moving until she began to relax.

"Maria, why don't you go take a shower? You'll feel better," Dix said, then kissed her lips.

"Maybe you're right." Maria looked deep into his eyes. "I

love you." She kissed him back, then stood, stretched and walked into the bathroom.

As soon as Maria was in the shower, Dix decided to check the house again. He looked out of the windows, searching for anything that might be out of place. As he left each room, he turned out the lights. He kept the outside lights on so he could see anyone that might try to sneak up to the house. The outside lights would also make it harder for anyone to see inside the darkened house.

As he wandered through the house, Dix felt angry about Maria's bad memories. *I won't let anything harm her,* he thought. *I'll do whatever it takes.*

Dix studied the mysterious letter from Ingel. The short letter read:

Dear Dix,

By your reading this letter, you will know that I am dead. I had hoped that things would have turned out differently. I am afraid you are in danger. Now that I am dead, they probably have seen you with me and find you a threat. Take precautions now.

Klaus told me to trust you, that you would do the right thing. We are not sure who all the players are, so you must be careful. Those that you think are your friends may not be.

The names of those in our organization are on the list I have enclosed. Those still alive can be trusted, but they fear for their lives. Show them the seven gold coins I have included and they will talk to you. It seems that we provided the money for our own deaths.

The Chlodwigs, Rodrik and Etta, are on the list. You will find them in Bressanone, Italy. They are keeping a package for me. Take it to Munich.

Reach for the stars and you will shine like the brightest of the twins. Protect yourself.

Ingel

The last line puzzled Dix. *What the hell is he trying to tell me?* he wondered. *A package? Take it to Munich? Is the package the information he told me about that he got from Klaus? What does "shine like the brightest of the twins" mean? It's odd that he'd tell me where to find the Chlodwigs and then give me such a cryptic message.*

Dix finally concluded it was a code—one that Klaus would have told Ingel to use. Not an elaborate code, but a statement that Dix would be able to decipher quicker than anyone else—giving him an advantage of a little time. The second piece of paper contained a list of names, including Ingel's, six of whom were now dead.

Dix decided to call Mariano. He studied the letter again as he waited for the phone to be answered.

"Pronto!" A woman's voice answered.

"Julia? Ciao. This is Dix."

"Ciao, Dix."

"Can I speak to Mariano?"

"He had to go out of town. He should be back sometime tomorrow."

"Please ask him to call me."

"Certainly. Is everything okay?"

"Yeah, I just need to talk to him about something."

"Okay, I'll give him the message. Ciao."

"Ciao."

"God, am I tired," Dix mumbled to himself as he replaced the receiver. "I can't concentrate." He slid the letter underneath his computer, then poured two glasses of red wine and took them into the bedroom.

Maria was drying her hair as Dix entered. "Feel better?" He handed her a glass.

"Much. Thank you." Maria sipped the wine. "Are you going to shower?"

"Yeah, I think it will make me feel better, too. I just can't concentrate." Dix sipped his wine and set the glass on the dresser.

The next morning, Dix was up early, his mind rested and relaxed. For almost an hour, he methodically went over the recent events, but he still couldn't identify what was really going on, who Ingel was going to expose, or what the Project Orion report was covering up? He had shown Maria the letter after his shower the night before, but neither could come up with satisfactory answers.

Dix carried a fresh caffè latte into the bedroom for Maria. He was surprised to see her looking out of the window as he entered the room. She turned toward him and smiled.

"That smells good," she said as he handed her the drink.

Maria grasped the warm mug with both hands and inhaled the aroma before turning back to the window. Standing by her side, Dix sensed a change in her. It was more than a good night's rest. It was something below the surface—as though she was radiating electric energy from within.

"It's a beautiful morning," she said. "This is good, Dix. I woke up this morning thinking about that painting Gergo Zámbori showed me, the painting in Ida Kohne's house, those soldiers smuggling art and all that talk about Nazi treasures. I got all excited."

Dix kissed her cheek, relieved that her mood was much improved. "I woke up thinking about Ingel, what happened to him, and his letter. Ingel wants me to get some kind of information to Munich. He said it will expose what his department has been doing since the end of World War II. He said Project Orion was a cover-up. But I don't know what it was covering up or how it ties into his department. He and Klaus both were interested in the G-7 meeting in Munich. All these things have been racing through my mind."

"Project Orion is familiar to me but I don't know why. I must have heard of it before. Why is that G-7 meeting so important?" Maria asked as she turned toward him and sipped her caffè.

"I don't know. That's what I'm going to find out. I'd like to see a copy of that report."

Dix discussed the events again with Maria, trying to make sense of it all. They had not yet figured out what Ingel's message meant, but knew more trouble was ahead. Dix needed Mariano's help and believed he was more involved than he let on. Mariano always seems to be around *whenever someone is killed,* Dix recalled. *And he knew the victims. But just how is he involved? He certainly knew Ingel was in trouble and that I was going to meet him. Like Ingel and Kohne, Mariano had seven gold coins too.*

Ingel's warning of danger played again in Dix's mind. He needed to find out what Project Orion was covering up. He studied Ingel's letter most of the morning, hoping to discover a clue. By midday Dix concluded that he would have to trust Mariano as there was no one else. But would trust him just so far—until he was sure.

Mariano agreed to come to Dix's house and arrived alone around 5:20.

Cordial as always, Dix met him at the door with a smile and cheerful greeting. Before Dix closed the door, he quickly surveyed the neighborhood to ensure that nothing was there that might threaten their safety. Then he led Mariano into the living room. Turning to sit in his chair, Dix watched Mariano unbutton his coat and reach inside. Then a chill rushed through him as Mariano withdrew a pistol. Dix's eyes fixed on the pistol, his mouth went dry and his heart pounded.

"Here you go, Dix," Mariano said handing him the 9mm Beretta. "You asked for it. Be careful."

"Thanks," Dix said, taking the automatic in his right hand. His thumb instinctively hit the magazine release button and the magazine dropped into his left hand. "I intend to."

"Fifteen rounds, staggered, one hundred-fifteen grain bullets," Mariano said, looking at the magazine in Dix's hand. "Don't use it unless you have too. It is a real son-of-a-bitch at 25 meters."

"I hope I don't have to." Dix grasped the grip like an old friend and felt the grooves against the palm of his hand. He pulled the slide to the rear and inspected the inside, then released it. "Double action, NATO standard. Nice."

"Caffè?" Dix asked, feeling a bit more relaxed.

"No, Sambuca."

"I'll get it, Dix," Maria said, appearing from nowhere, her eyes fixed on the Beretta.

"Ciao, Maria." Mariano stood when she spoke.

"Mariano, Ingel is dead." Dix watched his reactions.

"I know. I just came back from Budapest."

Dix felt cold again and he tensed at his statement. "You were in Budapest?"

"I went there yesterday when I found out about him."

"How the hell did you find out?"

"I have my sources. That's why I got you the Beretta."

"Mariano, what the hell is going on?"

Mariano hesitated, then gave him a guarded reply. "I'm not really sure. It's very deep and crosses many borders. That's all I can tell you."

Dix told Mariano what he knew—omitting Ingel's letter, Project Orion and the Chlodwigs—and gave him the paper with the list of names. Mariano had him recount in detail each event in Brussels and his meeting with Ingel. Several times Mariano asked Dix to repeat a particular event or topic that was discussed.

"Maria, have you heard of anyone purchasing any type of art recently that appeared to have been a good buy?" Mariano asked.

"No, I don't think so." Mariano's leap to this topic puzzled Maria. She hesitated, undecided about how much to tell him. "Wait, well, maybe. Lydia Marston had me look at a painting she bought. Julia and I went to her house when you were in Berlin. Usually, Colonel Marston buys junk and thinks it's good; he thinks he's an art expert." Maria rolled her eyes up. "I think someone told him to invest in art. Anyway, he has a couple of nice pieces, but he paid too much for them. The painting he and Lydia recently bought, though, was exquisite and they got it at a bargain price." She wasn't ready to tell him about her meeting with Sonja Abramovych and her connection to the Marstons' painting.

"Did she say where they bought it?"

"Yes, let me see... Udine, I think."

"Anything else you can tell me?"

"I've already told you about Gergo Zámbori, the art dealer in Budapest. That's about it." "Is this all related?" Dix asked.

"I don't know." Mariano sipped his drink and avoided eye contact.

"Did all the people on that list work for the G-7?"

"I don't know. I'll check."

"The other day you said Colonel Pasquali told you about a rumor of a recently discovered cache of World War II treasures. Do you suspect this somehow ties in?" Dix studied Mariano.

"No! It was just something Pasquali told me and I thought I might look into it for him since Maria gets around in the art world."

"Hey, you're holding back on me," Dix pressed.

"I don't really have much. Let me check out the names on the list and I'll call you tomorrow." Mariano finished his drink and chewed the coffee beans as he stood. "Be careful, Dix. You could be in trouble."

"Right. Thanks for the Beretta."

"Let's hope you don't have to use it."

Dix closed the door behind Mariano and watched him drive off. He turned to Maria and said, "He didn't tell us everything. Why would he suddenly ask us about art if it wasn't tied in?"

"I don't know, but he gets defensive when you bring it up."

"I know. Let's sit down and put our pieces together. Then I'll give Colonel Marston a call."

"Do you think he might know something?"

"Well, he may give us some answers without knowing anything. Of course that guy is a little dumb sometimes. I don't know how that plow jockey made colonel." Dix shook his head and wrenched up the corner of his mouth.

"Dix, be nice."

12

The call Dix made to Colonel Marston added information but seemed to fit a different puzzle. Marston verified that he had purchased the painting in Udine. He told Dix that one of the soldiers, stationed at one of the NATO sites at Portogruaro, had helped him. The soldier, a sergeant first class, apparently had a girlfriend in Udine whose uncle was selling off some of his mother-in-law's belongings. The woman, a widow, had died a little over a year before, leaving all her possessions to her daughter and son-in-law. The estate had been settled, and they were now selling off her things.

Marston went on and on about the man, his family and finally the paintings and a few other items he was interested in. Marston portrayed the son-in-law as a poor, old, weather-beaten farmer. Scratching out a meager living from his small farm and vineyard, the man had fallen on hard times and needed the money to make some repairs on his house.

"I know what it's like to be a farmer," Marston said. "I grew up on a farm in West Virginia and there were times when there was barely enough money to put food on the table."

"Did you go to his farm and see what else he had for sale?" Dix asked.

"No, the old man said his place was hard to find. He would be in town in Udine within a few days of when we talked, so I met him at the Italian Army Caserma there."

"Do you have a phone number for him?"

"He doesn't have a phone; the sergeant coordinated everything. Do you want me to send word to him for you?"

"No, not yet. I suppose you paid him cash?" Dix knew the answer before it came.

"Yeah, he preferred it. He said he would have to pay taxes if he took a check. He said he knew the painting was worth more, but he lowered the price for a cash deal."

"What did the old man look like?"

"Oh, hell, I don't remember. Just a little, old, weather-beaten man who spoke with a slight Austrian accent. He wore a tattered brown suit and boots. Probably didn't have much more than that. Drove an old blue Fiat. Why did you want to know?"

"Just curious."

"Dix, it was on the up-and-up," Marston replied. "I believed the old man; he seemed sincere. Besides, the sergeant knew him. He said everything was okay."

"What's the sergeant's name?"

"Sergeant First Class Drefan Brainard."

Dix thanked the colonel for the information and told him Maria thought he made a good buy. The best strategy, Dix thought, was to pump the colonel's ego to keep him at ease and leave him receptive to future conversations. Dix ended the call with a little fib, telling him Maria wanted to see what else the man might have and he would call back soon. That seemed to satisfy the colonel and avoided arousing suspicion.

Not as gullible as Colonel Marston, Dix suspected that the old man's story was phony, and that Marston actually had purchased his painting through the black market. Intrigued, Dix had Maria call Gergo Zámbori to find out more about the art he had told her about and to learn about the former owner, a dead man from Udine.

Maria charmed the dealer into believing she was interested in some of the art. The Hungarian smelled money and knew she could produce.

"Yes, my dear, I can get more," he said. "His partner—he has a shop in Trieste too, you know—called me a few weeks ago and said they were still in business. What are you looking for?"

"Do you still have the painting you showed me?" Maria felt it was already gone.

"Sold it. But I have a few others, as well as some gold and silver items. Does that interest you?"

"Perhaps. I am really looking for paintings."

"Let me check around and I'll call you. Things pop up all the time. Yugoslavia, Germany, Russia—"

"Trieste and Udine?" Maria added to test his reaction.

"Oh yes, always a possibility."

Maria continued with her spell, for several more minutes, extracting bits and pieces, not knowing what would be helpful or not. She ended by encouraging him to call when he found something. He assured her he would, and soon.

They compared notes for a few minutes then Dix said, "Maria, I think this black market art ties in somehow but I don't know how yet. I think you should let Mariano handle it. We've got bigger problems right now."

"But we're on to something here. This could be big."

"Maybe, but right now we've got big problems of our own."

"I can't let this go, Dix! I have to find out more about this. Do you know what it would mean if I found one of the Nazi caches?"

"Okay, Maria!" Dix knew it was no use arguing with her whenever she became excited over lost art. Her fervor would keep going for some time. Dix stood and said, "I'm going to do some research on the Internet."

Dix powered up the laptop as Maria pulled one of her reference books on the Nazi treasures from the shelf and sat with one leg folded under her in her favorite chair. The laptop's lights flashed and its screen came to life. Dix tried but soon lost interest in the Internet as his thoughts returned to Ingel and the letter he sent to him. Dix pulled the letter out and studied it once again.

Maria was frustrated with Dix, and believed she was onto something. Mariano's questions and interest in art, Dix's phone call to Colonel Marston and the story about his painting, her call to the art dealer Gergo Zámbori, Sonja Abramovych, and Ida Kohne's painting—all of this filled Maria's head. She reviewed the history of the Nazi's art purge during World War II. Not knowing what she was looking for, she thought back to the Titian painting she saw in Ida Kohne's house. *A civil servant can't afford such a painting.* Her thoughts swarmed. *The Marstons' purchase and Mariano's and Gergo's comments. There are too many coincidences.*

"Dix, I knew I had heard of Project Orion. It's in here." Maria looked up from her reference book. "Project Orion was the code name for the Art Looting Investigation Unit of the OSS's Counterintelligence Branch (X-2). They were responsible for the repatriation and compensatory restitution of the art looted by the Nazis during the war. The Project Orion Report gave details on the art taken during the war. Specifically, the report said all the known art treasures were returned or victims paid."

"Good going, Maria! If Project Orion's report was a cover-up, I wonder if that means Ingel's 'department' had some of the treasures. We've got to go to Bressanone to get Ingel's package. That could answer our question."

"Let's give all this to Mariano and tell him everything."

"I'm not really sure where Mariano is on this. I don't like it when he keeps me in the dark. Let's see what that package is in Bressanone and what else we can find out."

"You go to Bressanone, Dix. I've got to find out more about this mysterious art. I think I'll have Colonel Marston get me set up with the Austrian he bought his painting from."

13

It was about noon when Dix turned into the gravel parking lot in front of the picturesque Hubertushof Hotel near the Alpine village of Raas. The Bavarian-style hotel sat near the crest of the mountain overlooking the medieval town of Bressanone, Italy. Located south of the Brenner Pass in the South Tirol, Bressanone was almost equidistant from Bolzano to the south and the Austrian border to the north.

This hotel looked as if it was right out of a travel brochure. Brilliant against the white stucco walls, scarlet geraniums cascaded from planter boxes that lined the first and second story balconies. The chocolate-brown shutters invited sunlight into the five rooms overlooking the first balcony and the three rooms overlooking the second. An Alpine fresco adorned the wall area at each end of the second balcony in place of windows. Prior to World War II, Bressanone as well as all of South Tirol belonged to Bavaria. As a result, the culture was predominately Bavarian with German and Italian the spoken languages. The region was a highly regarded resort area for winter sports. Ski trails and lifts covered the mountains. Almost every type of winter sport could be found there.

Three picnic tables and four round tables filled the large

patio to the right of the hotel entrance. Two old men sat at one of the picnic tables talking and drinking wine. Various shrubs and trees filled the landscape with new spring growth. A lush meadow led to the top of the hill with only a hint of the Dolomites beyond. On the left side of the building was the café and bar, with a doorway serving the patio.

Dix chose this hotel because he had stayed here many times before. A former NATO nuclear storage site was located approximately a kilometer back down the mountain from the Hubertushof. This NATO site, since the removal of nuclear weapons in the early '80s, was used for security training. It was during these training exercises that, as a lieutenant colonel, he became familiar with the hotel and the excellent skiing and ice skating in the area.

Although a picturesque and familiar setting, more importantly, it was outside of Bressanone. Not knowing what he was about to walk into, Dix preferred to remain as unnoticed as possible—like a person sitting in the audience rather than on stage. In fact, this area had been the stage for many great dramas over the past century. Running through Bressanone was the A22, one of three major trade routes crossing the Alps providing Italy with trade to the north. This four-lane superhighway started just west of Verona and meandered north through the cleavage in the mountains at the Brenner Pass into Austria.

The A22 had been a main Nazi supply route through the Brenner Pass, a strategic location leading south into Italy. During Hitler's rape of Italian treasures, the convoys' main route was along A22. A Nazi Garrison, today an Alpini Caserma, or Italian Alpine Soldiers' Garrison, was located on A22 on the north the side of Bressanone.

Tired from the drive, Dix wanted to relax. He had made the trip, the same as always, in just over three and a half hours. Unlike previous trips, the ocean of grapevines stretching for miles along the highway and the green terraced vineyards climbing the hillsides did not pique his interest; nor did the quaint farmhouses or occasional dreamy castle perched on a hilltop. He acknowledged their beauty, regretting he had no one to share it with, but pleasure was not the purpose of this trip.

As Dix grasped his overnight bag and headed for the entrance, the recent events swirled around in his mind. He was still no closer than he had been to unraveling the mystery behind the deaths, Ida's comments and the gold coins. The events worried him. He knew he could take care of himself, it was Maria he worried about. *She's not in danger,* Dix reassured himself. *How much trouble can she get into at the library? An overdue book at best. She's talking with Colonel Marston and just doing research. She knows how to avoid trouble and keeps a low profile.*

Mariano had informed Dix before he left for Bressanone that all the people on Ingel's list had worked for the G-7, but no new information had been forthcoming. Dix continued to feel uneasy about Mariano and his connection to all that had been happening. All he could do for now was to exercise a cautious trust.

Dix needed to find Rodrik and Etta Chlodwig, but it was the time of day, *riposo*, when the shops were closed. The owners of the Hubertushof were locals and would know many of the local people in this tourist area. His best chance of finding the Chlodwigs, he decided, would be in the hotel restaurant.

As he opened the twin glass doors, Dix was greeted by the clanking of dishes. The cuckoo clock to his far left sprang to life, adding to the clamor. The waitress recognized him, and led him to a linen-draped table near a wall with traditional Bavarian woodwork. After he was seated, she brought him the cup of coffee he requested.

Dix was in no hurry as the shops probably wouldn't reopen for at least another hour, so he began to ask her about shopping in town. The waitress became more talkative and friendly with each question. She remembered Dix from his many previous visits. She also liked to practice her English with the English-speaking guests. Her command of the language was good, except when she became flustered or excited—then it could blend into a combination of German, Italian and English. Her German still heavily influenced her English syntax. When he decided the time was right, he casually asked, "Do you know of the family Chlodwig?"

"Umm, no I don't think so. Wait a minute." The young woman held up her hand, turned and stepped to another waitress.

Dix watched with interest as they spoke, but he could not hear what they were saying. Following their brief discussion, the second of the two waitresses approached Dix.

"You want to buy feather pillows and bedding, ja? The family Chlodwig owns the best shop for these things."

"Yes, can you tell me where the shop is?"

"Ja, go to the center of town. Immediately across from the two clock towers, you will see the street. Go between the buildings. Take this street, go to the second street and turn left. Their shop will be twenty meters on the right."

"Thank you. Do they make the pillows and bedding?" Dix asked.

"Ja, you pick out what you want and the fabric. The next day it is ready. They do not open until three o'clock."

The waitress told Dix that the Chlodwigs were well-known

for their feather pillows and bedding. She was proud that people came from Italy, Austria, Switzerland and Germany to buy their wares. Not only that, their visits were also good for the hotel business.

Dix thanked the waitress for her help and sat quietly for a while. He watched as the staff cleared the tables and cleaned the floor. *That was too easy,* Dix thought. *I've got to be very careful. I may not be the only one paying the Chlodwigs a visit for things other than pillows.*

Dix took his time, enjoying the coffee and watching the others come and go. Finally, he checked his watch, compared it to the clock on the wall and decided it was time to leave.

As Dix drove into the old walled city, the famous white tower and baroque cathedral loomed in front of him. The colorful facades with their large frescoes soon came into view. He never failed to marvel at Bressanone's churches, monasteries, cloisters, and castles that had stood in the town since the eleventh century. Dix observed the townspeople and their activities as he followed the waitress's directions to the Chlodwigs' shop. As he drove by, a man and woman entered the shop and he could see three other people inside. Dix found a parking space by the square near one of the clock towers, a couple of blocks from the shop.

If someone was following him or waiting for him, Dix needed to determine that before going in. He feared that the Chlogwigs might be watched and was certain they would be cautious. He had to be delicate in his approach as they no doubt knew about the deaths. As he walked toward the shop, he continued scrutinizing the area.

On one corner by the street he was about to enter was a bar that served refreshments, pastries and light snacks. On the opposite corner was an ice cream parlor. Dix paused in front of the bar and discreetly scanned inside, then surveyed the area outside once again. Everything appeared to be normal; no one lingered about or even seemed to notice him. Dix continued with his guarded stride.

When he reached the old, red-brick shop with its large window display painted dark green, he pretended to window shop before entering. Samples of the pillows and comforters with different types of feathers and down were artistically arranged. A small sign gave a greeting in German, Italian and English and described the materials. It also indicated that these languages were spoken in the shop.

The same three people were in the shop that he had seen before. Two women—one middle-aged and plump, and the other in her early twenties and slim—seemed to be working near the back of the shop. The other, a man, was talking to an elderly couple. As he stood there, another couple entered. *The two women in the back appear to be mother and daughter,* he thought as he kept looking at the window display. *The older one is probably Etta. The man talking to the couple must be Rodrik. Everything looks okay from out here. I'll go in and look around until the others leave.*

"Buon Giorno!" Dix said as he entered. He preferred to speak in Italian as his command of that language was far superior to his German. And of course it was considered more polite to talk to them in their native language.

"Buon Giorno!" the man replied, then continued talking with the couple.

Glad to be left alone for the moment, Dix took the opportunity to assess his surroundings. The shop was a large, open, L-shaped room with a wood floor. Lamps with big green shades, like inverted funnels, hung from the high ceiling. A layer of down and a few small feathers coated the shades as well as most of the other stationary objects. Not a single nook or cranny had escaped the ubiquitous down and feathers.

Shelves lined the wall to the left side. Various types of cloth lay in stacks in sections of the shelves, while completed works and various samples filled other sections. Two sewing machines and a work table were against the wall.

Several waist-high bins, approximately four-feet square, sat beneath each light. Most of the bins contained feathers and down from chickens, ducks, and geese. A couple of bins had samples of guinea, pheasant and turkey feathers and down. One bin contained samples of horse hair.

A doorway on the left side of the back wall, partly concealed by a brown curtain, led to the back office and additional storage space. Dix was not able to see around the corner into the rest of the shop. He could only guess that it contained more bins and shelves.

The two women continued to work silently. They would sew for a bit then stop, turn and lift the lid of a bin to remove some of the contents, stuff it into what they were working on, then sew again. The younger woman finally stopped and picked up a feather duster to dust the area.

Dix continued his shopping charade. He examined the various pieces of cloth then moved to the bins of feathers and down. The couple concluded their business and Dix observed them leave. The older of the two women looked up briefly and quietly spoke to the other as they continued to work. Dix moved about the tables and bins, examining the contents. Then the man approached Dix.

The short, stocky Tirolean smiled and his dark eyes sparkled. He wrung his hands.

"Signore, may I help you?" he asked, releasing his hands

and putting them in his apron.

"My name is Dix Connor."

"Pleased to meet you. I am Chlodwig, Rodrik Chlodwig," he said as he extended his hand.

"Do you have a few minutes to talk? I am a friend of Ingel." The man immediately released his hand and the smile dropped from his face.

"Ingel?"

"Yes, a German, blue eyes and light brown hair. He is about this tall," Dix said, indicating a height of about five feet ten inches. "He told me to show these to you." Dix held out his hand, palm up, exposing the seven coins.

"Ingel!" he said louder and placed his hand on Dix's back. "Come into my office. We will talk about Ingel over a glass of wine. How is he these days?"

"That's what I came to talk to you about."

"Truda, you and Mama watch the shop for a few minutes. I have some business," Rodrik said, turning to the girl and older woman. The Chlodwigs had a routine, a signal of caution. It was subtle and one that would not be noticed by anyone else. Rodrik had just given the alarm to Etta by repeating the name "Ingel," then putting his hand on Dix's back like he was an old friend and taking him to the back room for a drink of wine. It was an unmistakable signal to them.

The old man led Dix casually through the curtain-draped doorway into the back of the shop. He had set his office up in one corner near an old cast iron stove, out of sight from the front of the store. An old wooden desk supported stacks of papers and a ceramic cup holding pens and pencils. A desk pad with fountain pen and blotter covered the center of the desk. The desk was free of the omnipresent down and feathers, an obvious sign of its recent use.

A small table was to the right of the desk. On the table sat a wine bottle, three-quarters full, a small wine glass and three used coffee cups, a sugar shaker and spoon. Down had already found its way into the glass. Two chairs were in front of the desk.

"Please, be seated," he gestured, with an outstretched arm toward the chairs. Then he stepped behind the desk.

Dix sat in front of the desk with his back to the doorway. His eyes remained fixed on the man.

"Let me see, I have a clean glass here somewhere," he muttered as he opened the door to a cabinet and retrieved the glass.

Dix, accepting the man's hospitality, watched him without speaking. Rodrik looked inside the glass, then blew in it to eject the down that had settled in the bottom. He took his time and gently poured the wine, then handed it to Dix. He poured a second glass for himself.

"Saluté!" he said as he held up his glass to Dix.

"Saluté!" Dix replied. Mirroring the man's gesture of raising the glass, he took a sip of the wine. He felt completely at ease in the relaxed atmosphere.

Rodrik sat down and slid the chair forward. In one slow, controlled motion, he raised his hands and placed them on the desk.

"Don't try anything or Etta will blow your head off," he said in a low voice.

Dix tensed. He looked over his shoulder and saw the plump woman standing just inside and to the left of the curtain, pointing a double-barreled shotgun at him. The unmistakable clicks of a shotgun being cocked roared in his ears.

Damn! Dix thought. *How could I have been so stupid? Ingel said they were frightened. I walked right into this. I am rusty! Goddamn it! I knew better than to let my guard down. Christ, I'm a stranger to these people! Shit!*

"You have come here to kill us, haven't you? You are the one they sent, aren't you?" Rodrik demanded.

"No! No, I'm a friend of Ingel. He said you're holding a package for him and he wanted me to take it to Munich."

"To Munich? Why? Why doesn't he take it himself? Why you?"

"Ingel is dead," Dix said. "He called me from Budapest to help him, but he was killed before I could get him back to Italy."

"Why did he call you?"

"Klaus Müller told him to trust me."

"Müller is dead and now Ingel, you say. How do I know you didn't do it?"

"Whoever killed Müller almost killed me. They tried to run us down in Brussels. Later someone killed him."

"Keep going."

"Ingel knew someone was after him and he contacted me for help. He warned me that I might be in trouble too. I got mixed up in this but don't know the details. I just tried to help Ingel and now he's dead. The person who shot him tried to shoot me as well. Ingel wanted me to take a package you're holding for him to Munich. That's it!"

"You still haven't told me anything. I haven't survived this long by being stupid."

"Rodrik, we must get him to the cave quickly. We will kill him there and seal it shut," Etta commanded in a low voice so as not to be overheard. "We must hurry!"

"This is your last chance. Convince me or your body will rot in Castor," Rodrik growled in a low voice."

Castor! Why did he say Castor? Dix thought, his mind racing.

"I'm waiting," Rodrik said threateningly.

Ingel's letter! Dix thought. *Ingel said "reach for the stars and you will shine like the brightest of the twins."* That's it! *The constellation Gemini, "The Twins!" The heads of the twins are Castor and Pollux. Ingel was telling me to use one of the twins' names, in this case, Pollux.*

"Pollux," Dix uttered, mentally crossing his fingers.

Rodrik shot a look to Etta, then back to the man seated before him. His muscles relaxed but his expression remained unchanged as he locked his eyes onto Dix's.

"I am sorry but it is very dangerous," Rodrik said.

Dix heard the shotgun click as Etta slowly released the hammers and opened the breach. Dix breathed a sigh of relief. He didn't need to turn around to see what she was doing. The sound told it all.

"Look, I have no idea what this is all about. Ingel just wanted me to take the package to Munich. Can you tell me what is going on?"

"I can't tell you much. I just provided storage and transportation. I don't even know who we worked for or who was in the organization, other than Ingel and Klaus. Klaus was… well, I guess you would say, our leader."

"Why didn't you know more?"

"We were kept compartmentalized. We only knew about our portion and we were always contacted by computer on the Internet. If ever I needed anything, I would contact Ingel."

"Who are 'we'?" Dix quizzed.

"All I know about is Klaus and Ingel. I am sure there are others. I just don't know who, how many or where. The organization kept it that way. I don't even know who paid us. I did what they said and I was paid well for it."

"How did you get paid?" Dix asked.

"Electronic transfer to an account in Switzerland."

"Can you start from the top and tell me everything you can? Maybe we can help each other."

The Tirolean poured more wine into the glasses. He sat back, then took a sip. "No one realized at first the danger we were in, but we do now. I do know Klaus was trying to stop it. He, like all of us, was in too deep to do anything about it by the time he found out what was going on. Plus, the money was a tremendous inducement."

Rodrik continued to tell Dix the little he knew and about his involvement. He used the word *expose* when he mentioned that Ingel was going to Munich to the G-7 meeting.

"Yes," Rodrik admitted, "Ingel did give me a package, but I never opened it so I don't know what is contains."

Dix detected caution in his statement. "Why not?"

"I thought it was better that way. Ingel would have told me to look at it if he wanted me to. When we found out Klaus was dead, we knew there was going to be trouble. We tried to get in touch with Ingel but never heard from him. Then you showed up asking questions."

Rodrik paused, suddenly holding up his hand as a signal to Dix not to speak. The sound of someone entering the shop came from the front.

Etta turned around and peeked through the curtain. She remained silent and didn't move. The two sat motionless, straining to hear. Then Etta turned around and nodded toward the front to indicate that a stranger was in the shop. She continued to watch in silence. When the small bell on the front door jingled, Etta turned back around.

"It was a man talking to Truda and looking at pillows. He's gone now," she stated.

"It is too dangerous here," Rodrik said in a low voice. "Where are you staying?"

"The Hubertushof."

"I know it. Go back there and wait. I don't have the package here. I'll have to get it. Go now!"

Rodrik stood and Etta preceded the two through the curtain. The bell on the front door jingled again as a customer entered the shop.

"Your order will be ready tomorrow," Rodrik said to Dix.

Dix followed his cue and allowed Rodrik to escort him out of the store, as was the custom when an order was placed.

The late afternoon sun hung low in the sky, casting an orange hue over the town. Dix still hadn't learned much more, nor did he have the package he came for. The word *expose* that Rodrik used played on his mind as he walked back to the car. Satisfied he had made some progress, he turned the corner, entered the ice cream store, and bought a cone of hazelnut ice cream.

In his third floor room at the Hubertushof, Dix opened the window to let in the fresh evening air. A soft breeze coming up from the valley carried the scent of the flowers into the room. Noticing the flashing red light on his phone, he sat on the edge of the bed and lifted the receiver to retrieve the message. He knew it would be from Maria. She told him she was staying at the Astoria Hotel in Udine for the night and gave the phone number. *Maria must be enjoying herself,* Dix thought. *She has probably spent the afternoon at the museum.*

Dix glanced at the clock by the phone, then dialed the number she left. She did not answer so he left a short message saying he would return home the next day.

Dix stared at the phone and thought of Francesca Martin. He lifted the receiver again and dialed her number. *Perhaps she could help me get to the bottom of this. She's well-connected and knows just about everybody in the political arena.* She picked up the phone on the third ring. Dix gave her enough information to get her interested—including the murders. He asked for her help and offered to share the story with her. She readily accepted, not only because Dix had asked but also because the story intrigued her. She thanked Dix for the opportunity, assuring him that she would keep it quiet and honor their agreement. She promised to call as soon as she found out anything.

With nothing more to do until he heard from Rodrik, Dix decided to go down to the dining room. Savoring pheasant, quail or even squirrel and white wine prepared by their chef would provide a delectable distraction.

14

Maria called Colonel Marston to ask his help in setting up a meeting for her with Sergeant First Class Drefan Brainard. Happy to oblige, he assured her he would call the sergeant immediately. Maria, anxious to proceed, reluctantly withstood his gloating about the good buy he made on the painting. Finally, she managed to divert him onto another subject and then was able to get off the phone.

The sergeant called Maria just before noon and arranged to meet with her later that day. They agreed to meet in Udine at the Hotel Astoria for dinner. Maria arrived by train at 3:10 in the afternoon. She wanted to check into the hotel, then visit the library and museum for research before the dinner meeting.

Sergeant Brainard sat at the linen-draped table across from Maria in the main dining room of the four-star Hotel Astoria. She had expected a conservative wiry fellow. Instead, she found him to be rather attractive. He was about five feet eleven inches tall, one hundred and ninety pounds and in good shape. *The only conservative thing about him is his short, dark hair*, she thought.

Too flashy—the gold chain around his neck, gold bracelet, gold ring set with a diamond, and gold watch. He practically glitters.

The two spent the first half hour sizing each other up and determining credibility. Brainard, proceeding with caution, had the advantage as Colonel Marston had touted her to be a dealer and an expert in art. He probed for information while revealing little. Maria knew only that he was a soldier with a girlfriend whose relatives were selling an estate. Within minutes of their meeting, she determined that he was dangerous and far more than what Colonel Marston portrayed. She believed his sideline job was hardly on the up-and-up. If she were direct and dug too quickly for information, he would bolt, or worse—kill her. The only way to get information out of him, she figured, was to appeal to his weaknesses. Short on time and the need for information, she opted to take the dangerous route.

Maria nursed her Campari as she watched Brainard refill his glass for the second time as the waiter approached. She knew the time was right to turn her charm on full blast. *He reminds me of some of Noriega's thugs,* she thought. *Some good looks and that's about it. Easily swayed by a quick buck and not too intelligent. A slime ball.* When the waiter left with their order, she continued.

"Drefan, I understand you sell gold jewelry on the side," she said as she looked at his Rolex.

"Yes, necklaces, bracelets, rings, pendants and a few custom pieces." He took a tissue paper from his pants pocket and laid it on the table. He gently unfolded it to expose a long ridge of gold chains—bracelets and necklaces. "Eighteen carats. High quality, the best in the world."

"They are beautiful," she said softly. She fondled several of the pieces, allowing her finger to gently drag across the mound, then brush his hand. "Maybe later."

He returned the jewelry to his pocket and continued. She knew his guard was slipping. Maria began to exploit his macho demeanor with her charm and beauty. She suspected him to be the type who liked women, but liked himself more. She allowed his subtle advances, extracting information when she could. The process became easier as the wine filled his head and the testosterone obscured his judgment.

"Colonel Marston said you were interested in paintings."

"Yes, good quality. Oils, watercolors, sketches…I have some friends in the States as well as Central and South America who have asked me to be on the lookout for some pieces. They generally buy all types of things."

"What are they looking for?"

"They're interested in quality. Let's just say Marston's piece is on the low end."

Maria studied his reaction. She had dealt with much sharper dealers than the man seated across from her. Confident her charm was working, she was not about to let up. She brushed his leg with hers and sipped her Campari. The man told her he did, on occasion, come across an Italian family that was selling some of their estate.

"If you can get there first, sometimes you can find some excellent art works," he bragged. "A lot of times the families don't even know what they have."

Maria encouraged him to see what he could come up with. She suggested his girlfriend might help as well, and he confirmed she would.

"Drefan, there is another little matter I hope you can help me with." She lightly touched his hand, watching his reaction as she let her hand linger on his.

"And what would that be?"

"Some works may be a little difficult to get out of Italy, since permission from the Italian government is probably going to be required for what we are talking about. When my contacts make a deal, they generally don't like to wait. Can you help me with this? I'll make it worth your while."

"Maybe."

Maria felt her strategy was working and didn't want to press any harder. She sensed that most everything he had told her was a lie, part of his well-rehearsed cover story. Moving too fast now could frighten him off or make him suspicious. She was satisfied that she had achieved her objective. She eased off the subject through the remainder of the meal. Confident that her charm had done the trick, she toned it down so she wouldn't have to fight him off after dinner.

Unexpectedly, Brainard said he had to return to Portogruaro and he apologized for his early departure. His sudden announcement was a surprise and a relief. Maria was thankful that she wasn't forced to refuse his company in her room. As they were leaving the dining room, he assured her he could arrange a meeting with the uncle the next morning. He promised to call when it was set.

Maria listened to Dix's phone message when she got back to her room. Looking at her watch, she felt it was too late to call him back. She smiled at the thought of him. She also thought of the last few hours with the sergeant. The role she played disgusted her. She had stooped to a level that she thought she had buried in Panama and never wanted to revisit. She drew a hot bath to relax and wash away the feeling that came with the evening. The tub was deep and the water was warm. Exactly what she needed before going to bed.

15

Struggling, fighting and pushing, Dix woke and sat upright in bed. He was drenched in sweat and panting heavily. Anxiety covered him like a shroud. He was disoriented, confused by what he was remembering and what his eyes were telling him. He felt vulnerable—not in control and in some foreign place. He wiped his face with both hands, slowly bringing them down his face, feeling the stubble of his beard scratch against his palms. His left hand crossed the one-inch scar on his cheek. He traced it with his forefinger. *Vietnam. What made me dream of Vietnam?*

His mind clearing, he read the numbers on the clock. It was 3:37 in the morning. *What's that stench?* he thought as his mind brought him back to reality and the hotel room. A pungent odor filled his nostrils. It was a foul odor mixed with smoke.

Stepping to the window he saw smoke, illuminated by the bright moon, drifting upward from the valley below. An amber glow emanated from the town. *Some poor soul's barn must be burning,* he thought. He heard fire engine sirens in the distance.

Now awake, he found his way into the bathroom. He

splashed cold water on his face and dried it with the soft white towel hanging by the sink. Dix filled a glass with water and slowly drank its contents. He returned to the comfort of the feather-tick bed and, without knowing when, fell asleep.

Dix poured himself a cup of coffee before he sat at the table in the dining room. As he took a sip, the waitress appeared from around the corner and stepped to his table. They exchanged morning greetings and light conversation. She aroused his interest when she gave him sympathy for not being able to get his pillows.

"What do you mean?" Dix asked, puzzled by her comment.

"The Chlodwigs' shop, it burned last night."

"What?"

"Ja, their shop is gone."

"I'll be back later!" he said, getting up and leaving the dining room.

Dix parked the Volvo in a spot on the far side of the piazza with the two clock towers. A fire truck was parked near the entrance to the street leading to the Chlodwigs' shop. A large hose snaked from a fire hydrant on the corner of the piazza to the red truck. Several other hoses emerged from the other side like giant tentacles. Two police cars, with their blue lights flashing, blocked either end of the street and protected the fire engine. Several policemen were controlling the crowd. An ambulance was parked near the fire truck. A stream of water flowed alongside the curb, disappearing into a drain down the block. The smell of the recently doused and partially smoldering building filled the air. The stench of scorched, burnt and wet feathers, combined with that of the building, was overpoweringly putrid.

Dix took a deep breath and watched the gathering crowd, looking for anything or anyone suspicious. He entered the bar on the corner and ordered a caffè màcchiato and began eavesdropping to try and find out what happened. The chatter went from who saw it first, to how big the fire was, to how it was bound to happen. Dix took his time, listening to the different stories and watching the people outside. News spread through the mill of people that the bodies of Rodrik and Etta had been recovered from the rubble. The news dumbfounded Dix.

Reaching for his cup, Dix noticed an ashtray. In the middle of the white plastic container, partly obscured by the gray ash and crumpled cigarette butts, was a gum wrapper. It was the same type of wrapper, folded the same way that he had seen the blond-headed man fold his gum wrapper at the reception in Budapest. The gum had been removed; the foil refolded and inserted back into the yellow wrapper, then it was folded in half.

His muscles tensed. *He's here!* Dix thought. *What's he doing here? Is he the son-of-a-bitch that's responsible for the killings? Is he the only one?* He looked around the bar, but no one looked familiar. Everyone was talking in a fast tempo with their hands beneath a cloud of cigarette smoke. Dix approached the door and searched for him in the crowd. He stepped outside and strained to catch a glimpse of the man, but there was no sign of him. Meandering through the crowd, Dix made his way to the barricade about thirty meters from the charred remains of the building.

He scanned the crowd along the barricade, but saw no one familiar. Dix cautiously approached a fireman and a policeman who were talking next to the barricade.

"Signore, were the bodies of Rodrik and Etta Chlodwig the only ones in the building?"

The fireman turned and studied Dix for an instant, then replied, "Only those two. No one else was in the building."

The deaths of Rodrik and Etta angered Dix. *What was worth killing them for?* Dix thought, struggling to keep his emotions under control. *Whatever is behind all this may have died with them. Ingel's package is probably among the ashes in the building.*

With no other leads and no package, Dix's only recourse was to find the blond-headed man. He had to be the connection. Dix worked his way back through the crowd, scrutinizing each person along the way. When he was ten meters from the bar, he saw the top of a man's blond head out of the corner of his eye. *It's him!* Dix thought. *You bastard!* Pushing against the crowd, Dix zigzagged a path toward him, but the blond-headed man disappeared. Dix stopped to methodically scan the square in front of him, but it was useless. The man had vanished. At an impasse, Dix made his way back to the car in order to figure out what to do next.

He returned to the hotel. *Only Rodrik's and Etta's bodies were found in the burned out building,* Dix thought. *Truda, if she is still alive, is frightened and hiding somewhere. I've got to find her; maybe she can provide some answers.*

Dix unlocked his room and headed straight for the phone. He sat on the bed and pulled the phone book from the nightstand drawer. As he flipped it open, a knock at the door startled him. He stepped to the closet to retrieve the Beretta from his overnight bag. Clasping the automatic in his hand, he placed it behind him and slowly opened the door.

A slim and attractive woman in her early twenties, wearing a large, floppy hat, stood in the doorway. Large round sunglasses concealed her eyes, and gold hoops dangled from her ears. Clutched in her hands was a small pillow.

He stood motionless. "Truda," Dix said. "Come in. Are you all right?"

Dix stepped aside so she could enter. He peered down the hall and into the stairwell to ensure she was not followed. He closed the door and flipped the latch. Truda removed her sunglasses, revealing red, swollen eyes.

"They're dead," she said, trembling slightly, struggling to maintain her composure.

"I know. I just came from town. I am so sorry...."

"My father told me to bring this to you." She handed him the pillow and replaced her sunglasses as she fought back the tears. "I must go."

"Where are you going? You could be in danger too."

"Papa told me if anything ever happened to him, I was to go to Switzerland immediately."

"Switzerland? But you—"

"Papa gave me the pillow late last night," she said. "He told me to deliver it before I went to work. When I found out what happened, I did as Papa told me and now I must follow his instructions to leave."

Dix watched her struggling with grief and fear, amazed that she was rational enough to make any decisions, let alone leave immediately without taking the time to grieve and bury her parents.

You must go to the Carabinieri," Dix urged.

"No. It isn't safe."

She refused to be any more specific about where she was going other than to Switzerland. Dix tried to give her his phone number and address but she refused. She finally agreed to contact him via the Internet. Dix gave her his e-mail address and had her promise to let him know when she was safe in Switzerland. Granting the promise was the last thing she said to him before she left.

Dix pitched the pillow on the bed, then returned the pistol to the overnight bag. He hoped that Truda would contact him when she reached Switzerland—if she made it that far. Maybe then she could provide more answers. Dix had come for a package but was leaving with a pillow—and no answers.

16

Just as Colonel Marston described him, "a little old weather-beaten man," Maria thought, studying the man who got out of a dilapidated blue Fiat. *Probably the same tattered brown suit and boots he wore for Marston.*

The three met at 9:15 in the morning in the piazza at the front of the Hotel Astoria. Introducing the old man to Maria, Sergeant Brainard backed away and allowed the two to talk. The man was very polite and spoke with a slight Austrian accent. He was animated, talking with his large hands with thick fingers. He smiled and flirted with Maria, telling her how lovely she looked. Occasionally, the old man asked a question and dropped his hands, clasping them in front. When the conversation turned to the real purpose of the meeting, the dialogue became more serious.

Opening the car to expose his inventory, he invited Maria to examine what he had. One by one, he withdrew six paintings—presenting each one with a story and telling her how long it had been in the family. A true salesman. With each painting, he made a grand gesture of wiping the dust from its top, then pointed out the signatures and angled it in the sunlight so as to show off its true beauty. *About the same quality as*

Marston's, she thought as he exhibited the third one.

The quality improved with the fourth painting. An unsigned fleshy nude scene from Greek mythology, dark with age and the surface slightly cracked, still did not arouse Maria's interest. *Probably from the early 1800s,* she thought, remaining cordial but getting bored. By the time he held up the fifth painting, Maria's attention was drifting and she was becoming impatient.

"*Battle of Cadore,* signed by Tiziano Vecellio, circa 1540," the old man boasted, pretending not to know it was the great master, Titian.

"A Titian!" Maria exclaimed, her attention snapping back. She brushed her hair aside and looked closer.

"Si! si," he said with hand gestures and a broad, open smile. "Titian. It was one of my mother-in-law's favorites."

She looked closer, devoting her full attention to the work, but her excitement quickly faded. "It is a nice copy," she said to the man and shot a look at Brainard. "I'm not interested in copies." Her impatience returned. She was not interested in the man's last painting.

He touched her hand and he asked her to look at the last one. When she agreed, although reluctantly, he pulled the final one from the car and started his performance.

The sixth painting was an oil on wood of peasants. Maria's excitement rose as she focused on the small picture in the man's waltzing arms. She grasped his arm and leaned forward to look closer. *It is!* she thought. *It really is a Bruegel!* Although the sun was high in the sky and an Adriatic breeze danced through the piazza, Maria felt a sudden chill. She did not hear his sales pitch. When she snapped back into reality, she realized he was standing quietly with a smile on his face, his hands clasped in front of him expecting a reply.

"This one is very nice. I am not interested in the others,

just this one." She forced a calm, businesslike reply.

The weathered Austrian glanced at Brainard, then at Maria. The negotiating started. Several rounds of poker-playing diplomacy culminated in an acceptable price.

"I will contact Sergeant Brainard after I confer with my client to see if this is acceptable with them. I'm sure it will be sometime tomorrow," she concluded, extending her hand to the man.

The arrangement made, he nodded to the sergeant. Then the two returned the paintings to the Fiat. Maria held the Bruegel, admiring the work until it was time for it to occupy its place with the others. The old man got in the car and pulled onto the street as Maria and Brainard looked on. Maria watched the vehicle meander down the street until it disappeared in the traffic.

She didn't like going through Brainard, but the old farmer kept to his story that he didn't have a phone and his farm was hard to find. In the old man she may have found a link to a Nazi cache. Her next step was to search the records of the art stolen during World War II that was still listed as missing.

Dix stretched out on the bed to relax and think. He held the pillow Truda brought, then tossed it up as if playing catch. Again and again he tossed the pillow into the air, watching it spin upwards, then fall into his hands. The rhythmic process of tossing and catching began to relax his mind so he could think. Making its final spin, a small white feather found its way free from its stitched confines and gently descended. Dix grasped the pillow and watched the feather float toward him. Taking a deep breath, he blew the dancing feather into a swirling tumble. He watched it stabilize and resume an altered course to the floor as he placed the pillow beneath his head.

Startled by the feel of something poking the back of his neck, he sat upright. *Damn!* He thought. *What the hell is that? There's something inside.* Examining the pillow with his hands, gently squeezing it in various places, Dix could not determine what was inside. He took his pocket knife from his trousers and, rotating the pillow to the seam closest to the object inside, gently slit the threads. As the opening grew, the firmly packed feathers began to ooze out until a fountain of white fluff spilled onto the edge of the bed and cascaded to the floor. A corner of a small manila envelope appeared.

Dix pulled the envelope from its hiding place and inspected both sides. He bent up the metal tabs on the flap and slipped it open. He looked inside then dumped the contents into his hand. Two computer disks slid out. Nothing else was inside, no note or instructions. "I'll be damned!" he said to himself. "Rodrik, you son-of-a-bitch! You did it."

It suddenly dawned on Dix that Rodrik had used his business as a front for transportation and storage. Castor, the cave Etta had referred to, was probably the storage place. The items were sewn into the feather pillows and mattresses made by this Tirolean family. Since the family was such a well-respected manufacturer of quality feather goods, their shipments would be able to move easily throughout Europe. The feathers would provide the perfect concealment—they were lightweight and offered protective padding. Some pieces of the puzzle were beginning to come together around the edges—like the border of a jigsaw puzzle—but not enough at the center to give Dix a clear picture. *If Castor was used for storage,* he speculated, *then it must have high security.*

Dix's mind whirled. *Limestone caves are common all over Italy and are used for everything from mushroom farms to wine cellars to commercial storage. The military even used them for ammunition and equipment storage. So it wouldn't be unusual for the Chlodwigs to use* their cave for storage. It wouldn't look out of place if it had a high-security fence like many others.

But what was the nature of this secret operation which required high security—and trafficked in a high-value product worth killing over? Dix considered an international drug cartel. Although possible, it was unlikely since none of the individuals killed fit the profile. *It looks like Ingel's department did have some of the treasures that were supposed to be returned. Is this the Project Orion cover up? How big is it? Who else is involved? Is there more? But who covered it up? It seems to make sense.* If that's it—and it was looking more and more that way—Dix was surprised that some of the people he had known had gotten mixed up in it.

Damn, this reminds me of Panama, Dix thought. *Chasing around the country, picking up bits and pieces looking for a needle in a haystack, people getting killed, going up against a ruthless organization. Now, the same covert high-stakes cat-and-mouse crap. At least we knew what we were looking for in Panama.*

Dix removed the gold coins from his pocket and opened his hand to look at them. He closed his hand and squeezed his fist. Pain shot through his second finger as a blood vein broke beneath the skin. He released his grip and pitched the coins onto the bed. He stared at the coins in amazement. *Damn* he thought. *That's it. The seven gold coins. I can't believe I couldn't see it before. It's not just gold coins; the gold is for "G" and the seven coins for "7." The G-7. That's what they were trying to tell me! It's the G-7, or they are using the G-7 as their cover. An organization inside the G-7.*

These are what I have come for, he thought as he picked up the disks. What ever the disks contained, he figured it had to be the information Ingel wanted him to get to Munich. He deposited the disks and coins in the envelope, placed the envelope in his overnight bag, and concealed it among his clothes and toiletry items.

Many people had died for the information on the disks. Dix didn't plan to be one of them. Eager to return home and examine the disks, he determined to make safety the top priority for now.

17

Maria, still feeling the euphoria brought on by actually holding one of Bruegel's paintings, sipped her cappuccino. Then she glanced at the clock on the wall of the bar and realized that the city library would be open in a few minutes.

Maria spent the next hour and a half in the library researching records and books on Pieter Bruegel's work. Stacks of books and files grew around her as she examined the contents of each. Occasionally she got up and retrieved an additional reference book from the shelf. Making notes and examining the pictures and descriptions of his work, she wasn't finding the painting the old man had showed her. She leaned back in the smooth oak chair to ponder where to look next.

"Trouble, signora?" the small gray-haired librarian asked, her hands on her hip and her head cocked to the side.

"Si! I'm researching the work of Pieter Bruegel. I can't find what I'm looking for," Maria replied over the stack of books as she leaned forward and brushed her hair back.

"I'll search the files in the repository for you," the librarian replied.

Signore Afferi! Maria thought, then replied, "Grazie, signora. I'll be back in a little while."

Occupying an orderly office with two large windows in a back corner of the museum, Signore Afferi looked up as Maria tapped on his door.

"Signora! Come stai?" Afferi came to life and greeted her with a bright smile.

"I have been fine. And you?"

"Bene! How may I help you my dear?"

"Signore Afferi, I've been at the library researching Bruegel."

"Please sit down, Maria," he urged as he turned a chair toward her. "Now, what are you trying to find out about Bruegel?"

"I saw a Bruegel, an oil on wood. When I tried to look it up in the library, I couldn't find it."

"Where did you see this painting?"

"I met an old man who was selling off some of the belongings of his mother-in-law's estate—"

"Signora, are you sure it was a Bruegel and not a copy? There have been lots of forgeries appearing lately."

"I'm quite sure."

As they continued to talk, Afferi became more and more energized. She asked question after question until he pulled a reference book from the shelf, opened it and placed it in her lap. "See if you can find it in here."

She searched without success, then closed the book and placed it on his desk. He quietly pulled out another. Again, without success. Afferi showed her books, records and catalogued pictures of the works, many of which she had already seen in the library. Finally, he retrieved a bulging file and a tattered binder and laid them on the desk. Then he opened a bottle of wine. He sat two glasses on the table and filled them.

"It's been a long time since I've looked in these files," he said nostalgically. "This is special. Many memories are here."

Maria smiled and lifted the glass and said, "Saluté!" then sipped her wine.

"Saluté!" he replied. "You have given me the opportunity today to enjoy the company of a beautiful woman, share good wine and revisit some exciting times in art. I am an old man. Your company gives me great joy."

"Thank you, Signore Afferi, the pleasure is mine." Although anxious to find out about the painting, she knew to be patient. Afferi would eventually give her what she wanted. She also knew of his past and he had given her many tidbits of information plus a few stories for her coffee-table book.

"Maria, my dear, call me Salvatore."

"Salvatore it is," she replied and gestured a salute with her glass. Then she sipped in unison with him.

"I'd like to tell you a story, a true story that happened during the final months of the war," he said as he leaned back in his wooden chair. "It's a crime actually, committed by a Nazi major against the deteriorating Nazi regime. The war has been over for a long time and many of the things that happened have been forgotten. People aren't interested anymore. It's been a long time since I've had a chance to share it with anyone."

"I'd like to hear it, Salvatore."

The old man began to tell her the story of an SS major, Ulrich Volker Fabian, as the Allies were closing in on Germany and the Americans were about to reach the salt mines at Alt Aussee. Maria was enchanted. His tale held her spellbound for almost half an hour. He showed her pictures, documents and drawings as he told his story to prove the validity of the fantastic tale.

He told her that no one really knew how much or what Fabian took except for the last day that he was seen. With those words, Afferi opened another folder and handed her a piece of paper, yellow with age, with Nazi letterhead at the top. It was a brief description of everything that the Nazis believed the major took on May 3, 1945, when he left the Lauffen Mine. Signore Afferi withdrew a sheaf of papers.

"Here is a complete list with photographs of what that letter describes. It is signed by the director of the mines at Alt Aussee, Doktor Pochmuller." He patted the binder as he spoke.

As Maria turned the pages of photographs, she occasionally paused to examine one. After a while her eyes fixed on an unsigned fleshy nude scene from Greek mythology, dark with age and with a slightly cracked surface. She stopped and sat upright. *That's the same painting the old man had in his Fiat,* Maria thought.

"Yes, my dear?" Salvatore inquired.

Not wanting to tell him she hesitated and forced herself to smile. "Oh! Nothing. It is just difficult to grasp the amount of treasures he got away with." She returned her eyes to the binder and pretended to focus on the page.

"Yes it is difficult. But back then, compared to the total amount of stolen treasures, what he took was nothing."

Turning another page, she recognized another painting. *Venus!* she thought, not hearing Afferi's comment. *That's the one I saw hanging in Ida Kohne's house. My god! What have I found?*

She had discovered in Afferi's records the Titian oil on canvas that she thought was so out of pace in the Kohne's home. *Relax,* she thought as she fought to suppress her excitement. *Calm down.*

Maria paused before viewing more pages of photographs. When at last she reached the Breugels, she continued with guarded anticipation. She turned page after page until her eyes fell on the same oil on wood of peasants that she had agreed to buy from the old Austrian. *That one too!* she thought, forcing herself to remain composed. *That old farmer must have the major's loot. This is incredible! But how did he get it?*

Salvatore told her that he went with Rodolfo Siviero to interview General Ernst Kaltenbrunner after his capture. During the interview, he told her, the general informed them of the hideouts for the high-ranking Nazis in the South Tirol. Major Fabian, who had been in charge of security at Alt Aussee, was responsible for setting up the hideouts and had escorted the treasures to them. The treasures were intended to provide a new beginning—the Fourth Reich. Fabian kept a journal, as most of the officers did, and probably documented his exploits.

"About a week after the Americans captured Alt Aussee, a charred body was identified as Major Fabian," Salvatore said. "I never believed it and I don't think Siviero really did either. But the American Army did."

"Why didn't you believe it?"

"Fabian was smart and clever. Kaltenbrunner had his hands full and the Americans were closing in on them. He had to trust Fabian. But Fabian saw that the war was over and I believe to this day that Fabian planned his retirement months in advance and staged his own death. He was setting up hideouts. He had the resources and the opportunity, and I believe he took advantage of that opportunity."

"That's fantastic!"

"Yes, it is."

"What happened to his journal?"

"Si, davvero, his journal! It was never found. Find it and you will find his caches and the stolen loot."

"I've heard stories over the years of discovered Nazi caches. I know some of them are false, but do you think some of the stories could possibly be true?" Maria asked.

"It makes for good storytelling, doesn't it? Yes, I think some of the stories are true. I know of several over the years that were true and the treasures were returned. I'm sure there were some caches that have been found but were never reported, and the treasures were sold on the black market. I believe, and a few others agreed with me," Salvatore continued, "that Major Fabian was responsible for much of the still missing items that were recorded as entering the mines at Alt Aussee."

"Do you think he was responsible for the disappearance of the Amber Room?"

"Si, could be. In a shroud of secrecy Major Fabian brought it to Alt Aussee from Königsberg in early October 1944. There is no record of it after that," he told her. "It sounds like Fabian—I believe it is something he would have taken."

Salvatore couldn't prove any of what he told her, he admitted. All he had to go on was circumstantial evidence and what he had learned after the war and his research over the years. He believed that everyone was in too big of a hurry to put the war behind them.

Flipping through one of the last binders, Maria gasped when she saw an oil on canvas of a landscape with a castle. It was a photograph of the same painting in Sonja Abramovych's photograph and of the painting the Marstons had recently purchased.

"What is it, Maria?" Salvatore asked.

"I've seen this painting. I know who it belongs to."

"I'll make you some copies of my documents so you can report it to the authorities. You will make someone very happy and someone else very mad."

"I know. The ones that I am going to make mad are acquaintances."

"Italy's Art Theft Investigation team is very good and will

use discretion. Your acquaintances will never know you reported it."

"Good. Would you please make copies of the *Venus* documents that are in the other binder?"

Salvatore paused and studied her. "My dear, whatever you have stumbled onto must be reported and you must get away from it. This smells of great danger."

"I know."

Concluding her meeting with Salvatore, Maria couldn't believe her good luck. The files he had made it clear that the two paintings the farmer had shown her the day before were part of what Major Fabian took. What she couldn't figure out was how *Venus* got into the Kohnes' hands. She was also convinced that there must be more. Either the farmer or the American sergeant had discovered Fabian's cache or they worked for someone who had. She was desperate to know.

Maria's first impulse was to notify the Art Theft Investigation team immediately about Sonja Abramovych's painting. But she wanted to find out more about the other paintings prior to turning that information over to the authorities. On further thought, she realized that as soon as she provided them with information on the other paintings, the authorities would track Marston's painting to the old Austrian man and Sergeant Brainard. For the time being, she decided it was best not to tell them anything.

Maria stopped by the library to thank the librarian, and politely perused the few documents that the petite woman produced. They added very little to what Signore Afferi had already revealed. However, two items in one of the folders from the repository did capture her attention—maps of the mines at Alt Aussee and Lauffen that were attached as exhibits to official tribunal documents. Both had scribble marks on them, indicating which chambers were full of treasures and a brief summary of the contents. Dr. Pochmuller's name was in the upper right-hand corner of each. She made a copy of the maps, thanked the woman for her assistance and returned to her hotel.

Back at the hotel, Maria listened to the phone message that Dix had left for her. She smiled as she heard his voice, then started to feel guilty for what she was planning. *If I'm right, and I'm certain I am, I need evidence,* she thought.

Maria took a deep breath, then lifted the receiver and called Sergeant Brainard. Using her charm, she enticed him to dinner by expressing a desire to purchase a gold necklace.

She relaxed for a while, then got up to get dressed. Just before leaving to meet Brainard, she decided to call Dix. She needed the sound of his voice and his strength to get her through the evening. He had been home only a few minutes when she reached him. He told her about what had happened in Bressanone and that he was just going to read the first disk when she called. She thought she would be back the next day, she told him, and would call when she knew for sure. Then she told him about her meeting with Signore Afferi.

"The painting in Ida Kohne's house, I saw it in his records. It was taken and recorded as lost during the war. I also saw in the records the painting the Marstons recently purchased."

"They were all mixed up with something that had to do with missing art from the war and have been killed over it. I'll go through these disks and hopefully will know more when you get here tomorrow." Dix, more interested in his accomplishment than Maria's, wasn't really listening to her.

Maria considered telling Dix about her plan but decided not. He told her what she needed to hear, and she replied, "I love you, too." She replaced the receiver, took a deep breath and slowly exhaled to regain control of her emotions.

18

Brainard was already seated when Maria entered the main dining room of the Hotel Astoria. She wore a low-cut white silk dress. She walked slowly and confidently toward the table, a hint of a lace bra showing beneath the sheer fabric. The sleeveless dress, low in the back and cinched at the waist, emphasized her figure. Her shapely tanned legs were bare and she wore open-toe high-heeled sandals. Delicate gold hoop earrings adorned her ears.

Brainard stood as she approached. Her beauty brightened his corner of the room. The waiter, escorting Maria, pulled out her chair and pushed it forward as she sat. "May I bring you an aperitivo?" he asked.

"A Campari please," Maria replied.

"Wine for me, red," Brainard said.

The waiter bowed slightly, then left.

The two exchanged small talk for several minutes. Maria expressed her excitement again about the painting. "I haven't been able to reach my friend in the United States yet," she lied.

He just smiled. "That's fine, I understand. I know that it sometimes takes a while."

She guided the conversation to the gold jewelry he sold. He withdrew the tissue paper from his pocket, laid it on the table and started to unfold one side. She brushed his hand with hers as she unfolded the other side to expose a shiny mound of gold. She traced the mound in a provocative way, selected a long length of gold chain, held it up for examination, then replaced it. She repeated the process several times. Finally, she selected a simple, yet elegant necklace, very expensive and attention grabbing.

"I want to wear it. Would you fasten it for me?" she asked, looking into his eyes.

Brainard stood and stepped behind her chair. He leaned over, taking in her light, fresh scent. Grasping each end of the necklace, he fastened the clasp. Then he returned to his seat and eyed the chain resting gently around her neck. He looked at the front opening of her dress which revealed an enticing portion of her breasts. He sat silently as she withdrew cash from her purse and placed it into his hand, holding the money momentarily. They hadn't even discussed price.

Throughout the meal she continued to exert her charm. The more she touched and flirted with him, the more wine he seemed to drink. She had been adding mineral water to her wine ever since starting the meal. She intended to stay in control. As dessert was served, she rubbed his leg with her foot several times. She sipped her coffee and allowed her hand to brush his. The third time he gently took her hand. *I know how to work you,* she thought, knowing the time was right for her next move.

"Expensive old masterpieces turn me on," she said softly as she leaned forward to expose her breasts in the lace bra. By the expression on his face, she knew she had him.

"I've something I'd like to show you," Brainard said. "It's old and beautiful. It's in an office not far from here. Would you like to go?"

This is it. Just as I suspected, she thought.

"Yes," she whispered.

The headlights of Brainard's car reflected off the buildings as they drove down the darkened side streets of Udine. He turned into a parking lot in front of a nondescript modern building in a commercial district. He stopped the car in front of the building. High-pressure sodium lights illuminated the area. Six curved marble steps led up to the front door.

They got out and Maria stood beside him, watching his every move as he inserted the key into the outer door. He turned the key clockwise and it stopped with a click. Opening the outer door for her, he followed and allowed it to close prior to disarming the alarm. She watched as he entered the code and memorized its sequence. When the green light flashed on, Brainard turned the key counterclockwise until it stopped after the second click. He opened this second door for her to enter the office. As he stepped in, he turned on the light to reveal an office tastefully furnished with two desks and a white leather couch.

Brainard laid the keys on the desk out of habit. He excused himself and left the room. As soon as he disappeared, Maria took a stick of gum out of her purse and carefully unwrapped it. Holding the gum in her palm, she pressed the key Brainard had used into the gum to make an imprint of the key—a skill she learned in Panama as the leader of the resistance. She returned the gum to the wrapper and placed it into her purse. She carefully laid the keys back on the desk. She pulled on the center drawer and, to her surprise, it slid open. Pens, pencils, scissors, paper clips and a ruler. She closed the drawer and opened the top right drawer. She saw a row of bank statements and a tape dispenser. She closed that drawer when she saw the door open.

She watched him as he unlocked the door across the room. He used the same key he had used to open the front door. "I'll be right back," he said before vanishing behind the door.

Maria opened the top right drawer again and read the name of the bank on the statements—Banca Nazionale Del Lavoro. She closed the top drawer and opened the one underneath. A black book at the back caught her eye. She took out the book and opened the back cover to flip through the pages. Noticing a pocket on the inside back cover, she opened the flap and withdrew a small envelope. A key was inside. Hearing Brainard's steps, she quickly returned the book to the drawer, dropping the key into her purse.

Brainard entered with an easel in one hand and what looked to be a covered picture frame in the other. He set the frame on the easel and removed the cover.

She sat motionless, astonished, then stood slowly and moved closer.

"It's beautiful!"

"It's a section of a panel from the Amber Room," he said ceremoniously with his eyes fixed on her.

"I could never have imagined it would be so beautiful… such detail in the carving. The silver foil reflects the light into the amber; it's magnificent. The old photographs don't do justice to the detail of the workmanship. It is simply gorgeous. This is unbelievable!"

"I thought you'd like it."

"Where did you get it? People have been looking for the Amber Room since the war."

"My boss has connections."

She became lost in the ecstasy of the moment. *It can't be,* she thought. *A panel from the Amber Room, here? Like this? Im-*

possible. But it is and it's real. It does exist and I'm looking at a piece of it!

Slowly fear began to replace her euphoria. She struggled, forcing herself to remain calm and recapture her self-discipline. *This isn't just penny ante black market. This is serious shit! Don't blow it!*

"This really excites me, Drefan," she said as she moved closer to him.

He embraced her, drawing her close. She leaned into him.

"Let's go back to my hotel, Drefan," she whispered into his ear. Unsure whether she could go through with her plan, she tried to remain calm.

"You're trembling," he said.

"It's the excitement," she lied.

"Let me cover this up."

Shit! Maria thought. *The key. He's not going to put the panel back.* She watched him replace the fitted cover. Maria picked up her purse as he guided her out of the office and turned off the light. She memorized his movements as he locked the door, activated the alarm and then locked the outer door.

She caught sight of the office hours painted on the glass. *I hope those hours are right,* she thought, noting the nine o'clock opening time.

As he escorted her to the car, Drefan placed his arm around her and she leaned into him. He opened her door and she got in. As she watched him walk around the front of the car, she inserted her hand into her purse and felt the small envelope with the key, then checked the stick of gum. *The goddamn key!* Maria thought. *Not part of the plan.*

Brainard steered the car out of the parking lot and onto the street. He pushed a button on the stereo, switching from the local pop station to a jazz station, then clasped Maria's hand. She looked at him and forced a seductive smile, then turned back to watch the road.

They had traveled almost four blocks when she said, "Drefan, please pull over."

"Why?" he asked. "What's the matter?" He looked at her, glanced back at the road and, then back to her.

Maria watched as the car began to slow and approach another street light. As the street light passed by her window she rolled down the window. "Please, stop. I need some air."

"Why? What's the matter?"

"I'm going to be sick. Please pull over. Now!"

The car rolled to a stop. She sprang out and faced away from the car. She bent forward and pulled her hair behind her ear, then held her necklace and the top of her dress close to her body. She opened her mouth and inserted two fingers of her right hand into her mouth and down her throat. She gagged and her body convulsed. Once more, she inserted her fingers. Again, she gagged and her body convulsed. Her stomach tensed and the liquefied, acidic contents filled the back of her throat. She felt it, then tasted the foul liquid. Her body took control and purged her throat, the contents splattering on the ground.

Brainard got out of the car and walked to her. The revolting smell penetrated the night air. Brainard hesitated, then handed her his handkerchief. Maria took it and wiped her mouth.

"I'm sorry, Drefan. I guess it was the combination of too much excitement and too much wine." Her face flushed, she made sure he could see the tears in her eyes.

"Are you all right?" he asked.

"I'll be fine. I just need some water and to lie down for a while."

Maria knew she had succeeded. She knew that the sight of a woman vomiting would repel any man. She couldn't just go through the motions, she had to vomit. The bad breath caused by the caustic contents of her stomach only guaranteed her success.

"I'm sorry, please take me to the hotel. I'm sorry. I'll make it up to you, Drefan." Maria spoke in a soft voice, Making sure that he got a whiff of her breath. *The thought of going to bed with him is enough to make me vomit!* she thought as she got into the car.

19

Seated in front of his computer, Dix inserted the disks and clicked on the menu bar to open the files. A window popped up requesting the password. He took a guess and typed the word *Pollux*. He breathed a sigh of relief as the window disappeared and a list of files appeared on the screen. Dix clicked on the first file labeled "Background: Europe." It gave a synopsis of the Third Reich's aggressive program to loot Europe of its art. "The program, known as the Einsatzstab Reichsleiter Rosenberg (ERR), was headed by Alfred Rosenberg and used the mountain Castle of Neuschwanstein as his headquarters and main storehouse," Dix read. "The objective of EER was simply to loot Europe's art. The Führer's plan for the EER was to take possession of the best art and establish the Third Reich's cultural capital at Linz, Austria."

This introductory file outlined the contents of the disks and referred to various other files. It focused on the last year of World War II in Europe and was taken from the paper files of SS Intelligence Chief, General Ernst Kaltenbrunner. It summarized the operations carried out during the last year of the war for the survival of high-ranking Nazis and the preparations for the Fourth Reich.

Dix jumped from file to file examining the contents. The files described locations and operations in Europe, Paraguay and Argentina with the same detail. One contained maps of the salt mines at Alt Aussee and Lauffen. Another described the operation to reopen the mines. Locations inside the mines containing the treasures were depicted on the maps. Still another file showed treasure routes from Italy, with temporary storage sites, through the Brenner Pass from Verona north to Bolzano and on through the pass. The other route was from Padova to Mestre to Portogruaro to Udine then to Salzburg.

Dix opened a smaller file and read the heading: Reichsmarschall Hermann Wilhelm Goering's Personal Selections. It outlined what the mines shipped to Goering's rural palace in Karinhall and Bertchtesgaden. The file noted his visits to the mines and how he, at first, made his choices. He took the best of the modern art, which Hitler disliked. The document stated that Goering recognized an international market for the "degenerate" art. Toward the close of the war Goering became more aggressive and made selections before Hitler.

The information on these disks is what people are willing to kill for, Dix thought. If the information is correct, I'm holding the secret to many unknown caches.

So captivated was Dix by this information that it was after midnight before he realized that he hadn't eaten since lunch. Taking a break, he headed into the kitchen and attacked the refrigerator. The light illuminated the various fruits and vegetables of almost every color of the rainbow as he opened the drawers. Sliced ham, cheese and salami were in the top drawer. A dozen eggs, still in the carton lay on the second shelf, guarded by an assortment of sealed, plastic containers of leftovers. Various bottles and jars filled the doors and an additional two shelves. Milk and an assortment of juices filled the entire lower left side. The freezer bulged with packages of pork, fish, chicken,

Italian sausages, frozen french fries, peas, carrots and those ubiquitous mystery packages, leaving barely enough room for the ice trays. It seemed as though the bloated appliance scarcely had room for the light.

Stooping, resting his left hand on the door and sorting through the subject matter before him, Dix thought, *Maria makes it look so easy. How does she create meals out of all this stuff? I wonder what she had for dinner?* He studied and fingered the containers again. He made his decision. "Peanut butter it is!" he said to himself as he retrieved the grape jelly from the door. He made the sandwich, thick with the crunchy, brown spread and poured a glass of milk.

Setting his dinner on the table, he recalled one of his reference books and one that Maria had searched recently. Both books contained information on the looting of treasures during World War II. He pulled the books from the shelf and returned to the table, probing their contents as he ate. *Damn! That's a good sandwich,* he thought as he took his first bite. *Nothing can beat a sandwich like this.* He washed it down with milk.

Reviewing the information on Monuments, Fine Arts and Archives (MFA&A) of the U.S. Army during the war, Dix read that most of the caches were recovered. He read the accounts of the 3rd Army when they captured the mines at Lauffen and Alt Aussee, Bertchtesgaden and the Castle of Neuschwanstein. The book contained numerous pictures of recaptured treasures and described the magnitude of Goering's collection at Karinhall. Most of the pictures showed U. S. soldiers inspecting paintings, sculptures, chests of jewels, tapestries, and stacks of gold bullion and coins.

Pausing to lick the peanut butter oozing from the bottom of his sandwich, he thought of Maria and smiled. *Dix, don't do that! she'd say, then slap at my arm.* Wiping his hands, he opened Maria's book and found information about the Art Looting

Investigation Unit of the U.S. Office of Strategic Services (OSS). He came across the line, "The unit published a comprehensive account of the looting of treasures by the Third Reich, their concealment and subsequent restitution." He sat back with his mouth full of sandwich and thought, *It looks like they were trying to put the lid on this. They closed the books on it and tried to entomb it in the bureaucracy.*

He finished his sandwich and milk and returned to his computer for a final look before giving in to his need for rest. As he switched disks in the drive, he yawned and reviewed the long day, starting with Truda's knock on the door. He reflected on the deaths of his friends and the Chlodwigs. Somehow they had become involved with a ruthless organization that was profiting from the atrocities caused by the Nazis. Their only way out was death. It looked as though this organization would stop at nothing; it would kill anyone in its way. He hadn't yet looked at the subdirectory on the second disk. The title "Hamilton" had not piqued his interest. Ready now to continue his investigation, he opened the file and began to read.

An untitled introductory file contained a summation of actions of U.S. Army Captain Robert Hamilton of the Art Looting Investigation Unit (ALIU), code named "Project Orion," of the OSS's Counterintelligence Branch (X-2). Hamilton was in charge of Project Orion and had signed the documents that all treasures at the mines had been repatriated or restitution made. Orion's final report, however, omitted a number of caches that Hamilton knew about. Hamilton and a man named Schmidt formed an organization called Pegasus. This organization had kept secret the omitted caches and was either selling or trading the treasures they contained.

The untitled file had no letterhead or date and seemed as if it was an addendum to the other documents. It contained detailed descriptions about the hideouts, locations, who was taking care of the sites and the Nazi Underground network for the area around the south Tirol. An inventory of gold and silver bullion plus precious stones and art works was listed for each cache.

Each site was named after one of the celestial bodies. Dix scanned the list of code names: Altair, Big Dog, Pluto, Bear, Lynx, Wolf, Algol, Alcor, The Twins, and then Pollux, and Castor. *How could so many sites be kept secret after the war? They must have held a tremendous fortune.*

The last file in the subdirectory contained an account of Major Fabian's actions on May 3, 1945, and the subsequent investigation. There was also a copy of a report by the U.S. Army, dated two weeks after the May 3, 1945 report, about the circumstances surrounding the death of this same major. This report included a complete list of the officer's personal effects found in his quarters as well as a list of what was found with the charred body. All items were signed by the investigating officer and reviewed by General Kaltenbrunner. There also was an investigation of the disappearance of Fräulein Griselda von Englehoven, the second Secretary to SS Intelligence Chief, General Ernst Kaltenbrunner. The report said, "The secretary was last seen on April 30, 1945. No trace of her was ever found. Her personal belongings were in her apartment and inventoried."

Dix leaned back in his chair and stretched. The events of the last twenty-four hours had completely exhausted him, and he was finding it difficult to concentrate. The best plan of action for the moment, he decided, was to get some rest. He would look at the files again tomorrow.

20

An insistent ringing roused Dix from a deep sleep. Glancing at the clock, registering the numbers 7:31, Dix picked up the phone expecting to hear Maria. The chipper female voice on the other end was familiar, but it was not Maria's.

"Dix, it's Francesca Martin," the voice said.

"Francesca!" he replied, her name jolting him fully conscious. "Oh! Francesca, I had a late night last night."

"Sorry to wake you, but what the hell have you gotten yourself mixed up in? My contact at the G-7 office was pretty tight-lipped when I mentioned your name."

"Beats the hell out of me! But I'm going to find out."

"What I found out is pretty limited...." Francesca said. "Dix, you're being accused of killing some of their people and stealing classified G-7 documents."

"That's a lie—it's a setup!" Dix protested, more to himself than to her. "They want to frame me for what they did. If I get killed, all the better for them."

"What do you mean?" she asked.

"What the hell? I've got to get out of here! Francesca, I haven't killed anyone, nor have I stolen documents—but I've got a pretty good idea who did. I want you to find out all you can about what happened during the final days of World War II and the art treasures that the Nazis stole, especially, the art at the salt mines and General Kaltenbrunner."

"Salt mines? General Kaltenbrunner and the Nazis? Dix, are you awake?"

"I'm talking about the salt mines at Alt Aussee and Lauffen where the Nazis stashed the treasures they stole. Kaltenbrunner was the SS intelligence chief and his office was at Alt Aussee. During the last year of the war, he was in charge of the operations to prepare for the Fourth Reich."

"Okay, got it."

"Also, research everything on the Monuments, Fine Arts and Archives of the U.S. Army from about May 1945 on and the Art Looting Investigation Unit of the U.S. Office of Strategic Studies from September 1945 on. See what you can find out about Robert Hamilton."

Francesca agreed to his request and confirmed that she was still going to the Munich Conference.

"Francesca, don't let anyone know what you are doing or that you talked to me."

"Okay, but this is already getting risky."

"I'll call you when I get to a safe place," he told her, realizing he couldn't stay home and wait for the Carabinieri to knock on the door.

"I'll dig up all the information I can. Good luck, Dix. And for God's sakes, be careful!"

Francesca's news compounded Dix's problem. The Carabinieri would be on the lookout for him, and that significantly limited his freedom to move about. Dix reached for the phone to call Mariano. *Wait!* Dix thought. *He can't be in on this, but no chances; I'll call him later from a public phone. I've probably got less than twenty four hours, and maybe less than twelve, before the Carabinieri will be knocking at my door.* He hoped Francesca's warning gave him enough lead time to stay ahead of them and put the remaining pieces of the puzzle together.

Dix decided to call Maria, thinking that he would drive to Udine and figure out what to do from there. He dialed the number but she didn't answer. Dix left a message for her to call. "Damn it, Maria, where are you?" he said to himself as he stood. "She's probably still at breakfast, making friends with everyone as usual."

Dix headed down to the kitchen, opened the shutters, and peeked out. Seeing nothing unusual, he fastened the shutters. A slight breeze of fresh air carrying the fragrance of flowers entered as he opened the sash. He made a pot of coffee, then turned on CNN. He brought in the newspaper and mail and laid them on the corner of the table. The aroma of coffee permeated the room. He filled a large mug and added cream before sitting down at the table.

The phone still had not rung by the time his coffee was finished. The house was quiet except for the sound from the broadcast. His anxiety increasing, he made a bowl of cereal and poured a glass of orange juice. He alternated between eating cereal, glancing at the clock, and reading pieces of mail. Occasionally the headlines on the news caught his attention. When the mail was finished, he read the paper. Finally, unable to wait any longer for Maria to call, he headed for the bathroom to shower and shave. He needed to leave the house as soon as possible.

21

Maria could barely restrain her eagerness to investigate the contents of the safe deposit box. She planned to be at the Banca Nazionale Del Lavoro when it opened. Sipping caffelatte, she was anxiously waiting for a key to be made of the impression she had taken the previous evening. That key would gain access to the building where she and Brainard had gone. She would go to the bank and then take a taxi to the building where she would return the safe deposit key—or at least what she hoped was the safe deposit key—before anyone discovered it was missing.

The minutes dragged. She finished the caffelatte then had a traditional breakfast of roll with butter, marmalade and juice as she waited for the key to be made. She perused the morning paper and ordered another caffelatte, all the while visualizing what she was going to do at the bank.

Approaching the bank, Maria scanned the area, and looked for signs of trouble. Several people formed a line, waiting for the doors to open. She ascended the steps and took her place with them. *So far so good,* she thought. She saw no familiar faces as she waited. Within several minutes she heard the distinctive sound of keys rattling against the thick glass door. A young man opened it and stepped aside as the patrons entered.

The clerks had not yet settled into their daily routines and were finishing last-minute preparations for the workday ahead. Maria entered confidently, acting pushy and impatient, like the others. She counted on that approach to add frustration and confusion to get in and out quickly, and avoid much of the bureaucracy. She also knew that a lengthy visit would make her more vulnerable to discovery. She hoped that the clerk in charge of the safe deposit boxes would not be familiar with who usually accessed the boxes. Her scheme, she realized, wasn't foolproof, but she counted on her timing, boldness and aggressive posture.

Maria approached the desk of a young man who had just dropped a stack of papers into his inbox. She removed her oval sunglasses and told him what she wanted. He guided her to the room of steel boxes, took her key and opened number 746. He slid out the large covered tray and took it to the private room as Maria trailed behind. He placed it on the table and reached for the clasp. Maria touched his hand as a signal for him to stop and then thanked him.

He smiled. "Let me know when you are finished." He closed the door behind him, and left her alone.

Maria lifted the clasp and opened the lid. The box contained only a black, leather bound book. The leather was cracked and dry with age. A flaking gold Reich Adler was embossed on the cover. She took the book out and opened it. *A journal,* she thought as she turned the pages. *I think this must be the journal of the Nazi major that Salvatore told me about.* As she flipped through the pages, she realized the importance of the book and the danger it brought. She decided to go back to the seclusion and safety of her hotel room. She summoned the clerk and held the journal close to her as he escorted her back to the room full of other boxes. She thanked him as he returned the key to her, smiled and, using all her discipline, walked confidently out of the bank.

Maria locked the door as she entered her hotel room. Her heart pounded, her mouth still bitter from the adrenaline rush. She sat on the bed. Her hand began to tremble. She had experienced this same kind of fear before, and it reminded her of Panama.

She opened the journal and began to flip through the pages. Only making out a few of the handwritten German words, Maria knew it was talking about the stolen treasures. It was the journal Salvatore told her about. *It's too valuable and too dangerous to get caught with,* she thought. *I know what to do.*

With quivering hands Maria wrapped the journal in brown paper, then called for a special messenger to deliver it to Dix at home. She didn't want to take a chance on anything happening to the journal. Now she had not only the information Mariano had required but also the proof to go with it. She would ask him to go with her to the Art Theft Investigation team to make her report and he could do the rest.

While waiting for the messenger to arrive, Maria returned Dix's call. On the fourth ring the answering machine picked up. She left a message telling Dix that she was sending a very important package by courier and for him to wait for it. She told him her train didn't leave for about two more hours and again emphasized the importance of the package. She said she would call him just before she left and tell him what time to pick her up. Ending the call with her normal "I love you," she hung up the phone.

Maria then dialed Mariano's number. She got the answering machine there too. She left a message stating that she had some information for him and she would call him back later that afternoon. A knock on the door startled her as she hung up the phone. She sprang around and stood motionless.

A young man's voice came from the other side of the door, "Messenger!"

With a sigh of relief, she opened the door slightly and peeked out. Only the messenger was in the hall. Maria gave him instructions along with the package, paid for the delivery and generously tipped the young man.

"Grazie, Signora! You're very kind," he said, impressed with the size of the gratuity. "Be assured, I am very diligent and I will deliver your package very quickly." He handed her the receipt.

Closing the door, Maria smiled and exhaled. She was relieved to have the journal out of her hands and on its way to Dix. Charged with energy, she couldn't just sit in the room for another two hours. It was a beautiful sunny day and the city was filled with nice shops. She decided to go to the piazza.

Strolling past the storefronts, Maria entered a shop whenever something caught her eye. In one shop she tried on a few sun hats. In another she looked at shoes. She finally selected a stylish red pair to try on. The shoes cradled her feet as if they were custom-made. She paid the clerk, then headed back to the hotel.

Opening the door to the room Maria saw the flashing red light on the phone. She dropped the sack containing her new shoes on the bed and sat beside the phone. She lifted the receiver and listened as Dix told her not to leave, that he was coming to Udine to pick her up after the package arrived. He said that he wanted to research some of the old military records at the Italian Caserma in Udine and that he would call her when he was leaving. *That's odd,* she thought. *Why does he want to research the military records here? Still, staying in town another night would be nice,* she thought.

Maria sat at a round white table shaded by a large white umbrella in front of a restaurant on the edge of the piazza. She finished lunch and leisurely had dessert. The dessert was one of her favorites, a dish of lemon gelato with a glass of mineral water. Gradually spooning away the refreshing frozen dessert, she felt as if she was in paradise. Taking another small spoonful, she saw Drefan Brainard approaching her table. She tensed, but remained in control.

"Maria," he said as he slid a chair out and sat beside her, "you're good. I don't know how or when you did it."

"What are you talking about, Drefan?" she replied with caution.

"You took something that doesn't belong to you." He grabbed her arm.

"Sergeant Brainard, please, you're hurting my arm," she said, trying to free his grip.

"We're going to take a little walk."

Brainard squeezed harder, bringing tears to her eyes.

"You're hurting me!" Maria said.

"Quietly come with me or I'll break your fucking neck!"

Forcing her to stand, he dropped several bills on the table to cover the meal and guided her away.

"Where's the book you took from the bank?" he said. "I want that book!"

"You're crazy. I don't know what you're talking about!"

He forced her along the granite sidewalk around a corner to a secluded back street. His left hand was firmly around her arm, his right hand pushing in the small of her back. The advantage was definitely in his favor. They approached a black BMW 735 with someone sitting in the driver's seat.

"You took a safe deposit box key from the desk last night and you went to the bank this morning," he said.

"How could I have taken a key? You were with me the entire time!"

"Except when I left the room to get the panel. I've been to the bank this morning. The clerk said you were there. He described you perfectly."

"Bullshit!" Maria said with as much anger as fear as she turned toward him.

Her sudden, forceful lurch caught him off guard, and he lost his grip on her left arm. Instantly, Maria brought her knee up with full force and thrust it between his legs. Feeling her knee abruptly stop, she knew she had hit the target. Brainard grimaced with pain and fell to his knees. Maria then sprang to a full run. She had not seen the old man get out and walk behind the car. She ran straight toward him. As soon as she reached him, he grabbed her hair with his left hand and stopped her in midstride. He followed up with his right hand, cold cocking her.

The BMW gently bounced as it crossed an intersection. Jolting in the back seat, Maria came to. She lifted her head slowly, disoriented and still groggy from the blow. In a few seconds, the pain in her scalp returned and her cheek throbbed. Brainard sat beside her, still looking queasy. She looked at the driver of the car—the man who had knocked her out, the same old man with the Austrian accent from whom she had agreed to buy the painting.

22

Dix found it difficult to concentrate as he navigated from file to file on the computer. Waiting for the package delayed him and caused him to become increasingly anxious. At any minute the Carabinieri could be at his door or the blond-headed killer could decide it was time to make his move. With each noise from the house, bark of a dog or passage of a car, Dix jumped up to investigate the sound, only to discover nothing. The routine began to drain his energy. He was out of practice for this sort of thing, but he could not afford to be sloppy. More than once he picked up the Beretta only to put it down again.

He was ready to leave for Udine as soon as Maria's package arrived. He normally wouldn't have lingered, but her insistence on the package's importance compelled him to wait. *What could she have sent?* he thought, returning to the computer from his last round of security patrol. *Why would she send a package by messenger?* He leaned back in his chair and munched an apple.

The front gated buzzed, startling him. Grasping the Beretta again, he sat the remainder of his apple on the table and cautiously moved to the window. His eyes scanned the limited exterior view to the front wall. The neighborhood was quiet and nothing out of order. He leaned over to expand his view and saw a young man in a messenger's uniform and cap holding a package. *Finally!* he thought. He scrutinized the entire neighborhood again, trying to spot anything unusual. Satisfied that all was normal, he laid the pistol on the table and walked out to the gate. He signed for the package and tipped the man. His curiosity increased as he gazed at the brown-paper covering. *It feels like a book,* he thought. He scanned the area once again and then began to unwrap the package as he walked toward the house. About half way up the walk he stopped. *It's an old journal,* he thought. Opening the dried-out leather cover with its embossed Reich Adler, he flipped through the pages. His German wasn't good enough to decipher the handwritten text. The few words he could pick out told him the journal was a World War II officer's journal.

His eyes caught the familiar name "Griselda." *Griselda...*he thought as he flipped toward the front pages and found the name again: Griselda von Englehoven. *I read that name in the file,* Dix thought as he continued into the house. *Where'd Maria get this? What is she into?*

He laid the journal on the table next to the gun and lifted the receiver to call Steve Galtero, a Special Forces officer he had worked with in Panama and they had remained friends with ever since. Steve was still in the Army and stationed with the 10th Special Forces in Germany. A dedicated and professional officer, Steve was one person that Dix knew very well and could trust. As he dialed the phone, Dix peered out of the windows to check his security again. The house and neighborhood was peaceful with no one in sight.

When Steve answered, Dix explained the situation to him and told him everything he knew. When Dix asked for his help, Steve readily agreed. Dix also told him about the journal.

"The journal is written in German. I hope you can translate it," he stated. "See what you can find out about the OSS, especially Project Orion—names associated with the report—and what they did during the final days of the war with regard to the Nazi loot from May 1945 on."

"I'll find out all I can," Steve said. "I know a guy in the Executive Civil Service. He once told me that his uncle was in the OSS during the war."

"Good. Check that out, but be sure to keep this as quiet as you can. And what ever you do, don't say anything about me or use my name."

"Got it," Steve replied. "The guy's uncle is retired now and lives in Germany, I think. Maybe we could talk to him."

Steve agreed to meet Dix and Maria in Udine. He said he would try to catch a flight to Aviano, that evening if he could, otherwise he'd be on the overnight train. As soon as they ended their call, Dix dialed Maria's number at the hotel to let her know he was on his way. Again she didn't answer, so he left a message that he would see her in a couple of hours.

After replacing the receiver, Dix turned around and accidentally knocked the apple to the floor. As he bent to pick it up, the window pane next to him exploded inward, followed by two more panes. Instinctively, Dix hit the floor, covering his head with his hands. Glass shards rained on him. He lay motionless. His ears strained for sounds but there was nothing. Then he realized he hadn't heard the shots. Rolling on his side, he looked up and saw three bullet holes, one in the cabinet door and the other two in the wall. "Shit!" he said to himself as he crawled over to his the Beretta.

Lifting his right hand to the top of the table without raising his head, he gently moved his hand across the flat surface that was littered with sharp pieces of glass. His fingers inched along until they touched the cold steel. When he identified the coarse grooves of the handgrips, he grasped the pistol firmly and pulled it toward him. He crawled forward to the wall at the left of the window, then slowly rose to a crouch, bringing the pistol up. Glass crunched beneath his feet. He was ready to return fire.

A car engine roared. Out of the window he saw a car speed away. He caught a glimpse of the license tag as the car turned the corner. Brussels and the crosswalk flashed in his brain. *That looked like the same dark blue Mercedes that tried to run us down,* he thought. *The tag was government.* He turned and sat down, his back to the wall beneath the window. He breathed in deeply and exhaled. His hands trembled. *Damn, that was close!* he thought as he surveyed the damage and the apple on the floor, speared by a piece of glass. *Time to get the hell out of here!*

Surprised that Maria wasn't in the room when he arrived, Dix figured she had just stepped out and would return at any minute. The plush room had been made and fresh towels delivered. Her clothes were still there. The red light was flashing on the phone. Thinking it might be a message from Maria, he was taken aback to find that it was his last message to her. Dix sat in the chair next to the bed and opened the sack to see what Maria bought. "Shoes, I knew it!" he said to himself as he inspected the red leather shoes. "She's shopping, damn! That's where she is. She ought to be back soon. She knew I'd be here about this time."

An hour passed and Maria still hadn't returned. *Even Maria wouldn't be shopping this long,* he thought. He inspected the room again for a note she might have left for him, but there was no note. Then he went to the front desk to see if she had left any messages. Again nothing. This was uncharacteristic of Maria. The knot in his stomach tightened, and his imagination soared. He began to think that Maria may have been taken to get at him. *Did whoever that tried to shoot me know that Maria was here?* he wondered.

He cautiously walked through the hotel and talked to the staff, again drawing a blank. He decided to widen his search by going into the piazza. He passed shops where he was sure she would go. Finally, he recognized the name of the shoe store. It was the store listed on the sales slip with the shoes in Maria's hotel room. Dix asked the salesclerk about Maria. She remembered her, said Maria was alone and that she left after buying the shoes. He thanked the woman and walked out of the store.

Dix made his way to the restaurant at the edge of the piazza and sat at a round table outside. There were many people in the piazza and he had a good view of the area. He hoped they might spot each other if she passed by. He felt reasonably confident that no one would make an attempt on his life with so many people around. The sun had disappeared behind the mountain, its rays replaced by evening twilight. The sound of church bells rang through the square. All the umbrellas were collapsed and the staff was preparing for evening guests. "A beer, please," Dix said when the waiter arrived.

Within a few minutes the waiter returned with the beer and a glass. Dix asked him about Maria. "She's a very attractive woman in her late thirties, dark hair above her shoulders." Dix gestured with his right hand to indicate the length of her hair.

He shook his head, "I'm sorry, signore, I can't help you. I haven't seen her." He turned and walked away.

Dix struggled with what to do next. Ignoring the glass, he lifted the bottle to his lips and gulped a mouthful. *I can't go to the Carabinieri, that would be walking into their hands,* he thought. *Damn, she seems to have vanished. She's not at the library or mu-*

seum, they're closed. Where the hell is she? What's happened to her? He took another mouthful from the bottle.

The twilight turned into darkness and small flames danced atop the candles on each table. Lights from the restaurant spilled onto the piazza. It was a mild evening with a slight Adriatic breeze fluttering about. It was a night to enjoy as people started to find their way into the piazza to do just that. Some came to shop, some to dine and others to stroll beneath the stars. But for Dix it wasn't that kind of night.

He returned to the hotel room, hoping that she would be there waiting for him. She would certainly wait when she saw his bags.

His expectations evaporated the moment he opened the door. She was not there and it appeared that no one had been in the room. He sat on the bed, looking for some clue. He checked the bathroom again—her toiletry items were still there. He picked up her cologne and smelled her fragrance.

He sat by the phone and dialed the front desk. Hearing the woman's voice, Dix said, "If my wife asks for me, I'll be in the restaurant on the piazza."

The piazza was dark and the only light was that what spilled out of the shops and the candles on the tables. Dix sat at a prominent table. The flickering candlelight illuminated an attractive woman's face as she sat talking with a man at the adjoining table. The subtle glow of her smooth skin and dark hair caused Dix's heart to sink. *She smiles just like Maria,* Dix thought. At that moment a different waiter brought him a glass of wine, breaking his trance. As he placed it on the table Dix asked him about Maria. "She's a very good-looking woman in her late thirties, slender body, dark eyes, dark hair above her shoulders."

He shook his head and gave the same cordial response as the other waiter. "I'm sorry, signore. I don't remember seeing her." As the young man left a short, stocky man about Dix's age, wearing a blue and white Polo shirt tucked into his denim pants, approached the table.

"Hi, Dix!" he said with a slight nasal New York accent and a broad smile. "I thought that was you. The clerk in the hotel told me where to find you."

"Steve!" Dix said, startled. "Thanks for coming. How was the flight?"

Steve Galtero, a muscular, first generation Italian-American, had trained Maria and the Free Panamanian Resistance that she led for a top-secret operation in Panama. Steve had a leathery, weather-beaten face with deep creases in the wrinkles of his cheeks. He was full of spirit and curiosity, like a kid at the circus.

"I got on the first flight out, a C-130. It wasn't too bad for a cargo plane. I'm just glad the flight wasn't any longer. Where's Maria?"

"God, I'm glad you're here. She's disappeared."

Dix motioned to the waiter to bring another glass of wine for Steve, then began telling him what had happened since he had talked to him on the phone. "She's just vanished," he said as a new waiter sat the glass in front of Steve.

"Signore," the young man said to Dix, "you asked about the woman?"

"Yes!" Dix answered, focusing his full attention on him.

"I was here at noon and served her. A man took her away. He said he was her husband. I could tell they were arguing but

I didn't think anything of it."

Dix pumped him for information but learned no more than he had already been told. The waiter described the man that took Maria but said that he didn't see them actually leave. "Wait, I do remember seeing a black BMW speed around the corner a few minutes after the man and woman left," he said after several more questions. "Many people were in the piazza. I thought the car was going to hit someone, the way it sped away.... They could've been in the car. The car was going too fast—I'm not sure."

"Dix, let's go back to the hotel," Steve insisted. "You're slipping. You shouldn't be sitting out here in the open. It'll be to our advantage if we aren't seen together."

"I guess you're right. I was just trying to find Maria. I thought that she might see me here or I could find out what happened."

23

In the hotel room Steve told Dix what he had been able to find out prior to leaving. "I have one of my officers doing some checking on a few things. The man I know in the civil service told me very little. He was very evasive and didn't want to talk, but he did tell me that someone had stolen some classified G-7 documents. I tried to extract information from him using a routine of consolations and offering to help, but it didn't work. He was uptight. I think he was agitated about something more than the G-7 papers. I wouldn't have gotten that much if I hadn't told him I was writing a paper on the OSS during World War II for a class I was taking. I told him that I thought his uncle could give me some information for it."

"I didn't know you were taking a class." Dix said.

"I'm not," he replied with a grin.

"The fuckers are setting me up to take the fall and they've nabbed Maria as the bait to trap me."

"It's kind of looking that way."

Steve showed Dix all the information he was able to get before leaving, most of which didn't seem to provide any clues. "I haven't contacted the former OSS guy yet. According to his nephew, he is on a Mediterranean cruise and won't be back for two more weeks. His name is Robert Hamilton. He retired from the CIA ten years ago."

"Robert Hamilton?"

"Right. What is it?"

"That name was in the files I told you about."

"Let's see what you got."

Dix showed the journal to Steve. At first he flipped through the pages, front to back then back to front. He began reading it and soon confirmed that it was a journal from SS Major Ulrich V. Fabian. "I can barely make out the officer's first name. It's his accounting of his actions starting in July 1944," Steve said as he looked up from the journal.

"Fabian was from the elite Grossdeutschland Regiment and was assigned to General Ernst Kaltenbrunner's staff," Steve continued. "He was special assistant to the general and in charge of security at Alt Aussee. He was also establishing hideouts in the South Tirol for high-ranking Nazis and personally escorted treasures to these hideouts. This is good shit!"

"The journal and the disks go hand in hand," Dix said, referring to the information in the computer disks.

Steve continued to translate the journal, becoming more and more engrossed. Several times he fell silent and Dix had to ask him what it said. "Fabian had a girlfriend, Griselda von Englehoven. She was the Second Secretary to the general."

"Maria must have stumbled onto the journal and they took her for it. Maybe she isn't the bait to get me and the two are just a coincidence." Dix said.

"It seems as though our major was preparing for his postwar years." Steve grinned and took a pouch from his back pocket. Opening the foil he exposed a dark brown mass of chewing tobacco. He fingered the moist strands and placed a golf-ball sized wad into his mouth. Chomping, then positioning it properly in his right cheek, he continued, "This journal is really getting good. Fabian was skimming from the hideouts he was supposed to set up and the treasures he had collected. Closer to the end of the war he became more aggressive. He listed locations, what he had stashed where, and even sketched maps to his stockpile of loot."

"And Maria stumbled onto their journal," Dix said. "But who are they and where would they have taken her?"

As Dix and Steve continued to talk, they finally surmised that the journal contained information on war treasures that had never been discovered, *except* by whoever had the journal.

"If the magnitude of the treasures in the journal is correct, it would be too massive to move around," Dix said. "They're probably using the original locations as much as possible."

Steve grunted his agreement and spit into a glass.

Dix set up the laptop and opened the files. Showing them to Steve, he cross-referenced the journal and the disks where the SS Major and the secretary were mentioned as well as their relationship. The major was dead and the woman disappeared. "I think the major killed the woman based on his last few journal entries," Steve said, then spit tobacco juice into a glass. "Dix, check this out."

"What is it?"

"I missed this before but in this last part... it says he got some penicillin from an American Army Captain."

"No shit? Really? What's that all about?"

"Probably nothing. Those old Nazis wrote down everything."

"What else does it say?"

"I can't make out the rest of his paragraph. Something has obliterated the ink. Shit!"

"The biggest questions are how does it tie to the G-7 and

why were their people being killed?"

"First things first," Steve said as he chewed the wad in his mouth. "Our immediate problem is Maria. Let's get her back, then figure out the G-7 part."

Without any more to go on, they were forced to wait. Maria was the pawn and they wouldn't kill her until they got the journal back. Steve had Dix again go over every step he had made from the minute he arrived at the hotel. Dix recounted each detail including how the shoes were on the coffee table and the room was clean.

The clean room struck Steve as odd. "Why didn't they search the room?" he said.

"Maybe they didn't know this was her room," Dix replied.

"They knew. Wait here. I'm going to check something." With that Steve got up and left.

Within about fifteen minutes Steve returned to the room. "The chambermaid that cleaned this room had already gone home but one of the other chambermaids said she commented on how torn up the room was," Steve said as soon as he closed the door. "It took her so much time to straighten up that she was behind the rest of the day."

"So they did search the room."

"Yeah. Without finding the journal. I suspect that Maria will tell them you have it," Steve said, then held the glass to his lips and spit tobacco juice into it. "She's tough but not stupid. They'll contact you."

"The bastards know I'm here and I have the journal. How are we going to turn this around and not get killed in the process?"

"When they contact you," Steve said as he began to lay out a plan, "they will probably demand a meeting very quickly and in a deserted place. That makes you and Maria vulnerable after the exchange and gives us little time to prepare a defense. If the gunman is part of their organization, he has the advantage."

"A shooter, that's what I'm worried about. He's the variable we can't account for."

"Me too. When they make contact, insist on a public meeting place. They'll resist but concede. That'll balance out the scales if not tip them in our favor. I'm counting on them not knowing about me. And a public place would minimize the chance that they would start shooting."

Steve wanted the meeting to be in the piazza or bar, depending on when they asked for the meeting. He would conceal himself and provide protection.

"After the meeting and exchange, we've got to get out of the area quickly or get killed." Steve unfolded the map and began studying the streets for the best egress route.

After a meticulous study of the map, Steve and Dix tried to account for every possible scenario they might face—from the exchange of the journal for Maria to their escape to the Carabinieri. Returning to Bressanvido was not an option.

"I don't want you to go unarmed, Dix," Steve said, opening his bag and retrieving a Beretta.

"I've got one."

"Good. Hide it but be able to get to it quickly."

"This one will be my backup then," Steve said as he flipped the Beretta onto the bed, then took out another black pistol.

"What the hell is that?" Dix asked.

"It's a Heckler and Koch, .45 caliber with twelve-round magazine. It's experimental, called the Mark 23, MOD 0. They gave it to me to try out, then I've got to give it back with my comments."

"Let's see it," Dix said, holding his hand out for the pistol.

"Nice. Silencer and laser-aiming module come with it,"

Steve replied as he separated the three components and handed them to Dix.

Cradling it in both hands, Dix examined the weapon, then grasped the grip with his right hand. He pulled the one-piece machined steel slide to the rear to reveal an empty chamber, then released it leaving the hammer cocked. Feeling its near perfect balance, he extended his arm and took the correct sight picture with the three self-luminous tritium dots.

The gun snapped as he squeezed the trigger. Dix relaxed his stance and brought the .45 close to his chest again to examine the reinforced polymer frame once again. Steve handed him the laser-aiming module and showed him how to attach it in the molded grooves of the frame. Next, he handed Dix the seven and a half inch long silencer and screwed it onto the threaded barrel.

"This son-of-a-bitch is nice," Dix said with a grin, twisting his wrist to check for any shift in balance. "Is it custom-made?"

"No, but it will equal any custom-made pistol." Steve said as he took it from Dix's hand.

Their preparations completed, all they could do was wait. An occasional noise would come from the hall, usually someone passing by outside the door. As the night wore on, the noises decreased in frequency, and the two dozed off with the door securely locked and chained. Dix was on the bed with his shoes off while Steve lay on the floor, his feet to the door and the Heckler and Koch beside him. They were ready to spring into action.

The phone rang at 6:43 in the morning. Dix looked at Steve before he answered.

"Yes," Dix spoke into the receiver.

"Yes." Dix gestured to the phone indicating it was the call they were waiting for.

Steve moved next to Dix and leaned his head close to the receiver as Dix tipped it out for both of them to hear.

"You have the journal and we have your wife," said an American voice. "We are offering a trade."

Steve looked at Dix and mimicked for him to talk to Maria before he agreed.

"First, let me talk to Maria."

Dix's stomach began to tighten after an agonizing silence.

"Dix, I'm okay," said Maria, gasping and frightened.

"Maria!" Dix burst out. But there was no response. The silence returned. Steve squeezed his arm as a reminder to stay in control.

"Now the meeting," said the American voice. "There is an old farmhouse without a roof and one wall—"

Steve leaned forward and gestured a forceful no. Bar or restaurant, he mouthed. Dix nodded.

"No," Dix said. "A public place. A bar or restaurant. I don't want any accidents."

Silence came over the phone. His heart pounded.

"The bar at the far end of the piazza. L'Oro bar, 7:15. Come alone. Bring the journal."

"Right," Dix replied and before he could say another word the phone went dead.

24

The piazza began to fill with people making their way to their favorite place for morning coffee. Dix walked by the restaurant where Maria had been seized. The tables had already begun to fill beneath the clear morning sky. The umbrellas, open like giant mushrooms, shielded the tables from the bright sun. Dix continued across the piazza to the bar for the exchange.

The bar had a large, glass front and high ceiling. A massive curved counter with a black marble top recessed well into the room welcomed the patrons. A group of people gathered in front of the counter, talking and drinking their morning beverage. A young, unshaven Italian man greeted each person who entered. In a rhythmic pattern he banged, clanked and chinked behind the counter, operating the large red and chromed caffè machine and serving different coffees and pastries. Glass shelves attached to a mirror behind him supported various bottles of liqueur and wine. Dix sat down at a center table in a row of five tables in the seating area to the left of the counter. He faced the door.

Steve sat at a table to the left of Dix so he would be perpendicular to the meeting. He slowly removed the Heckler and Koch from his pants, shielding it with a newspaper, and laid the pistol on the table beneath the paper. He took a bite of his roll, then sipped his caffè, looking relaxed and unconcerned.

    Several more men entered the bar and placed their orders. Dix studied each man carefully. Several times he adjusted the newspaper that concealed Fabian's journal. No one in the growing crowd showed any interest in Dix. Then his eyes locked onto the short-sleeved khaki shirts and diagonal white leather straps across the chests of two Carabinieri as they entered one side of the piazza. The gold emblems on their white hats glistened in the sunlight and holsters gently patted their hips as they strode forward. Guardedly watching their advance, Dix then saw a Carabinieri Fiat utility vehicle stop on the opposite side of the piazza. Two more men in khaki shirts exited the blue vehicle and walked toward the other two.

    Dix shot a look at Steve as the knot in his stomach drew tighter. Steve's eyes communicated the same attentive fear as Dix. The two watched as the four Carabinieri turned and entered the restaurant across the piazza. As the last one entered, Dix glanced at Steve again, both men's eyes reflecting relief.

    The din in the square had reached its morning peak. Church bells rang, echoing throughout the neighborhood. A flock of pigeons sprang into the air with a flutter. The square was filled with the sounds of people talking, children playing, music spilling from the restaurants and other city sounds. A lively buzz rose from crowded bars: the clamor of dishes, tables and chairs being dragged on the patios, and conversations sparked with laughter. It was business as usual.

    Dix's anticipation grew more intense as the minutes ticked off. The slightest element could foil the transaction, even an accident or the early departure of the four Carabinieri or late arrival of others—all played on Dix's mind. He scanned the crowd again, searching for anything unusual. His eyes found Steve.

Steve wiped his mouth with the napkin and his eyes telegraphed for Dix to look outside toward the far corner of the bar. Steve moved his hand close to the newspaper so that, if needed, with a short, quick move the weapon would be in his hand. He lifted the cup to his lips and studied the crowd. Then he looked toward the sidewalk in front of the bar.

Dix watched the three figures emerge where Steve indicated. His eyes locked onto Maria flanked by two men wearing sport coats and open collars. One was an older man and the other a younger, physically fit American. Each locked an arm around Maria as they passed in front of the bar and entered. Both men held their free arm close to their waist. Dix's heart pounded. As they drew nearer, he saw the bruise on her cheek and her split and swollen lips. She wore no makeup and her hair was disheveled. Her crumpled clothes told the rest. She was expressionless; the normal sparkle in her eyes was gone.

His blood boiled as he fought the urge to use his Beretta on the two men. He scrutinized them. Then locking on to Maria's eyes, he tried to reassure her but she seemed unreceptive. He saw her focus on Steve and her eyes darted back to him, telegraphing confidence.

The three stopped in front of the table facing Dix. "Connor?" the American said as he sat, then tugged on Maria's arm, signaling her to sit.

The old man remained standing with his arms clasped in front of him. He looked around the crowded room, then back to the table in front of him.

"Yes," Dix replied coldly.

"You have the journal?" the old man demanded with a slight Austrian accent.

"Yes." Dix gently slid the newspaper from atop the leather-bound volume. He glanced up at the old man then back to the American.

"Good. We're all going to take a little ride. Let's go!" said the old man, then parted his sport coat and exposed his other hand holding a small automatic pistol. The American offered a glimpse of his own weapon.

Dix shot another glance to Maria, then looked up to the pistol the Austrian revealed, his thick fingers around the grip and his index finger filling the hole of the trigger guard. Dix studied the man for several seconds, then shifted his eyes back to the sleek automatic protruding from his midsection.

Steve watched the growing mass of bodies in the bar and the thickening cigarette smoke. He examined the old man with wrinkled skin and a beard of gray stubble. The he shifted his eyes to the American. He saw the man's right leg vibrate nervously. Beads of sweat formed on the man's face.

Steve nonchalantly lifted his roll with his right hand, took a bite, placed it back on the saucer and gently slid his hand to the newspaper. He picked up the cup with his left hand and sipped the contents. Timing was critical and had to be in sync with Dix's—each had to be ready to back up the other instantly.

In a cold emotionless voice, Dix objected to the old man's assumption. Staring deep into the American's eyes, Dix pointed his Beretta from beneath the table at the man. "We had an agreement, an exchange. This is what you came for. Now let's go our separate ways."

Dix slid the journal slowly in front of him with his fingertips. He held his hand in place for several seconds.

"Let's go, now!" Brainard ordered as he slid the book closer to him and gestured with his pistol.

Steve snapped the safety off and pulled the hammer back on the Heckler and Koch, the metallic clicks distinct and unmistakable. For an instant, no one moved.

"I don't think so!" Steve said, allowing them to see the threaded barrel of his gun beneath the paper he was holding. "No sudden moves and we all walk away."

Dix followed Steve's lead and snapped the safety off his gun, then with his thumb pulled the hammer back.

The old man and the American registered expressions of surprise when they heard the Beretta's clicks. Their bodies tensed.

"Don't think about it! I'll have two slugs in you before you can flinch," Dix said.

Sweat beads trickled down Brainard's face as he looked at the old man. Neither spoke.

"Even if one of you makes it, those two Carabinieri will never allow you to leave the piazza." Steve nodded in the direction of the two Carabinieri who had emerged from across the piazza and were walking toward the bar.

The American slowly stood. He looked at Dix and then at Steve. He lifted the journal and silently backed away from the table. The two men concealed their weapons as they made their way back into the crowd and out the door. Steve remained alert as they disappeared around the corner. Dix grabbed Maria and held her close.

"All right, let's get out of here," Steve said.

Brainard and the old man, determined to eliminate loose ends, began following the trio as they made their escape. Steve, following his evasion plan, drove the car and meandered through the city. Dix navigated, checking the map to ensure they would avoid dead ends and potential choke points. Maria watched for the trailing car, calling out its presence at each turn. She assisted Dix with identifying the streets as they passed. Zigzagging, never going in any one direction for more than a few blocks, Steve managed to lose the two, then headed out of Udine. He drove east for seventeen kilometers on a country road to the hill town of Cividale. Steve wanted to ensure they were not followed. If they were, driving east would not give away their true destination.

Along the way, Dix had Steve stop so that he could call Mariano and brief him on the situation. When Dix was finished, Maria got on the phone. Maria answered Mariano's questions about what had happened to her; she provided every detail that she could remember. She told him about the office Brainard had taken her too. "I saw them loading a truck with a variety of paintings," she said. "I didn't hear them say where the truck was going. They did very little talking in front of me." She emphasized that the journal proved what she had told him and that it gave the locations of missing treasures. "These men are ruthless. They planned to kill Dix and me as soon as they got the journal back," she continued. She didn't tell him about Steve.

While the two were on the phone, Steve went to a salumeria nearby. He returned, within minutes of the phone call to Mariano, with two bottles of red wine, four one-liter bottles of water, some bread, cheese, prosciutto, salami and two roasted chickens. They needed food, but stopping to eat wasn't in the plan. They had to get to a hiding place quickly.

Adhering to Steve's plan, the three circled around country roads out of Cividale, heading first north then turning west along tree-lined roads. They slowed only when an occasional tractor or farm truck impeded their progress.

Their zigzagging course finally ended in the town of Spilimbergo, a small village on the west bank of the Tagliamento River—approximately thirty kilometers west of Udine. This was an area that Dix knew well from his days in the Army. NATO forces trained extensively in this region of northeast Italy and Dix had spent time there during military exercises studying the terrain and driving the country roads. He counted on having a better knowledge of the geography than someone who might be after them.

They settled in a small, older pension. Their adjoining rooms were on the second floor of the sun-bleached beige stucco building. Not the quality they normally chose and certainly not one they would recommend to their friends. For the time being it was what they needed—a temporary hideaway.

Maria took advantage of the modest bathroom, trying to wash away the last twenty-four hours. Her body suffered from the ordeal and needed rest. It had been a long time since she had gone without sleep and she definitely was not accustomed to the treatment she received. After a relaxing shower, she drank a glass of mineral water and lay on the bed. She smiled and squeezed Dix's arm as he kissed her forehead. Her breathing slowed and needed sleep came quickly.

While Maria slept, Dix called Francesca to find out what she had learned. "The OSS made several reports on looting of art. They documented the actions of the Nazi leadership and had a good account of the magnitude of Hitler's operation," she told him. Much of Francesca's information confirmed what he already knew about the OSS and their report. She attempted to convey the quantity of the treasure that had been amassed as documented by the two organizations but fell way short. She reported that the OSS took the lead. Their documents stated the treasures were catalogued and returned. "The reported missing loot was determined to be destroyed and restitution was made," she continued. "I did find out that over a thousand documents found in the Stasi files previously thought destroyed are going to be turned over to the Americans during the Munich meeting. They are supposed to contain old records of General Kaltenbrunner and information about the last days of the war. There's a lot of excitement over the documents. Since they are considered classified, though, no one would be specific about the contents."

As Francesca relayed this information to Dix, he thought back to a conversation he had with Klaus Müller in Brussels at the NATO conference. *Klaus told me about those files. He said they had a lot of people worried. He also said that a lot of art was never recovered or repatriated and that the missing art was a serious issue, that a cloud of death hangs over the treasures.* "Good," he replied. "Keep searching for any more information about the two organizations and especially the files."

Steve called John, the officer who was researching information for him on the OSS. He briefed Steve on the information he found and had it assembled and ready to fax to him.

"Well, sir," the officer said, "the way I see it is that at the end of the war, no one cared. The 3rd Army was in charge of most of the treasures. The magnitude was more than anyone could imagine. Patton had a time keeping his soldiers from taking stuff for souvenirs, and there were some who made off with a few pieces. Most were caught and court-martialed. Only a couple soldiers got a way with it, just souvenirs. Nothing big."

"Good, John, thanks. I'll call you back in a few minutes with the fax number."

"Sir, there are a few documents that are... well, sensitive."

"I understand."

"Sir, look at the report on the OSS findings. It was signed by a Robert Hamilton. After I put all this together, it seemed fishy to me. It was as if he was closing the book on the whole thing. He said it was all returned or restitution made. I can't find anything that shows it was or who did it. All I can find is that Hamilton said it was done. I found where some of it was returned but there's no way that all of it could have been returned. It just didn't add up to me."

"Okay, John, I'll take a look. I'll call you back."

The two men exchanged the information they had received as Dix prepared the laptop to receive the fax. The information on Hamilton was the most captivating so far. As soon as they reviewed the information being sent, Dix said he wanted to compare it with what he had seen on the disk. Finally, with the computer ready, Steve called to have the information sent and told John to find out all he could on Robert Hamilton, including his address.

After several minutes of clicks, hums and flickers of light, the computer fell silent. Dix disconnected the laptop from the phone and with great anticipation, opened the file that John had faxed.

Dix and Steve huddled around the computer. They studied the new information and compared it to the files on the disks. During the final days of the war after Germany capitulated, the Europeans just wanted to go home. But for many there was no home to return to. The Americans also wanted to get on with their lives. Captain Robert Hamilton, U.S. Army, led the investigation into art looting and prepared reports on the treasures. His position and his access to General Kaltenbrunner's files at Alt Aussee gave him the opportunity to capitalize on his situation.

"That son-of-a-bitch!" Steve expressed, leaning back in his chair. "John was right.

It seems as though our Mr. Hamilton took advantage of the situation and went into the treasure business."

"It looks like our OSS man in charge, Captain Hamilton, followed in Major Fabian's footsteps," Dix added. "There's nothing here that connects Fabian directly to Hamilton, but it is obvious that Hamilton was seduced by the treasures. It looks like he devised a scheme to make a cursory repatriation and restitution of the treasures. He was smart. He returned enough of the loot to make it look authentic, even sacrificed a few caches he discovered."

Dix and Steve concluded that Hamilton must have visited the locations of each cache and conducted an inventory of his newly acquired assets. Along the way he formed his organization. "Damn, he was slick!" Steve surmised. "He had the locations, names of those taking care of the hideouts, information on the underground and then he recruited them. Those that wouldn't go along with him, he turned in or killed."

"It looks that way," Dix said. "Remaining in the OSS and later the CIA provided him the perfect situation and cover for his operation. He could monitor any activities related to the treasures and take any necessary actions to prevent discovery. Holding the threat of exposure, they cooperated."

"My guess is, whenever anyone wanted out, he wouldn't allow it," Steve said as he chomped a fresh wad of tobacco. "He's probably the one who leaked information and had them arrested as war criminals. He knew how eager the Nazi hunter organizations were to arrest and prosecute. The publicity of their actions provided the inducement for the others to stay in line."

The connection that Steve and Dix couldn't make for sure was the G-7, but they suspected that the connection was Hamilton's nephew in the civil service. He was the obvious choice because Hamilton needed someone he could trust on the inside. They theorized that Hamilton started closing down the operation when the Berlin Wall fell and Germany moved toward reunification.

"Hamilton knew of General Kaltenbrunner's files but probably believed that as long as they were locked away by Stasi, they were of minimal threat to him," Dix said. "When they were later reported destroyed, he probably felt more secure. But the files' subsequent discovery and Yeltsin's plan to turn them over during the Munich meeting would expose him."

"And the popular belief in the West was that Communism and the Wall would never fall," Steve added. "Therefore, no one planned for it. When it did fall, Hamilton, like the others, was caught off guard."

"We need to call on Mr. Hamilton," Dix said, leaning back and looking at Steve.

"My thoughts exactly. I told John to get all the information he could on him. If he is on a cruise, like his nephew said, all the better."

25

Dix called Mariano to find out if Brainard or the Austrian had been arrested. To his surprise Mariano told him that they found Brainard's body in the office where Maria said she had been held. There was no trace of the Austrian or the journal. The Carabinieri confiscated a few pieces of art, but for the most part the office and storage had been cleaned out. "My friend Colonel Pasquali of the Art Theft Investigation team, wants to talk to Maria," Mariano warned. "I'm stalling him but I can't hold him off too long. You must tell me everything you know." He tried to convince Dix to let him handle it as he was going to get himself and Maria killed. "This is a matter for me, not you, Dix!"

Dix refused Mariano's help but promised to keep him informed. "When I know all the details, I'll tell you," he said.

"I can't keep the Carabinieri away and I don't have any information on who fired the shots at you at your house."

That statement struck Dix as peculiar because the subject had not been discussed. Dix's guard went up again. *How the hell does he know? Was that a slip or was he trying to tell me something?*

Day turned into night as Steve and Dix planned their next move and waited for information on Hamilton. Maria stood beside Dix, resting her arm on his shoulder she said, "Let's get something to eat. Not cold chicken or sandwiches—real food."

"I could use something myself," Steve said as he stood and stretched.

"There's a pretty good restaurant a couple of blocks from here, in the center of town," Dix said. "They have good pasta and pizza too."

Maria indicated her agreement by reaching for her compact and refreshing her makeup in an attempt to conceal her bruise.

The three walked along the dark street. They turned the corner and saw the restaurant, light flowing out of the glass front into the dark town center. The center was merely a wide triangle formed by the two main streets, perpendicular to each other. Darkened buildings lined the streets. The incandescent bulbs illuminated the four patrons in the restaurant. A tractor passed by, its diesel engine spewing black fumes into the air as it disappeared into the night. Satisfied that it was safe to proceed, the three continued. Half way across the triangle, an Italian Army truck rumbled past, replenishing the diesel exhaust in the night air.

Seated at an old wooden table with a red-and-white checked tablecloth, at the back of the room, the trio had wine and pasta for dinner. They drank the proprietor's wine. He boasted that it was the best his vineyard had produced. For a few moments the world seemed far away in the rural setting of this working man's restaurant.

Maria began to tell Dix and Steve what she had learned before she was taken hostage. Her account of how she set up the meeting and posed as a buyer angered Dix.

"That wasn't very smart, Maria," Steve said.

"I needed to get proof of what I suspected to give to Mariano."

"Well, you damn near got killed!" Dix scolded. "Mariano is more involved in this that he lets on. Let's not tell him everything just yet."

"All right. I told you that I saw Ida Kohne's and the Marstons' painting in the records I researched. Do you remember?"

"Yeah," he vaguely recalled.

"There was more," she continued. "During that meeting with the old Austrian man, he showed me two other paintings—a Bruegel and an unsigned fleshy nude. They were all listed as missing since the war."

"Go on," Steve said.

"Signore Afferi told me a story about the Nazi major whose journal we had. That proved Signore Afferi's story."

She told them the story just as Signore Afferi had told it to her. They listened intently. She ended by saying she believed, since they had the journal, Brainard and the old man had found the Nazi major's treasure or worked for someone who had.

"Mr. Hamilton seems to be a significant player," Steve said. "and we've got to find out and prove his part in this."

The trio fell silent as the sound of two motorcycles grew louder. Dix became uneasy. It wasn't long until two large, blue Moto Guzzis parked in front of the restaurant. Two Carabinieri dismounted and placed their helmets on the handlebars. One lit a cigarette and the other wiped dust off his knee-high, black leather boots. They straightened their uniforms and adjusted the white leather straps that were diagonally across their chests.

They waited as a blue Fiat arrived and two more Carabinieri got out.

"Shit!" Dix whispered. "Trouble."

The four para-military policemen entered the restaurant and gazed around the room. Dix turned his head to shield his face from the inquisitive eyes of the Carabinieri. They sat down at a table near the center of the room.

Tension rose in Dix, Steve and Maria as the four men were between them and the door. The new arrivals seemed to pay no attention to the three of them across the room. Dix glanced again at them.

"Shit!" he whispered, as he nodded toward the one facing them. "I know that one, the sergeant."

"Stay cool," Steve said. "Maybe he hasn't seen you or doesn't recognize you."

The shortest of the four Carabinieri, with a large crooked nose, stood and slowly approached them, his tall leather boots thumping on the floor as he walked.

"Signore Connor, I thought that was you," he said, smiling and extending his hand.

After they exchanged cordial greetings and a few brief comments, Dix calmly introduced the sergeant to Maria and Steve.

"We are on security detail for the refugee camp on the river training area," the sergeant said, with his weight on his left leg and his hand resting on his holster.

"How are things going at the camp?" Dix said.

"It's a mess and people are coming from all over the Balkans."

"We were visiting friends and stopped here for dinner before going on home," Dix said.

The man remained relaxed and cordial, with no indication that he knew Dix was wanted. After several minutes of friendly conversation, he rejoined the others.

"I forgot all about the refugee camp the Italians set up," Dix whispered so as not to be overheard. "It's not too far from here."

"That was too close," Steve said.

"I know their routine. They are finished for the night," Dix said. "They just came into town for dinner. They can be prima donnas at times. I think we'll be okay for tonight but tomorrow after their morning meeting, it could be a different story."

The three remained calm and completed their meal. Maintaining a careful watch on the four Italian gendarmes, they drank another glass of wine, giving the appearance there was nothing out of the ordinary. As the tension eased somewhat and their arrest didn't seem eminent, their conversation turned to lighter topics.

"The sergeant that came over here"—Dix nodded toward the Carabinieri—"he was providing security for us several years ago when we were on a NATO exercise. As a matter of fact, the training area was a few minutes from here down along the river bank. About twelve-thirty one night I woke up to people yelling and shouting. The entire site was rousted out of bed. As soon as I got out of the tent I saw one hell of a fire. The entire site was lit up."

"What happened?" Steve asked.

"The sergeant over there and a few other Carabinieri had decided they needed a little light in their tent. They lit a candle and set it too close to the side of the tent and went to sleep. The candle either fell or was knocked over and it set the tent on fire, the grass and damn near the entire woods."

"Did they get hurt?" Maria quizzed.

"Just their pride." Dix replied. "The tent and its contents were reduced to ashes. As matter of fact Mariano was with me and I thought he was going to shoot them. Boy, was he mad."

"I never had the luxury of a tent," Steve said. "I think the Army figured Special Forces soldiers would burn up tents, too!"

Finally, trying not to arouse suspicion in the naturally curious Carabinieri, they made their way out of the restaurant. Dix gestured and spoke to the Carabiniere sergeant as they departed.

They continued their nonchalant demeanor for the benefit of those four still inside the restaurant until they disappeared around the corner.

"That was close," Dix said as they went around the corner. He took another look over his shoulder.

"Too close," Steve said as he wrestled the tobacco pouch from his pocket and fingered the contents. "We need to get out of here."

"We'll be okay for tonight." Dix watched Steve place the wad of tobacco into his mouth and chomp on it. "I know their routine. They've been with the refugees for a couple of weeks and are behind on other things—like us."

"First thing in the morning then. Be ready to go early."

26

Merging in with the dense early morning traffic, Dix, Maria and Steve took the northbound E14 autostrada toward Austria. They counted on the border crossings to be packed with traffic by the time they reached the border. They anticipated that the guards, even if alerted, would be looking for a male and female American. No one knew of Steve and his rental car, and they hoped that would improve their chances in getting passed the boarder guards. To better their odds, Maria would hide in the back, covered with their bags and clothes. The guards would be stressed with impatient drivers in cars and trucks waiting to cross. Having made the crossing many times in the past, Dix knew that the guards would only make a cursory inspection, if that much, before waving them through.

They inched closer to the Italian-Austrian border. Several cars and trucks were pulled over and the drivers were entering the guard's office to have their transport documents stamped and processed. As Steve approached, three guards were inspecting trucks and one was inspecting a van. Holding the two American passports out of the window, making it easier for the guard to see them, they anticipated a wave-through.

Their stomachs knotted when the guard told them to pull

over. Steve obeyed his instructions as if nothing was wrong, gesturing with his hand in acknowledgment and forcing a smile.

"Shit!" Dix whispered through his clenched teeth.

"Stay cool," Steve said as he guided the car into a parking space.

Steve adjusted the rearview mirror so he could watch the guards behind them as he contemplated a plan. Several minutes passed without any of the guards taking any interest in them. Cars, vans and trucks continued to pass the checkpoint. Drivers entered and departed the office in a steady stream. Several drivers took the opportunity to eat and to drink coffee. Five minutes passed and still no guard. Dix watched as the guard was replaced by another.

"Give me the passports," Dix ordered. "I've got an idea."

Approaching the guard, Dix held the passports in his left hand. To add to the confusion, Dix began questioning in English and gesturing with his hands as he approached. Shouting above the noise of the traffic, he captured the guard's attention. The man, unaware of why Dix was told to pull over, was confused by the situation. Dix continued asking in an irate manner as to why he couldn't proceed.

"I've been waiting for ten minutes!" he shouted. 'What's the matter? When is someone going to check my car?"

The guard, struggling to figure out what was happening, glanced at the car in which Steve sat and then back to the approaching Dix. When Dix stopped with his palms up, waist high in a questioning manner, it forced a decision. To Dix's surprise, the baffled man motioned for him to go. Dix turned and with a show of agitation walked back to the car.

"Let's go!" Dix said as he got into the car and closed the door. "Quickly, before they remember why they told us to pull over. Look natural and drive careful."

Steve immediately started the car and drove on as if there

were no problems. They expected to be pulled over at any minute as they proceeded through the buffer zone. He constantly glanced in the rearview mirror. Dix turned around in his seat to watch for any sign of trouble. A constant stream of vehicles, every make, model and color followed. An equal amount of traffic passed in the opposite direction heading into Italy. As the road turned, the Italian border disappeared behind the pine tree-covered mountain and the Austrian border appeared. They continued with caution, their apprehension easing. Steve held the passports out of the window again, making it obvious they were Americans. The Austrian guard eyed the two men, then motioned for them to proceed. Breathing a sigh of relief, they pulled away. Well out of sight of the last guard, Dix helped Maria get up from her hiding place. Her face was flushed and wet with perspiration.

It was late morning by the time the trio arrived in the Alpine city of Villach, approximately twelve kilometers inside Austria. The city was a major transportation hub providing access north into Germany or east through Austria and beyond. They rented rooms, one across from the other, in a small inn just off the main road. They chose Villach, reasoning that anyone who might be tracking them would presume they had gone on to a larger city. They needed to stop and find out the latest situation—if the Carabiniere sergeant had reported seeing them and if a search in the general area was under way. The inn was comfortable and clean but wouldn't make the Michelin Guide. It was, however, superior to the last one they were in.

Steve called John to find out if he had found Hamilton's address. "Hamilton lives in the small village of Seebruck, north of Chiemsee Lake," the officer told him.

The small Bavarian village was near the area that the U.S.

Army had taken from the Germans at the close of World War II and had used it as a recreation area ever since. John provided a complete description of Hamilton and added, "He has a small antique shop in Traunstein. The name of his shop is From the Past. He derives most of his business as a regular vendor at the bazaars sponsored at the military bases throughout Europe."

The two men talked for several minutes exchanging questions and bits and pieces of information. "Good job, John. Now find out all you can about his nephew in the civil service. Oh, and find out when the next bazaar is scheduled."

"Any particular one? Are you looking for anything special?"

"No, anywhere in Europe. I want to see what Mr. Hamilton has without arousing suspicion and to see if he really is on a cruise." Steve gave John the telephone numbers to his and Dix's rooms. "Call as soon as you find out anything, but don't leave a message. Try both numbers and if neither answers try every half hour."

Steve sat back in the chair and reviewed his notes before going to inform Dix.

Dix, Maria and Steve huddled around a map. Only minutes before, Maria had picked up the Esso map of Germany, unfolded the tattered cover and exposed the colorful geographical representation of the formerly divided country, and laid it on the coffee table. The map had proven to be a trustworthy ally to Dix and Maria on prior trips across Europe. Over a dozen cities were circled in pencil, past routes were highlighted in pink and yellow.

They reviewed the information they had gathered so far and began preparing their next move. As Steve relayed the latest news about Hamilton, Maria located Chiemsee Lake between Salzburg and Munich on the north side of E11 / A8.

She found Seebruck, then traced the road southeast around the lake to Traunstein. They discussed options for several minutes, then Steve stood and began pacing the room. "Damn, I'm hungry!" he said. I'm going down to that imbißstube."

"To where?" Maria asked as she looked up at him.

"To the imbißstube. That green-and-white snack stand we passed about a block from here. What do you want?"

"A wurst on a brötchen, mustard only, and fries. No mayonnaise on the fries," Dix said with a broad smile.

"The same for me," Maria added as she looked at Dix.

The phone rang just as Dix stood to open the room's window wider. He and Maria looked at each other with the same startled expression. He picked up the receiver and, when the caller identified himself, let out a sigh. It was John calling back to give them some more information.

"There is a bazaar sponsored by the military in Augsburg right now and From the Past is listed as one of the vendors. The next one will be in a month in Frankfurt."

"Thanks, John. I owe you a beer."

"Don't worry, I'm keeping track."

"I'll tell Steve."

The three sat around the map eating their food and discussing their next course of action. Dix pointed out on the map where he had marked the locations of Hamilton's shop and home in relation to Augsburg. All three were along the E11 / A8, which ran from Salzburg through Munich to Augsburg. Dix suggested they stop by Hamilton's shop on their way to the bazaar. "It'll take us a couple of hours to get to Salzburg—and Traunstein is about a half hour beyond," Dix said as he traced the route. "Then it looks like it'll take us another three hours to get to Augsburg from there."

"On the way back," Steve added, his expression showing he was already plotting his move, "why don't we stop by Mr. Hamilton's house and have a look around."

The doorbell jingled as the three entered the modest antique shop. A hint of lacquer, paint and polish was in the air. The front was filled with furniture of all kinds—desks, chairs, tables and mirrors. Two 1940s bicycles hung from the ceiling on the far wall and another leaned against a shelf of antique farm tools and wooden buckets. Old pictures, frames, paintings and odds and ends hung on the wall. A counter with a display case was to the right. A red-haired dog lay on the concrete floor in the shadow around the corner of the counter. A selection of gold and silver jewelry, gold coins and precious stones sparkled in the concealed lights illuminating the top shelf of the case. On the middle shelf was a selection of amber jewelry and more gold coins. Old watches and several small ingots of gold and silver lined the third shelf. Several gold chalices with necklaces draped over their brims were on each shelf.

"May I help you?" asked a woman's voice from deep within the shop. Her clogs clunked against the floor as she approached. Soon they saw a slender woman with blue eyes and blond hair pulled back in a ponytail. She wore tight fitting jeans and a yellow pullover top.

"We just want to look around," Maria said politely, as she noticed the woman was staring at her bruise. "I was in an accident." Maria gently touched her cheek.

"I'm sorry. It must have been pretty bad," the young woman said.

"Yes, it was." Maria smiled and nodded, then walked away.

Steve went his own direction, weaving through the furniture. He turned down a section that was filled with old military items—uniforms, decorations and equipment from several European countries and the United States. A number of plaques, citations and documents hung on the wall. Several flags, banners and guidons filled a rack next to the wall. He carefully investigated each section of the shop. He found a vacant work room in the back that seemed to be for repairs. Tools hung on the walls; cans of paint, lacquer, stain and cleaning solvent rested on separate shelves. A large paint-splattered table stood in the center of the room. An air compressor sat idle in one corner by the back door.

Next door to it, he found a storeroom filled with dust-covered furniture and several paintings. Steve figured these items were about to become inventory for the shop. The room was void of any storage space or counters. He continued his search, staying alert for the blond ponytail.

Continuing his browsing and scouting, Steve had almost made a full circle of the shop. The only area he hadn't looked in was the section where the woman stood. He figured that was the office, as he had not seen one elsewhere. He waited and watched. He nodded at Maria as a signal for her to engage the woman in conversation so he could look at the office. When the ponytail moved toward Maria, he made his move.

Dix and Maria continued their inspection of the shop, snaking through the furnishings. The hodgepodge of items increased in quality the further back in the shop they went. Maria noticed many museum-quality frames scattered about. She inspected two tapestries then found a wall full of quality paintings, most of which were unsigned.

"Are you stationed in Germany?" the young woman asked as she thumped up behind them. She apparently assumed that the two men were in the military.

"Yes, Frankfurt," Dix lied.

"Are you looking for anything in particular?" she said.

"Oh, I don't know," Maria replied, unable to resist. "You have several nice paintings. Is this all you have?"

"Right now, yes, but Mr. Hamilton gets things in all the time. He finds all kinds of art for people. If you would like to tell me what you are looking for, I could tell him when he gets back. He will call or send you a note if you will leave your name, address and phone number." She told them that she expected Hamilton to return at noon the next day from the bazaar in Augsburg.

Maria and Dix were starting to conclude that the woman was just an employee of the antique shop. She didn't seem to know where the merchandise came from. Her job was mostly to make the sales and gather information about customers.

"A lot of military personnel visit our shop and routinely purchase items not displayed in the store," she told them. "I get their names, addresses, phone numbers and anticipated dates of moving back to the States, if anyone makes special requests. Mr. Hamilton, in turn, checks them out and when he is satisfied that they are who they say they are—you never know—he tries to sell them what they want."

After several minutes Steve rejoined Dix and Maria who continued to talk to the young woman. With a nod he indicated that he was ready to leave. Dix and Maria thanked the woman for her help but declined her invitation to leave their names for Mr. Hamilton. They told her they would return.

The three raced west on E11 / A8 toward Augsburg. Learning that Hamilton was due back at noon the next day didn't give them much time. They exchanged information on the antique shop. Steve told them about the office. It was small—barely big enough for a desk, a file cabinet and one person. The shelves contained reference books you would expect to find in an antique shop. A computer was on the desk and its contents were of no help.

Dix sat in the back seat and dropped out of the conversation as Maria and Steve discussed Hamilton and his shop. He thought about how well organized and cunning Hamilton was. Through his connections, he had developed an extensive network to sell his goods. And he had developed a clientele of mostly military people. The more senior officers probably bought the more expensive items—more so than the tourists. Staying an average of three years in Germany before returning to the United States, their constant turnover assured new customers, as friends told friends of the antique shop. A number of customers probably returned during their vacations or as a result of reassignment to Europe.

It struck Dix that Hamilton must have developed an equally reliable and unobtrusive network for shipping antiques out of Europe. The more expensive items needed more care. As his customers returned to the United States, a way was needed to ship the pricier merchandise into the States undetected—a cover operation perhaps.

"Hamilton has excellent knowledge of how the military is organized and operates," Dix heard Steve say. "He probably knows many enterprising and underpaid soldiers, like Brainard, who would be willing to make an extra buck. By offering money to a low-ranking soldier, who was usually broke halfway through the month, he could probably get what he wanted."

"He may have started that way, but it's too slow and complicated." Dix said. "He would need a bigger distribution system."

"Why not just go straight to the transportation clerk and moving company rep?" Steve questioned, as he started following his line of thought.

"Yeah, you're right," Dix said. "They're on the inside and can track the shipment and fix the paperwork."

"Not in the household goods," Maria said. "I'd send it in that shipment that goes ahead of you and it is waiting when you arrive. Don't you remember when we shipped our stuff to Italy? It would be the same way going back. The military didn't really check. We could have had anything in there."

Realizing that Maria had hit on the fastest and least complicated method, Dix replied, "Sure. The movers pack up your advance stuff and turn it over to the Air Force to fly home. Hamilton could add his shipment on this end and remove it on the other."

The more they talked, the more plausible Maria's idea seemed. "Perhaps the shipping clerks at the major military installations identify an available shipment, prepare the paperwork, track the movement and notify their contact on the other end," Dix said. "The shipping company person then packs up whatever they want to ship and marks it so it looks like the rest of the shipment. They include it when they pick up the soldier's shipment and turn it over to the Air Force to fly back to the United States."

"If so, the bastard is good," Steve said. "Hamilton is smart. We've got to find and exploit any weakness or mistakes he makes."

27

Dix, Maria, and Steve entered the second of the large green-and-white beer tents housing the biggest part of the bazaar in the U.S. Army Kasern in Augsburg. More than two thousand people were winding their way through the rows of vendors selling everything from clothing, jewelry, leather goods, furs, paintings, statues and furniture to wines and liquors. Money exchanged hands at every booth and merchandise flowed out of the tents. Some vendors were taking special orders while several others were doing custom work on-site. Dix, Maria, and Steve easily blended into the moving throng of bodies as they made their way to the booth with the sign FROM THE PAST above it. They stopped three vendors short and across the aisle from their destination.

Steve proceeded to the far side of Hamilton's crowded booth, pretending to shop while Dix remained behind to observe and to watch for any familiar faces. Maria followed after Steve when he reached the booth. She took up a position at the near end of Hamilton's booth. Steve and Maria could see most of what Hamilton was selling. Neither gave any indication they knew each other. A clean shaven man of medium build—six feet tall and about one hundred-eighty pounds—

stood talking to a fashionable woman near Maria. They were talking as if they had done business together before. The man wrote in a notebook, smiled and played up to the woman. The man was unmistakably Robert Hamilton.

He reminds me of Brainard, Maria thought, *just an older version.* He had thinning, gray hair and had overdone it with the gold. He wore a gold chain around his neck, a square gold ring with the letter H in small diamonds on the third finger of his right hand and a plain gold ring on the third finger of his left hand—plus a gold watch. *Too much flash!*

As soon as the woman left, Maria engaged him in a discussion about an oil on canvas landscape he had on display. It was not the usual quality of painting Maria would buy. *Colonel Marston quality,* she thought as the man talked. *Marston would be thrilled with this.* This one as well as a similar one in his booth, though, were nice paintings and, for the price, excellent buys for the assembled crowd. As Maria charmed him, he showed her a much better quality painting that was already sold. He asked for her name, address and phone number, and told her he would try to find something she would like, that he would start looking right after the bazaar. Maria said that she would stop by his shop instead on her way home in a couple of days. She was careful with the old pro, using her knowledge to find out as much as she could and to appeal to him as one interested in higher quality art. At the end of their conversation, Maria accepted his card and turned to make her way back to Dix.

Dix observed the flowing mass of humanity wearing everything conceivable. A woman pushing a tandem baby carriage with twins bumped him. After looking down, smiling at the woman and moving out of her way, he continued to watch the crowd. He saw Maria turn around to make her way back as Steve continued to look at the merchandise. From the corner of his eye Dix thought he saw someone familiar. He shifted his head and, as the man approached, focused on the face ten feet in front of him. Dix tensed as he realized that the face he was looking at was Colonel Mariano Simione, Chief Intelligence Officer for Land South Headquarters (NATO). His good friend Mariano was dressed as sharp as ever in civilian garb. *Shit!* Dix thought. *What the hell is he doing here?* Dix shot a look at Maria, who recognized Mariano at almost the same instant. She stood motionless as he continued toward Dix. A shorter Italian with a large crooked nose, also in civilian clothes, took hold of Maria's arm and spoke to her. He guided her toward Dix as Mariano stopped in front of him.

"Doing some shopping, Dix?" Mariano asked in a sarcastic tone of voice.

"A little," he replied cautiously.

The two studied each other for several seconds. Mariano appeared confident and commanding. The sudden appearance of Mariano and the Carabiniere sergeant caught Dix off guard.

"Let's take a little walk, Dix," Mariano said as he took Dix's arm and guided him through the crowd. "Ask your friend to join us too."

Dix realized he could not bluff Mariano. He looked toward Steve who was trying to stay hidden in the crowd to watch the unexpected meeting. Dix gave a nod to Steve to join them. Mariano guided them out of the tent to an area where they could be alone. The Carabiniere trailed in the rear.

They sat at an aluminum picnic table under a large tree away from the bazaar crowd. Dix introduced Steve to Mariano as a friend from Germany. Mariano lit a cigarette and took a deep drag, then exhaled. The Carabiniere sergeant mirrored his superior's actions. Steve retrieved his pouch of tobacco and placed a wad into his mouth. He chomped and chewed, then positioned the tobacco in his right cheek. Steve turned his head and spat a stream of juice on the ground. Dix's stomach tightened as the juice hit its mark and splattered.

Mariano spoke first. "Dix, I told you to stay out of this. It was too dangerous." He took another drag on his cigarette. "Maria damn near got killed in Udine, so did you when they shot at you. Now you're about to spook Robert Hamilton."

Maria's eyes registered surprise when he mentioned that someone had shot at Dix. Dix was startled to hear him mention the past events and refer to Hamilton as if he, Mariano, had been with them.

Steve rubbed his burr-cut head with his right hand, then spat tobacco juice on a spider making its way across in front of him. His eyes focused momentarily on the unlucky insect struggling to get free as he listened to Mariano.

The Carabiniere sergeant, taking a drag on his cigarette, watched Steve. His eyes followed the stream of tobacco juice, then he exhaled the smoke and looked up.

Mariano told them that NATO intelligence had been watching Hamilton. "When his name came up a couple of times as a result of my investigation into circumstances surrounding a couple of murders, we wanted to find out if there was a connection. As a result, we got a little interested in him," Mariano continued. "We don't have proof yet on Hamilton, and we can't make the connection or see the motivation he'd have for the killings. The old Austrian man in Udine has disappeared along with the journal."

"Mariano, you don't investigate murders," Dix said as he realized there was more to his story. "What are you investigating?"

"I'm not actually investigating the murders. I'm investigating why. Some highly sensitive NATO and G-7 documents, both of which are related, have disappeared. We believe the documents were taken to conceal something in some old Stasi files. These files are going to be turned over to the West at the upcoming G-7 meeting in Munich. That's all I can tell you—and it's all off the record."

Dix asked, "Why didn't you tell me this before?"

"Well, I had to make sure you weren't mixed up in this. Circumstantial evidence was going against you. You knew everyone that was murdered," Mariano continued. "You began popping up at every place the murders occurred and you have been accused of stealing the documents."

"Me? You know that's not true!"

"I had to be sure, Dix. After I was convinced that you were not responsible for the killings and stealing the documents, I tried to keep you out. When you wouldn't listen to me, I kept my eye on you."

"You didn't clear me?" Dix protested. "Goddamn it, Mariano, I thought you were my friend!"

"Calm down, Dix. As I said, I kept my eye on you. It was an opportunity that presented itself and we had to take advantage of it. If the focus was on you and everyone was looking for you, we figured Hamilton or whoever was in charge would slip up. Then we would have the assholes by the balls."

"With friends like you, who needs enemies? You could have at least told me!"

"It wouldn't have been as convincing. Now calm down and tell me what you've got."

Dix took a deep breath. Still nettled by his friend's doubt in him, he began to realize that Mariano was possibly right. He inhaled deeply again, then told Mariano all that he and Steve had learned about Hamilton. Dix concluded with their suspicion that Hamilton later went into the art business to sell off treasures that were supposedly lost or destroyed in the war. He added that they had no proof. Dix didn't mention the disks he had received from the Chlodwigs.

The information Dix, Maria and Steve pieced together made it obvious that Hamilton was involved and why the people were killed. Mariano confided in them that the murders and missing documents have led to an increased tension in international relations.

"The looting of treasures from the war is a touchy subject," Mariano said. "It's a wound that many don't want to reopen."

"We're going to pay a visit to Hamilton's house before he gets back home." Steve spat more tobacco juice on the small puddle he had formed previously. "We couldn't find any records or information in his shop about his operation, so it must be in his house."

"No! It's too risky," Mariano protested. He remained expressionless. "Turn over what you've got and I'll take it from here. Otherwise, I'll have the MPs arrest you."

"Mariano," Dix said boldly, "we're doing this for Edgar, Klaus, and the others. Then we're taking what we find to Munich for the G-7 meeting. You're going to get the whole lot."

"He's no fool." Mariano sounded irritated. "Hamilton will have guards. If he has any information there, it will be locked up."

They continued their verbal tug of war for several more minutes. Finally, Mariano reluctantly agreed, but only if he went along. He told them that by going with them they would be quasi-legal. The U.S. and European countries had sanctioned him to take appropriate actions deemed necessary whenever and wherever required. "My investigation started late last year," he told them. "It's classified with restricted access. Ruggero

Baldassare contacted me, but he was killed before he could give me all the information on the operation. He was a maritime liaison for the Italian government and was also an advisor to the G-7. It was only recently that we suspected Hamilton was the key, but we haven't been able to prove it. My investigation stalled until you and Maria stumbled into the operation and unknowingly gave me information to get the investigation moving again."

Mariano further told them that because of the sensitivity, few knew of his investigation. Even the lower echelons of the governments hadn't been told. He warned that it would set his investigation back, if not derail it altogether, if Dix were arrested before he had all the evidence. Worse, it would be almost impossible to keep everything quiet if Dix was arrested and Mariano was with him.

Steve detailed his plan to Mariano. He wanted to be at Hamilton's after dark, slip in and out before anyone knew he was there. His plan was simple enough. All they needed to do was to get to the house, check it out and move in when the time was right. They would get his records and go straight to Munich.

28

Maria told them what she had seen at Hamilton's booth. "His furniture definitely included quality antique pieces," she said. "From what I've seen in his shop and here at his booth, some pieces are reproductions and some are not. I think Hamilton did that on purpose to camouflage his operation or at least give an appearance of being legitimate. Still, I believe that some of the furniture he is selling probably is from the Nazis' loot."

"What did the Nazis have to do with furniture?" Steve asked.

"During the war the Nazis stripped everything in their path, looting municipalities and private collections right down to the bells in the towers. That included furniture."

"Yes, that's true," Mariano said. "But are you sure these items are from the loot Hitler's soldiers took? Can you prove it?"

"No. Well, I mean I can't prove it right now." Her mind raced. "But I think I can. I didn't think anything about it at the time. But just now as we talked about the Nazis and Hamilton, something caused me to think back to when Signore Afferi showed me his files."

"What do you have?" Mariano quizzed.

"At Hamilton's shop I noticed a light area on the back of some of the paintings and some of the furniture. Sometimes this light place was underneath the furniture. Most people wouldn't notice it or they would dismiss it as a small rubbed place that didn't matter. At the time, that's what I thought. But now I'm curious. The paintings apparently have the same rub spot on the back of the frames and in about the same place. I saw it again on the landscape painting at Hamilton's booth."

"What's the big deal with a rub mark on the back? They're bound to have rub marks on them if he hauls them around all over the place," Dix said.

"I'm thinking those places may be where he sanded the wood after he removed a label or mark. If something was there, the wood would be lighter in the place where the label had been and its outline would be darkened by the glue. If he removed the label, he would need to sand the spot and then touch it up or make it blend in with the surrounding wood. Making it look like a rubbed place was about his only option. I'd like to examine what he has more closely. He may have missed an ERR label."

"What's an ERR label?" Steve interrupted.

"It's a small label that the Nazis put on everything they confiscated—with the initials ERR on it. They stand for the Einsatzstab Reichsleiter Rosenberg. Alfred Rosenberg, Reich Minister for the Occupied Eastern Territories, set up the ERR with one objective during the war—the looting of European art," she said. "Everything the ERR took had a label, even the paintings. The label identified the item as property of the Nazis'."

"On the disks, I remember reading about the ERR," Dix said.

"What about the paintings?" Mariano said. "Tell me about the ones you saw."

"The ones I saw were mostly unsigned or signed by lesser known artists. They were from about the early twentieth century back to about the mid-eighteenth century. He had all types on display—from fleshy nudes, landscapes, and portraits to fruit and flowers—in all sizes."

"We need hard proof," Mariano said. "Hamilton would surely have checked them over very closely for any identifying marks."

"I'm sure he did. Hamilton seemed to push a little on his ability to locate better quality works," she added. "Several people accepted his offer. He was more brazen than I anticipated. Maybe he has been at it so long that it is second nature to him." Maria brushed the hair from her face and took a sip of Coke.

"Or he's getting careless," Steve said.

"Or maybe he's trying to get rid of the stuff as fast as he can and go out of business," Mariano said as he stroked his mustache.

"I'll be right back." Dix stood. "I'm going to call Francesca to see if she has any more information."

"I'll go with you. I'll check with John to see what else he's found out," Steve said as he turned and spat tobacco juice.

Maria continued her discussion with Mariano. She stretched and leaned back. Mariano withdrew a pack of cigarettes from his pocket and offered one to the sergeant. The sergeant lit Mariano's, then his. Maria sipped her drink again as the soft breeze swept beneath the large tree where they sat. She told Mariano about the records she had researched and the paintings she had seen—Ida Kohne's and the Marstons' as well as the ones in the old Austrian's Fiat—were all listed in those records.

"They were all listed as missing since the war," she said. "The one the Marstons have was taken from a Jewish family during the war by the Nazis. The only survivor of the family is Sonja Abramovych. I met with her when we were in Brussels. She told me the heartbreaking story of what happened to her and her family during the war. I want to help her and do whatever I can to get her painting back."

"Do the Marstons know?"

"I don't know the answer to that. But since the Marstons have her painting and we know the Marstons, as well as Ida Kohne, please keep my name out of it."

"Not to worry. The Art Theft Investigation team is very good and will preserve your confidentiality."

"Would you go with me to meet with them when we get back to Vicenza?"

"Yes. We'll see Colonel Pasquali. Besides, he wants to talk to you as well."

Francesca told Dix that things were heating up at the G-7 committee's office. The Germans, Italians, French and Americans were pissed. She told Dix they still weren't talking but continued to blame him for stealing the documents and killing some of their people. "There is a lot of talk about the files that are going to be turned over to the West in Munich. Everyone believes they contain information that will embarrass the U.S. and several other countries. I have a Swiss friend," she said, "that told me the Swiss are uneasy also. They think the files will give information on their dealings with the Nazis during the war."

"What do you mean?" Her statement puzzled Dix. "I thought the Swiss were neutral."

"That's what most everyone thought, but they cooperated with the Nazis so they wouldn't get invaded. They did quite a bit for Germany during the war."

Francesca continued to relay the details she was able to find out. She told Dix that the G-7 was having a reception, dinner and party the night before the meeting. The reception and party along with the general session the next day were to be held at the Bayerischer Hof Hotel.

"I need you to get us invitations to the reception and party. Then get us reservations at the Vier Jahreszeiten Hotel. It's on Maximilianstrasse only a few blocks from the Bayerischer Hof. Put them in Steve's name—Steve Galtero—they may be checking the hotels and I don't want to walk into their hands."

"Right. I know the hotel," she replied. "The invitations shouldn't be much of a problem; it's the hotel rooms that will cost me a favor. Give Steve my phone number and have him call me when he gets to Munich."

"Francesca, one more thing. I need a disguise."

"God, Dix, be careful. This cloak and dagger stuff is what gets people killed."

"I will. Just make it a good disguise. You'd better use a different name on Maria's invitation."

"Okay. My cousin is in the theater. I'll give her a call."

"Be discreet. Thanks, Francesca."

"Oh, Dix, I did find out something else strange," she said."

"What is it?"

"Several people on the committee staff have suddenly retired and they weren't just U.S. staffers. After checking into it, seems they retired because of the files."

"Really?" Dix said as he took in this new information.

"I've done some other checking around," she continued. "It appears that some of the bigger museums and a couple of auction houses have gotten their hands on some art works that were known to be stolen. It looks like the Nazi treasures seduced a lot of people."

"Yeah, a lot of people in some pretty high and powerful places."

217

"Dix, one more thing," she cautioned. "The G-7 has convinced the authorities that you are armed and dangerous. They just mentioned you and no one else. I'm afraid they will shoot first and ask questions later."

"It figures—the sons-of-bitches."

"They're trying to shift the investigation away from the committee to you. One of my contacts suggested that you are even trafficking in stolen art. The G-7 is putting pressure on the authorities for your arrest."

"They're starting to panic," he responded. "With panic comes mistakes."

29

It was early evening and the sun was still high in the sky over the small village of Seebruck. The five drove around the sprawling estate of Robert Hamilton. The property was surrounded by a high concrete wall finished in white stucco to match the house. An electronically-operated, wrought iron gate provided the only access. A magnificent two-story house with a clay tile roof and wide eaves stood in the middle of the property almost one hundred meters from the walls. The porch, reaching the second story and supported by round columns, provided a grand welcome to visitors. Trees, shrubs and flowerbeds were professionally arranged to compliment the architecture. Statues and figurines punctuated the manicured lawn. A large fountain splashed into a shallow pool. The drive curved around the fountain to the front entrance of the house.

A four-car detached garage was off to the right toward the rear. Behind the house was a swimming pool with two statues of nudes kneeling on one knee pouring water into its far corners. Between the pool and the house was a wide patio area for entertaining with a covered bar and kitchen area.

They parked in a secluded spot and walked to a small tree-covered hill that allowed them to observe the estate until it was time to make their move. The sun sank lower in the sky and a breeze swirled in the pine trees. Two squirrels played in the pine needles beneath the trees. A wild rabbit hopped nearby, stopping occasionally to nibble. Dix nudged Steve when he saw the gate open. They focused on the entrance to the drive. A blue Mercedes eased through, then proceeded to the house.

"Give me the glasses," Dix said, taking the binoculars from Steve without waiting and putting them to his eyes. "That's the same Mercedes I saw speed away from my house and in Brussels."

Dix watched the car come to a stop in front of the house. When the car door opened, he saw the blond-headed man.

"Shit!" he said. "It's him—the blond-headed man. I'm sure he's the one that's been killing everyone."

Steve focused on the man and took the glasses back from Dix to get a better look. A second man emerged from the house to greet him. Dix looked back at the Mercedes. He trained his eyes on the rear of the car. He took the glasses back from Steve to get a good look at the license tag.

"Government plates," Dix said in a cold voice. "I *knew* it was government plates. They're U.S. State Department plates from the embassy. That's how he moves in and out undetected."

Dix understood after identifying the plates how the blond man could vanish then reappear virtually anywhere. The car, with government plates, could move about without being stopped and pass through any border crossing without question. Hamilton was using U.S. Government resources for other things, and it stood to reason that he would use a government vehicle to conduct his business affairs.

Steve took out his 35mm camera with telephoto lens and started taking pictures. He took pictures of the car and license plate, the blond-headed man, the man who greeted him and the house. These photos would supplement the information on the disks and any records that they might find inside the house.

"Simple plan," Dix said sarcastically as they watched the two men disappear into the house. "No problem, in and out, you said."

"Well, things have a way of changing." Steve smiled crookedly, then spat tobacco juice on a beetle making his way along the pine needles. "I'll just modify the plan. Don't fire 'em up unless you have to!"

They continued to observe the estate and to figure out where the study was located. From their vantage point, they could not tell if there was a burglar alarm or other security devices. As the sun dipped lower in the sky, it reflected off something bright on the porch. The last few minutes of sunlight revealed the security camera.

"Dix, did you see the reflection?" Steve asked.

"I saw it. I saw the security camera. That means there are more."

"Dix, Steve, geese!" Maria whispered loudly as she pointed to the nearly two dozen birds.

"Shit!" Dix exclaimed between clenched teeth.

The geese were the security guards of the estate. They were more efficient than dogs. Geese had been used by the Army for security details for years. If an intruder attempted to enter their territory, geese would become extremely loud, honking and flapping their wings. They would also become very aggressive and peck at the intruder. The clamor they raised would alert any person inside the house.

The geese and the security cameras were unexpected complications they'd have to contend with. As they continued their surveillance on the house, the sun disappeared and the landscape became dark. Outside lights from the estate illuminated the exterior of the house and high-pressure sodium lights lit the perimeter. It was impossible to approach the house in any direction undetected.

Steve turned to Mariano and said, "Go to town and get a bag of grain. Get about ten to twenty kilos of corn, wheat, or oats from a feed store. Then get back as quickly as possible."

Mariano nodded then motioned to his sergeant to stay with Steve. He then slid back from his position and moved toward his car.

While Mariano was gone, Dix and Maria continued to watch the house. Steve and the sergeant searched the area for the electrical supply line and for a possible weak point in the security.

"No activity from the house," Dix reported to Steve as he and the sergeant approached.

"I found where the electricity from the property connects to the main line. I can disconnect it, but it won't do any good. We spotted a back-up generator by the garage."

"Twenty kilos of corn," Mariano said as he returned. He took a drag on his cigarette then motioned toward the bag with his hand as he watched Steve kick the bag before kneeling beside it. "I bought a big bag of rolls from a bakery to go along with the corn."

"That's good. They'll have a nice little feast," Steve said as he took a drink of water from the bottle. Then Steve told them his plan. "I'm not happy with it, but given the circumstances it's all I can come up with at the moment."

Steve removed the Heckler and Koch from his bag and laid it on the bag of corn. He told the others to get their weapons and check them. Then he retrieved his backup Beretta and laid it on the bag. In a continuous, almost mechanical, movement, Steve slid the aiming device onto the grooves in front of the trigger guard, then screwed the silencer onto the end of the threaded barrel. He placed two extra magazines in his front pocket.

Dix, Mariano and the sergeant each withdrew a 9mm Beretta. Maria watched the three men drop the magazines from the pistols and pull the slides back. She picked up Steve's backup and mimicked the actions of the men. The three stopped and watched her expert moves with the Beretta. They remained silent until she finished.

"Maria, I—" Dix spoke what the others thought.

"Dix," she cut him off, "just for protection."

He knew from past experience that it was no use arguing with her. *She sounds just like she did back in Panama,* Dix thought. *Tough and determined. She was never one to stay behind.* He held his tongue momentarily as she slapped the magazine back into the pistol and put it into her back pocket.

Steve found a weak spot in the security of the house on the side they were on, about halfway back along the property near the small stream. A tree grew on the outside of the wall about six feet away. The branches that grew over the wall were cut back to a height of about eight feet. He believed that by taking out the light closest to that spot in the wall, the area would become dark and unobservable to the camera dedicated to that area. He would have only a few minutes to get from the wall to the side of the house. Steve counted on the cameras not being able to see the area within three feet of the side of the house as he felt they were intended to spot someone on the grounds further out from the wall. The camera at the entrance was a different matter. It was intended to show who was arriving and getting out of a car before they entered the house.

Mariano and the sergeant waited as Steve took Dix and Maria to a spot on the wall about thirty meters forward of where he planned to cross over. They gathered old limbs from the surrounding area to pile up next to the wall. Steve added an old tire he found nearby and several pieces of a log that someone was cutting into firewood. They built up the pile until Maria could stand on it and reach the top of the wall. As Maria peered over the fence, she saw geese coming toward her. They weren't honking but they were quickly moving to that part of the wall to investigate the noise they had heard. Dix started pitching pieces of rolls and corn on the ground next to the wall and in the shadow so as not to be seen.

"When they get here, Maria," Steve said, helping her stand as he handed her a handful of corn and rolls, "don't make eye contact. Keep your head down and be still, as though you're meditating. Pitch out more corn and rolls. Let them get used to you and as they do, move up slowly until you're on the wall."

Steve had them feed the birds for a half hour before Maria tried to move onto the wall. "Remember," Steve cautioned, "if they arch up their wings and stick their beaks up and forward, back off. They are becoming aggressive and warning you out of their territory. Just be calm and don't get into a hurry."

"Okay," she said with a nod.

"When I make it to the house," Steve said, "give them the rest of the corn and rolls, then ease off the wall and let them go for it. Go up to where we crossed the wall and go over. Make your way to the house from there. Go way around the entire flock."

Steve tied a rope around a tree limb that hung over the wall. Steve, Mariano and the sergeant had to climb the tree and, using the rope, swing to the top of the wall, pass the rope to the next one waiting to swing over, then ease themselves down the wall. That was the easy part. Steve had learned through many years of experience that the simplest of tasks can sometimes cause big problems. In this case, after they crossed the wall it looked simple enough—sprint the hundred meters in the darkness undetected.

Steve checked his watch then moved down several branches. He looked around to check on the two feeding the geese and decided it was time to act. He pulled out his .45, gently pulled the slide to the rear and guided it back into place chambering a round. Mariano and the sergeant replicated his actions then flicked on the safety with their thumbs. Steve looked around at the others one last time before he started. Assured they were ready, he rested his arm on a branch for support and took aim at the high pressure sodium light. The silenced Heckler and Koch snapped and recoiled. The light popped out. Darkness slammed around them. There would be only a few minutes of confusion while whoever was monitoring the security cameras tried to figure out what happened. If they were watching TV or engaging in some other activity or entertainment as Steve guessed, it would give him more time.

Steve swung onto the wall. Gaining his balance he flipped the rope back to the waiting sergeant. He grabbed it with his right hand, strained on the rope and swung across. Steve steadied him when he reached the top of the wall and, as the stocky Carabiniere passed the rope to Mariano, Steve lowered himself to the ground. He turned and remained still as he inspected the area. The sergeant joined him on the ground, followed by Mariano. It was still quiet; the geese had not detected the intruders. Steve scrutinized the area one last time, then motioned for them to go.

At a sprint, Steve led the other two—with Mariano on his right and five paces to the rear and the sergeant on the left and four paces to the rear. Steve leaped across the stream followed by the sergeant, then Mariano. The sergeant slipped on the wet grass and fell to the ground with a grunt. The grunt attracted the attention of one of the feeding geese. It turned and arched its wings and extended its neck with head forward, then started honking. The rest of the flock joined in as the one goose advanced on the intruders. "Shit!" Steve said to himself. "It's going to hell in a handbasket!" Mariano helped the sergeant up, then continued toward the house.

Steve pumped his arms and pushed his body to full speed as he raced toward the house. His lungs expanded and contracted, bringing in large amounts of fresh air then forcing the used air from his body. He strained with every muscle to gain more speed, more ground. The corner of the house got closer and closer. Pumping and pushing, he was almost there when two large black dogs emerged from the darkness, their ferocious teeth displaying hostility. Their growls of warning roared in his ears. Bringing his body to a stop, Steve crouched and swung the Heckler and Koch in front of him in one continuous motion. He used both hands to steady the pistol and squeeze the trigger. It snapped, then he shifted his aim and squeezed off another round. It snapped again. Verifying that both animals were on the ground, Steve continued toward the corner of the house as the honking birds advanced.

Steve looked over his shoulder and saw Dix and Maria, behind the flock of noisy birds, running toward him. He turned his head to check on his companions and saw a figure standing in the darkness. The moon illuminated the nickel-plated pistol in his hand. At that moment a blinding flash followed by a thunderous roar shocked Steve. Instinctively, he hit the ground and tumbled as two more blasts filled the night air. Rolling, then bringing the Heckler and Koch up, he squeezed the trigger and felt the recoil. Steve watched the man's body jerk and flip backwards. When the body remained motionless, he looked around to see the Carabiniere sitting up with his left arm streaming blood. Mariano was moving toward the sergeant. The honking geese had stopped and the frightened animals were retreating to the darkened stream. Dix and Maria were still moving forward.

"He's okay!" Mariano blurted as he looked up from the sergeant while he placed a handkerchief on the wound. "It's in his upper left arm, not serious."

"Okay!" Steve said, his lungs pumping for fresh air. "Go to the back of the house. Watch out. They know they've got company now!"

"Dix, go with Mariano!" Steve said. "Maria, stay out here and cover our ass!"

Steve crouched and moved slowly along the side of the house. Mariano and Dix did the same and then disappeared around the back. Steve continued foot by foot. A shot rang out, then two more echoed from the back of the house. Steve froze. He strained to listen, but all he could hear was his own heavy breathing and pounding of his heart. He advanced to the front entrance. He crept up the steps, his eyes constantly scanning. He reached the door and flattened himself against the wall. He hesitated, examined the exterior one more time, then with a quick peek he looked inside. Seeing only paintings on the wall and furniture filling the brightly lit room, he slowly opened the door.

He crept in and saw Dix's reflection in a mirror in the far end of the house. Steve continued when he received an acknowledgment in the reflection. He made his way through the front room to join Dix to secure that end of the house. A shot exploded, followed by three more. Steve couldn't see what was happening. He inched forward. Then he saw the figure of a man. Raising the Heckler and Koch, he squeezed off a round. The pistol snapped and the body collapsed. The room fell silent again.

Then the deafening blast of another shot behind Steve filled the room. His lightning-quick reflexes twisted him and took him to the floor. He didn't feel any pain. The room was quiet once again. His body had not been hit. He inched up with the Heckler and Koch at the ready. Maria was standing and looking at Steve. He stood, then saw the body sprawled on the floor in front of her. Blood was oozing out of the dead man's head, turning his blond hair red. A silenced pistol was still clutched in the dead man's right hand.

They searched the rest of the house for anyone else. Satisfied they were alone, Steve told Maria to keep a watch out for anyone approaching.

"A simple plan," Dix said, ribbing Steve as he walked into the room. "Don't fire 'em up unless you have to! Looks like we had to from the get go."

"Well, the assholes wanted to play rough." Steve grinned and tightened his right cheek, then began chomping on the tobacco. "I really didn't appreciate the dogs!"

Steve immediately put Dix to work searching for Hamilton's records. Mariano entered with the sergeant and started inspecting the house. The sergeant held his left arm with his right, keeping pressure on the wound under the handkerchief Mariano had applied as a bandage.

"You all right?" Steve asked the sergeant.

"It hurts a bit. The bleeding has stopped. I'm okay."

Their next step was to watch out for Hamilton's return. Mariano insisted that they take Hamilton alive, if possible. Not knowing how much time they had until Hamilton returned, each went to their assigned tasks. Steve began to drag the bodies out of sight so that anyone approaching the house wouldn't be alarmed.

30

Dix entered the study. An impressive collection of oils and watercolors hung on the walls; porcelain vases accented the furnishings. A large walnut desk supported a computer. Dix sat in the desk chair and pushed a button to start the computer. Its lights blinked on and the hard drive whirred into action. Dix opened the center drawer and saw pens, pencils, paperclips, scissors, several business cards—all the usual items one would expect to find. The computer monitor screen finally blinked and filled with color, then a window popped up asking for a password. Dix leaned back. *What would he use?* Dix thought. *The cache locations in the files on the disks were named after the celestial bodies. So why not here too?* He leaned forward and typed in "Big Dipper." The window flashed "Access Denied," then flashed "Enter Password."

"Shit!" Dix exclaimed. He reached for the keyboard again and entered "Sun." Again he received the same response. "Damn it!" he said. He paused, then tried "Milky Way," but it was no more successful than his first two attempts. He flipped the keyboard over to look underneath, hoping Hamilton may have taped the password to its bottom. Nothing.

He checked the immediate area for a possible clue to the

password. Again nothing. He returned his attention to the drawers, hoping to find the password written down somewhere. He pulled on the top drawer on the right side, only to find it locked. He pulled on each of the other drawers, but they too were locked. Opening the center drawer, he took out a pair of scissors and worked them between the top right drawer and the frame of the desk. Using all of his strength, he managed to pry the top drawer open.

Dix began to search through the folders, one by one. Periodically, he read in detail some of the pages he pulled from the files and set them aside. Others, he just scanned. When finished with that drawer, he forced open the bottom right drawer. The wood cracked and splintered. At the rear of the drawer, he saw a bulging file with "Pegasus" typed on the tab He pulled the file from the drawer, laid it on the desk and opened it with anticipation. Pegasus, Dix recalled, was the organization that Hamilton had formed with a man named Schmidt. The file contained the background details of Pegasus, since its beginning in 1945.

Hamilton had catalogued the contents of each cache, the location, and person in charge. There was an accounting of the gold on deposit with banks in Switzerland, Paraguay, Argentina, Sweden, Spain and Portugal and how it was subsequently laundered to other bank accounts. Another page showed jewelry sold, with and without stones. A large amount of the loot had been sold to museums throughout the world. It was the same information Dix had read on the disks he got from Rodrik Chlodwig.

Just at that moment, Dix heard the sound of footsteps. He looked up as Maria entered the room, examining the paintings on the wall and the vases on the shelves.

"It's like museum," she said. "I can't believe this! There are paintings by Metzinger, Baumeister, Schwitters, Munch,

Kirchner, van Gogh, Picasso. There's priceless art all over the place."

"I know, it's amazing. I'm finding a lot of records in the desk with information on his operation. But nothing that isn't already on Klaus' disks. There might be more information on his computer, but I can't get into it."

"I'm going to keep looking around. Maybe you'll figure out a way to access it."

Working his way through the files, Dix realized that Klaus Müller had either made hard copies of the files he was looking at or Hamilton had electronic copies in his computer that Klaus had copied onto disks. *Now Ingel's story on Castle Hill makes more sense! Klaus must have threatened to use his copies to expose the organization, if they didn't let him out. They killed him but he had already passed the disks to Ingel. Then the organization killed Ingel. Now I have those disks and they must know it—or believe I do!*

As Hamilton's organization grew, it became more expensive and he needed to convert more and more of the loot into cash. The gold wasn't difficult. Much of it was in the banks to which he had access. The gold that was not in the banks, he either sold or had made into jewelry and then sold. The jewels were more difficult. Some were sold with the gold and silver he had made into jewelry while other pieces were sold through outlets, like his store, or through a number of soldiers, like Sergeant Brainard, who were scattered across Europe. Dix sat back in the chair overwhelmed at the magnitude of the operation and the amount of the treasure Hamilton had managed to sell off.

Although the records were a little sketchy, Dix was able to determine that the Pegasus operation had established a trade route into the Soviet Union. At the end of World War II, when the Russians were advancing on Berlin from the east, Captain

Hamilton went to Berlin to investigate reports of looting by the Soviets. He discovered that they took the opportunity to reclaim those treasures they felt were rightfully theirs. The Soviets added restitution to the list and helped themselves to even more of the remaining Nazi treasures to stock their super museum. They had in fact plundered a substantial amount from the territory they recaptured from the Germans. Much of the treasures the Russians took had remained locked away ever since. It was Hamilton's trip to investigate the Soviet's plundering of Germany that he made the contacts for the treasures.

Dix discovered in another file that Hamilton, through his position with the CIA, located and traded many of the treasures. Hamilton also used his position to arrange for his nephew, Al Blakemore, to progress rapidly in the civil service. He eventually landed a spot on the G-7 committee, where he could alert Hamilton on what was to be discussed at each meeting. When the discussion of certain works of art or the art itself posed a threat to Pegasus, Hamilton would arrange for that piece to be "discovered" and returned. If anyone refused to cooperate, Hamilton would leak information about that person or treasure. It was apparent that Hamilton understood he would lose his cover and access to the inside information through his various contacts and travels throughout Europe when he retired. By getting his nephew situated with diplomatic access, the operation would continue to flourish using the G-7 resources. The files didn't indicate the extent to which Pegasus was using the G-7 resources, but it was clear that these files were not current. Dix suspected that the more up-to-date files were electronic and stored in the computer. He also suspected that the financial records and records of Hamilton's customers would also be electronic.

Next Dix found notes and papers further detailing how

the operation worked. "Maria was right!" Dix mumbled to himself. "Hamilton was using the military to ship some of the stuff back to the States. He duped young soldiers for a couple of hundred dollars to include a box or small crate in their household goods shipment back to the States. He knew they would go along. They could make easy money and no one would get hurt, so they agreed. The soldiers had no idea the risk they were putting themselves in. What an asshole."

A final folder contained certificates and letters of appreciation Hamilton had received from governments and military officials across Europe for his contributions and assistance. None of these people were aware of his secret agenda. He had made himself well-known and respected, no doubt, to gain access to places where he could sell off his merchandise. *Quite an operation!* Dix thought. *I've got to get into his computer.*

"Dix, you've got to see this!" Maria burst out with excitement. "Come on! It's simply magnificent!"

Startled by the interruption, Dix looked up as Maria approached again, then got up to follow her. She led him down a hall and through a door leading to a basement that seemed more like a bunker. It had reinforced concrete walls, a steel blast door and a fire suppression system. The decorated room was a mini museum. It contained Hamilton's private collection of the most valuable works—paintings, sketches and drawings in oil, watercolor, ink and pencil.

"This is incredible!" Maria exclaimed. "They're all here, da Vinci, Monet, Degas, Renoir, Rembrandt, Dürer, Velázquez.... The collection of artists goes on and on."

Speechless, Dix followed her from painting to painting—landscapes, still lifes, nudes, genre scenes and so on. Statues, vases, figurines, tapestries and bronzes were displayed throughout on walls, shelves and pedestals. There were also exquisite works in gold, silver and every kind of precious stone. They quickly concluded that the collection needed to be documented. Dix was eager to return to the computer, so Maria called Mariano and Steve down to help her. The sergeant stayed upstairs to keep a lookout for Hamilton.

Steve got his camera and photographed everything to go with their notes. It was a laborious process but one that needed to be done in order to recover the art and to put Hamilton away. By the time Maria, Steve and Mariano finished, Hamilton still had not returned. The unnerving part of waiting on Hamilton was at hand.

It was morning when Maria sat upright and caught Dix's alerted expression. She then looked at Steve and Mariano, both slumped in the wingback chairs asleep. The geese were honking and fussing. She peered into the monitor that showed the front gate. It was open, then a red Mercedes van eased into the drive.

"Steve!" Maria called out. "Mariano. He's here!"

The four men sprang to life. Steve and Mariano dashed to the back door and slipped out. Dix and the sergeant took their places inside the front door as Maria focused on the screen and watched the gray-haired Hamilton slow the van to a stop in front of the garage.

The unsuspecting Hamilton opened the van door and started to get out. Steve crept up behind him and gently placed the silencer behind his left jaw. When the cold steel touched his skin, Steve pulled the hammer back with his thumb, allowing the click to roar in Hamilton's ear.

"Welcome home, Mr. Hamilton," Steve said in a low voice. "Nice place you have here. Would you like to join us inside?"

Hamilton didn't reply but submitted to Steve's tug on his shirt.

31

Seated in a wingback chair, Hamilton raised his head and looked at each of his visitors. "Who are you and what do you want?" Hamilton betrayed no fear in his controlled voice. "You're not thieves. Which government?"

"Colonel Mariano Simione, Chief Intelligence Officer for Land South Headquarters, NATO," Mariano said. Then he pointed to the others. "Lieutenant Colonel Steve Galtero, Dix and Maria Connor, and Sergeant Enzo Fiore."

"Connor, you have the lives of a cat," Hamilton remarked, staring at the man he had ordered killed. "I know of you too, Simione."

Mariano cut him off. He confronted Hamilton with everything they had pieced together from the disks and the information Dix had found in the desk.

"Tell me about Pegasus," Mariano began, "and who is Schmidt?"

"If you have all that, why are you asking me?" Hamilton shot back.

"What's the password to your computer?" Dix demanded.

"You've got what you want. There's nothing else in the computer."

Dix punched Hamilton in the face, tipping the chair back and sliding it to one side.

Dazed and a bit surprised, Hamilton said, "Fuck you!"

Again Dix punched him. "Don't try my patience, you son-of-a-bitch! What's the password?"

Hamilton was a little slow to come around. Blood ran from his nose and his left eye began to swell. With slightly slurred speech, Hamilton began, "I knew this day might come. I've lived very well and have amassed a large fortune...." Hamilton rambled on about the unification of Germany and the breakup of the USSR, saying many new opportunities were at hand. The treasures in the former Soviet states were waiting to be taken and he had the connections to get them. There was an emerging market in those countries providing wealth to those who had been without. With this new wealth came the desire for the things he had to offer. "I can make you rich," Hamilton said as he looked at each one of them. "Ten million dollars each, right now if you join me. In the future there will be many more times that. Join me!"

"It's not yours to have, Hamilton," Dix said. "What's the password?"

"I've told you, there's nothing in the computer."

Dix slugged him again, this time in the abdomen. "In 1945 you screwed over the Army and the rightful owners of the treasures. Since then, you've continued feeding off the military to help your organization."

"You've killed a lot of good people over this stuff," Mariano added. "Hamilton, I'm afraid you're going to start paying now."

Hamilton gradually provided more information. But each time he was asked for the password, he refused to answer and suffered more blows from Dix and Steve. When the questioning turned to the operation in Italy and to the journal, he denied knowing anything about either. Finally, after an hour of questioning and more slugs, he began to reveal more and more. He started back at the end of the war when he began the operation he called Pegasus.

He told them that one night after he had inventory Altair one of the caches he concealed for Pegasus, he went to eat at the farmhouse of Nefen and Hedda Reinhard. "Nefen and Hedda were the caretakers of that cache and ran a safe house established by the Nazis for the Fourth Reich. I had been there three or four times before and had struck an agreement with the Reinhards. It was money and their freedom that had convinced them to work for me. I arrived at their farmhouse a little later than usual that night. They were feeding a young, attractive man in tattered clothes. He was trim and fit with his hair cut short. They introduced him as a neighbor who farmed the adjacent property. His hands were soft, not rough and calloused like a farmer's would be." Hamilton paused. "Could I have some water?"

Mariano nodded and Maria went to the kitchen. She poured a glass of water and brought it back. "I'll tell you what you want to know," Hamilton said as she gave the glass to him. He took a sip before continuing.

"The man the Reinhards were feeding said his wife had been killed when the Allies were closing in on the Nazis near their farm. He was wounded in the side by a piece of shrapnel. I checked the man's side and saw where the blood was seeping through the bandages and staining his shirt. I asked him why he wasn't in the Army," Hamilton said, then gulped the water. "He said he was declared unfit for military service. For the time being I left it at that. Hedda told me he had a temperature and his wound was getting infected. She said that medical supplies were practically nonexistent for German civilians, but word had spread that the Allies had plenty of medicine and antibiotics. She asked me for help. I just stared at the man, who

237

then put his hand in his pocket and pulled out a clenched fist." Hamilton paused.

"Go on," Mariano ordered.

"He offered me a handful of diamonds for some fresh bandages and antibiotics. He specifically asked for penicillin. I barely knew what penicillin was," Hamilton said. "I told the man to go to a hospital, because it was difficult to get supplies. The farmer told me the hospital didn't have any supplies either and he was afraid he would be mistaken for a soldier. I told the Reinhards that I knew the man was lying but went along with it. I was intrigued by the diamonds and wanted to learn more before deciding what to do."

The man had been watching Hamilton and by not turning in the Reinhards, he figured Hamilton was going into business for himself. "Schmidt was how he introduced himself," Hamilton recalled. "He said he had much more and no one knew where it was hidden."

"Go on!" Mariano said.

"To make the long story short, Schmidt said the treasures he had wouldn't be found in General Kaltenbrunner's files. He convinced me that he knew of more treasure."

Hamilton stopped, took the glass again and had a sip before continuing. "He was very sharp and aloof, but I knew that Schmidt was really a Nazi—most likely an SS officer trying to escape. When I brought the bandages and medicine, Schmidt showed me a black leather-bound book. The notes in the journal convinced me that he was indeed telling the truth about the additional treasures. The journal revealed more information than I was able to find out from General Kaltenbrunner's files. Schmidt was very cautious with the journal and warned me that, if I ever crossed him, he would turn the journal over to the Americans. I knew that would be the end of my operation and time in jail. Schmidt also knew that if I turned him in, he would be jailed and possibly executed. Each of us had something on the other and we both wanted what the other had to offer. The limited mutual trust went only so far, as we each knew the other was capable of murder."

Hamilton knew that his time in the Alt Aussee area would soon end. "The area was going to be turned over the Russians after the war," Hamilton said. "Meeting Schmidt was what I needed."

The two men entered into an agreement and Pegasus was born. Hamilton was in the American sector and Schmidt was in the Soviet sector. Schmidt didn't want to be discovered by the Soviets and most of the hidden treasures were going to be in the Soviet zone. In addition, Hamilton developed his contacts when he found out the Russians were plundering treasures from the Germans. Hamilton had extensive knowledge of treasures in Russia that were hidden away in bunkers. When the time was right, Pegasus would gain access to those treasures as well.

The arrangement they made had remained in place ever since. The aloof Schmidt retained control of the black leather-bound book. He provided the supplies to the operation and Hamilton provided the organization and distribution system. "Both of us profited handsomely from this arrangement," Hamilton said. "Our contact with each other was through the Reinhards."

When asked more about who Schmidt really was, Hamilton said, "Schmidt...just an old Nazi." He gave no other details.

"Did you ever meet with him again?" Mariano probed.

"When the Reinhards died, Schmidt and I met at the funeral and agreed to keep the arrangement alive under the same conditions. We developed a new way to communicate, using a system of coded messages in the newspaper whenever contact was necessary—for a purchase, sale, or other reason. With the development of the Internet, we shifted to e-mail. That's everything I know and that's probably the journal you are talking about," Hamilton said. "That was the only time I saw it. I've never crossed Schmidt and never tried to find out where he lived. I haven't seen the old man in probably fifteen or twenty years. He has some young, good-looking American fellow working for him now and he makes all exchanges."

"This guy is good," Dix said leaning back, glancing at Maria, then Steve and Mariano. "He discovered the treasures, set up an organization using handpicked people from the Nazi regime, kept a low profile, and for almost fifty years sold off the treasures that the world thought were destroyed or forgotten about."

"Yeah, and right under the noses of the Europeans, using the American military community as an outlet," Steve said as he stood. "He was operating from the center of where it all began and under the nose of the U.S. Army—the organization that discovered the treasures and thought the issue of treasure was resolved."

"He retires from his government job to live like a king," Maria added.

"Right," Dix said. "He has the organization and distribution system and all the information on the loot."

"Yes, he developed a hell of an organization," Mariano added. "I guess the others in the organization, such as Ingel, Ruggero Baldassare, Edgar Kohne and Eric Sherard, were responsible for certain caches, made deliveries for packaging and sold or exchanged the loot in their areas of responsibility. Their diplomatic credentials allowed them access to almost every part of the world."

"Something like that." Hamilton said.

"Then when the events in Europe began to change and caught everyone off guard," Mariano said, glaring at Hamilton. "You saw it was time to move or to close down your organization. So you started tidying up the loose ends. When Yeltsin said he was going to turn over the documents, you panicked or at least made a few mistakes. Most likely you saw Ingel, Kohne and the others who wanted out as loose ends."

They learned from Hamilton that the discovery of the files Yeltsin was going to turn over was detrimental to his operation. The files which contained detailed information on the Fourth Reich caches, were from General Kaltenbrunner's office. They had been removed in the final days of the war. They were discovered with some items that belonged to one of the secretaries—a girlfriend of Major Fabian. The files never made it into the Army's hands. Hamilton didn't know how the Army, during their investigation, had missed the files the girlfriend had. He surmised that the secretary had planned to give the files to Major Fabian, but that never happened.

During the pandemonium that occurred when the Allies closed in on Alt Aussee and the files were discovered outside of the general's office, they probably were not considered that important and were set aside. Hamilton learned of the files several years after the war while working for the CIA. During a clandestine operation he accidentally came across them with some other Stasi files.

"I tried to destroy them several times when I worked for the CIA," Hamilton said. "When the USSR began to collapse and the wall fell, what order there was turned to chaos. There were too many files and boxes of documents to track. The Russians and East Germans had no method to their nonexistent filing system."

They learned from Hamilton that the Russians had vast rooms of old manuscripts, books and crates of treasures from the war and no one knew or even cared where anything was. Yeltsin decided to turn these specific files over much earlier than originally planned. They had been shuffled around and were disorganized. If Yeltsin hadn't moved up the return date, Pegasus would have been closed down.

Hamilton had developed Pegasus over fifty years, converting the Nazi underground to his own use. They needed money and freedom, and Hamilton supplied that in exchange for their assistance. As they grew older and their families grew, he developed the children as well. He used many tactics to recruit them. For some, it was the promise of money and power. Others were coerced by the threat of revealing their parents. Pegasus reached around the world. His people were strategically placed in governments and business. Pegasus owned substantial interests in a number of businesses from banks and finance companies to art galleries, auction houses and transportation companies. Several of those businesses were under Pegasus's control. All the businesses were legitimate corporations with only a few of the Pegasus people in key places to expedite transactions. The petroleum and finance business proved to be especially lucrative. The investments provided excellent returns and the international operations of these businesses gave exposure to many people willing to spend large sums of money for the more expensive treasures of Pegasus.

"The files will be destroyed in Munich," Hamilton smiled.

"How? By whom?" Mariano demanded.

"You and those disks you have will be destroyed, too," Hamilton added in a confident, cold voice. He stared at Mariano, holding firm for several seconds before shifting his eyes to each of the others. Then he laughed. Mariano slapped him.

Hamilton stopped laughing and stared directly at Mariano. "Beating a dying man will do you no good," Hamilton sneered. "I have pancreatic cancer. I've lived very well and created an empire. My nephew will be taking my place at the top when I die. You missed your chance to be rich and now you will die, too."

Hamilton went on to tell them that the files were never supposed to be returned, but Yeltsin needed the support and money from the West. He needed to gain credibility, and he knew that turning over the files would aid his cause. If he failed, the former USSR was destined to plunge into a war and drag the rest of the world into it. The looted treasures were always a sticking point and a topic at almost every high level meeting.

Hamilton confirmed that Dix had been under surveillance by the organization for several weeks because he knew several of the G-7 agents who were killed and had been seen with a couple of them. He was ordered killed when they believed he had Klaus Müller's disks. Mariano was also on the list because his investigation was coming close to discovering the operation. The G-7's success in getting the authorities in Europe to hunt for Dix would make it difficult for Dix's team to expose Pegasus in Munich. The addition of an assassin further reduced their chances of success.

"There are still a few old Nazis scattered around the world," Hamilton continued, "Many of them have helped us and the files will expose them. We learned many lessons from the Nazis."

"How are the files going to be destroyed?" Mariano demanded, getting close to Hamilton's face and clutching his shoulders.

"They're going to take out Yeltsin and the files." Dix stood and began to pace. "Steve, you and Mariano and the sergeant had better head on to Munich to see what you can find out. Besides, we shouldn't all be seen together. Our chances of stopping them are much better if they don't know about you."

Considering everything that Hamilton had told them, Dix realized the motivation behind the organization. Killing Yeltsin would destabilize Russia and thrust the country and most of

Eastern Europe into chaos. A power struggle from within the Russian ranks would pit the hardliners against those seeking democracy and change. The starving masses would likely rebel against the government without Yeltsin, especially if the attack were blamed on the hardliners. Organized crime and corruption would escalate. Hamilton wanted anarchy in the region in order for his operation to survive in the East. His plan was to move into an emerging government and control it. That would give him access to the vast treasures that the Russians had confiscated and locked away at the end of the war. Access to the treasures and records would be a simple task in a chaotic government without Yeltsin. The elimination of Yeltsin and the files would solve Pegasus's problem. With Dix being wanted, it was certain he would be blamed for the attack.

Time was running out. They had less than twenty-four hours to find out how the files were going to be destroyed and to warn Yeltsin. Not knowing who could be trusted in Munich, they quickly decided that their only option was for Mariano and his sergeant to leave immediately and notify the authorities of the planned assassination of Yeltsin and convince them that Dix was set up by the G-7. Steve would go directly to the hotel to look at security and personnel. He hoped that an assassin might give himself away before the meeting. Mariano and Steve, not knowing how long it would take them to complete their tasks, agreed to meet the others at the hotel in Munich the next day. For the moment, Dix would continue to probe Hamilton for details.

The smug Hamilton refused to provide any more information on the Munich meeting. He preferred instead to talk to Maria about the treasures. It was as if the dying old man was having his last rendezvous with a beautiful woman.

Dix called Francesca to fill her in on Pegasus and what they believed was going to happen. After telling her their immediate plans, Dix asked her to find out when Yeltsin was due to arrive in Munich and what his itinerary was. Dix told her that the route Yeltsin would take from the airport could be where the attack would occur and to find out what the route would be. He wanted to know about Yeltsin's guards and whether there had been any recent changes. She had to find out who from the G-7 committee would be escorting him and anything on German security for the meeting. It was necessary for her to get a list of where the G-7 members were staying. Finally, he asked her to identify and locate all the reporters covering the meeting. The more information she could find out the better. Francesca gasped at this list of duties to complete in such a short time, but she promised to get it done.

Lastly, Dix told her that he and Maria would be bringing Hamilton to the hotel that evening. Dix wanted to be in Munich after sundown.

"I almost forgot, I've got all your reservations at the Vier Jahreszeiten Hotel," Francesca said. "I didn't change my reservation at the Bayerischer Hof. Do you want me to change it to the Vier Jahreszeiten?"

"No, stay there," Dix replied. "Steve is going to call you as soon as he gets to Munich."

"I don't have the confirmation back yet on the invitations. I expect to get it any time now."

"God, I hope so," Dix responded anxiously.

"Not to worry. Peter Morgenstein is on the approved invitee list. I know his niece and I called her. Peter is sick with the flu and they aren't going. You're going in his place. I had to do some finagling with my connections but I got them."

"Francesca, that's pretty risky. He's a prominent American writer. Don't you think that someone at the reception and party may know him?"

"I don't think so. Peter hasn't been to any of these things in years. His niece keeps him current on the VIP invitee roster—more for his vanity than anything else, I think. But, Dix, how are you going to get past security?"

"I don't know yet. That's the problem. They usually put the junior person at the security checkpoint. Those guys still read comic books."

"Then they probably don't read the stuff Peter writes and won't know him."

"I hope you're right. But they'll still ask for some sort of identification. That's the challenge. If I can get past security, I'll be good to go."

"Dix, please be careful."

"I will. Thanks, Francesca. See you in Munich."

"Ciao, Dix."

32

Hamilton sat quietly in the chair with his head down. His hands were crossed and resting in his lap. While Dix was on the phone, he thought about his life and the pleasures of times gone by. But cancer was consuming his body now and he had already made peace with himself. He had violated almost every one of the Ten Commandments, some several times, during his life. He asked for forgiveness—believing the cancer was God's way of punishing him. Most of the lives he had taken ended quickly. His fate was a slow and painful death. Although he was prepared to die, he was not prepared to spend his last few days of life locked up behind bars. The idea of isolation and unfamiliar surroundings frightened him. He had planned from the moment he discovered the disease to die in the comfort of his home. He reflected on the last several hours. The beautiful surroundings and the sparkle in Maria's eyes as she looked at the art had given him great pleasure.

Hamilton cleared his mind and watched Dix slide into the chair behind the desk. He looked around the room, then looked at Maria and Dix.

"Hamilton, I need that password," Dix said.

"Medusa," Hamilton said calmly, then stood.

"Careful, Hamilton!" Dix stood also and pointed his Beretta at him.

"No need to worry. Can I have some more water?"

"Maria will get it. Just stay there and sit down."

Maria went into the kitchen. Dix typed in the password. Hamilton took a small capsule out of his pocket and put it into his mouth before sitting. He gazed at the portrait that hung on the wall behind his desk.

Maria handed him the glass. He took a drink of water, then sat the glass on the end table. His body jerked as he gasped for air. Then he collapsed, his mouth beginning to foam. It was quick for him.

Dix hit the ENTER key just as Hamilton collapsed to the floor. Stunned, Dix sprang from the chair and knelt beside Hamilton. He knew immediately what Hamilton had done. The odor of bitter almonds rose from the foam in his mouth. "Shit!" Dix said, looking at Maria. But there was nothing they could do for Hamilton. They had to keep moving forward. Dix stood and returned to the computer.

The password had activated a macro in the computer. A program automatically sent an e-mail message that read "Perseus" to Schmidt and Al Blakemore, Hamilton's nephew. Dix saw the message but had no idea what it meant.

Dix stood as he tried to figure out what the computer was doing. It seemed to have assumed a life of its own. He watched helplessly as the computer lights blinked and then went out. Dix sat at the desk and tried to access the computer again, but couldn't. At that moment it occurred to him that Hamilton had given him a code word that activated a program. The program then corrupted all the files. Dix didn't want to stay around to see if there were more surprises left by the dead man.

"Maria," he said, "get your things. There is no telling what else he may have done. Let's get the hell out of here."

The two sprang into a run out the door. Each second counted. He grabbed Maria's arm and pulled her as they ran. Just as they cleared the fountain, the house erupted in a huge and thunderous fireball. The shock wave from the explosion knocked them down and showered them with debris.

Dix rose first and looked at Hamilton's house engulfed in flame. He then turned to Maria as she sat up. "Are you all right?"

"I think so. That was close."

"Too close. Apparently the computer was programmed to do more than corrupt files. Let's get to Munich."

Part Three

33

On the outskirts of Munich, Dix pulled into a rest stop and called Steve at the hotel. Steve told him where to park the car and where he would be waiting for them. While waiting for them to get to the hotel, Steve checked the lobby area for any police that could cause a problem and planned the best route to their rooms to minimize observation.

When they arrived, Steve escorted Dix and Maria into the hotel, bypassing the reception desk. They acted as if they were simply returning to their rooms.

Maria showered while Dix called Mariano, the sergeant, and Francesca to tell them they had arrived without Hamilton. Francesca, struggling with her excitement, told him she was on her way to their room. She told him that she had brought her cousin, Margherita, to fix his disguise. "Margherita works in the theater makeup department and is quite the artist."

Dix finally managed to squeeze in a word and told her to wait a half-hour so he could shower.

After Francesca and Margherita arrived, Dix ordered room service for all of them. They ate in their room while discussing their plans and listening to what Francesca had found out. She had obtained a list of suites and meeting rooms reserved by the

G-7. These areas were for working groups and lower level meetings apart from the main meeting room. Steve, Mariano and the sergeant arrived, at staggered times, in Dix and Maria's room.

Throughout the meal they discussed the events leading up to that point. Francesca outlined Yeltsin's route from the airport to the hotel. They each inspected the route and discussed the possibilities. Finally they ruled out an attack on the way to the hotel. Most likely the files and Yeltsin would be in separate cars, and it would be impossible for someone to know which car and would take too much time for them to search at the attack site. They agreed that any attack would probably happen in the hotel.

"Dix, the G-7 committee has the authorities convinced you are their man," Francesca warned. "Security will shoot first and ask questions later. They've got the Germans thinking the same way."

"The security detail and the German police had information that Dix was going to be at the meeting and would make another assassination." Mariano lit a cigarette and stood. "I couldn't convince them otherwise. They're still naming only you. I didn't see anything on Maria or anyone else, but anyone who is seen with you would also be arrested. Blakemore has done a good job on this. No one was buying into the G-7 doing the killings, but they did agree to give me limited support until they had proof. They're stupid!"

"We need to find out who else at the senior level is involved in Pegasus and what records they have," Dix said. "We've got to find out who is going to kill Yeltsin and stop him."

"Or her," Maria added. "It could be a woman in his party or a reporter or even the hotel staff."

"Just warning security that an attempt on Yeltsin is going to be made won't help much. There are threats against him all the time," Steve said.

"I told them and they said they would be investigating it." Mariano sounded frustrated with the police. "They're taking it in stride."

"He's right," Dix added. "Yeltsin won't be intimidated. When he gets the vodka in him, he's almost uncontrollable."

"His security people say his drinking is a nightmare," Mariano said.

"We've got another problem to contend with." Steve stooped and rested his hands on the back of Dix's chair. "Hamilton was smart. Even though we got the blond-headed gunman, you can bet your ass there's another."

"You're right," Mariano said.

"Mariano, Dix isn't the only target." Steve reminded Mariano that he was targeted too.

Moving on to the next topic, Francesca told them that she had obtained invitations for each of them for the reception and party, but not the dinner. According to the itinerary she had obtained, Yeltsin would arrive at the reception at 7:30 that evening and stay through dinner. He would leave the party at 11:00 and return the next morning at 8:30 for the meeting. He was scheduled to speak from 9:05 until 9:25 at which time he would present the secret files to the G-7 leaders.

Destroying the files and eliminating Yeltsin would happen just before he turned them over, they suspected. The triggerman would probably not kill his own people or the other world leaders, as they weren't the targets. They ruled out a bomb because a bomb would not destroy all of the records—unless it was a nuclear bomb. Therefore, they reasoned, the most likely scenario was that Yeltsin would be taken out separately and that someone else would destroy the files. Regardless of how all this was to happen, it would probably occur around the time the files were turned over to the G-7 or soon afterwards. One other possibility was that Yeltsin might turn the files over just prior to his speech. But the question then was, Who would he turn them over to? That could be a problem.

Francesca reported that there had been no recent changes to Yeltsin's or the G-7's staff, and she knew all the reporters who usually covered these meetings. Everything on that front seemed normal. The security at the hotel was impeccable. Steve had found no sign of a bomb. He had searched areas that offered the best chance for successfully killing Yeltsin, but had found nothing—no pieces of tape, no pieces of wire, no wires sticking out of fixtures or protruding where they shouldn't. And it was the everything-as-usual appearance that bothered Steve.

"These guys are really good," Steve said. "They've left no apparent clues. Still, there's bound to be something very small that has been screwed up or overlooked, so everyone must keep alert."

"It's time to get your makeup on, dear boy," Francesca said to Dix.

Margherita stood, picked up the makeup kit, then stepped to the dressing area by the bathroom.

"What do you want me to do?"

"Bring your chair over by the light," Margherita replied as she handed a towel to Francesca.

Francesca wrapped the towel around Dix's neck while Margherita laid out the moulage, theatrical prosthetics, Dermablend and makeup in preparation to transform Dix's appearance. Margherita studied his face and compared it with the photograph of Peter Morgenstein that Francesca had given her. Then she began working on Dix. She pulled the skullcap over his short, light brown hair. Next she built up the sides of his nose with latex then applied prosthetic jowls. After adding a couple of blemishes and bumps and a mole, she checked her work under the light and wiped her hands on the towel. Then she began to apply the liquid latex to make his skin look wrinkled with age. She worked and blended the latex in for a natural appearance. Next came thicker eyebrows. She allowed the latex to cure for a few minutes before applying Dermablend and makeup to blend the colors. She even applied a small thin gray mustache. She slipped the gray wig on Dix, then took out a set of stage teeth. Dix opened his mouth and she inserted them over his teeth like a retainer. The teeth were slightly crooked and misaligned. They appeared to be stained with coffee and yellowed with age.

"What do you think?" Francesca said as she handed him a mirror.

"Damn, that's good. What do you think?" he said to the others as he lowered the mirror.

They agreed in unison that Margherita's work was superb.

Francesca took the mirror from Dix, reassuring him that he resembled the real Peter. Next Margherita worked on his hands. They too needed to be wrinkled and to have age spots. When she was satisfied, she grabbed what looked like a wad of elastic. "Dix, slip this on," she said as she allowed it to unfold. "Slip your arms in the loops."

This device brought his shoulders forward and caused him to stoop slightly. She made a few adjustments, then slid a thick insole into his right shoe to make it look as if he had a slight limp. As the final touch, she slipped a pair of glasses on Dix. In just over thirty minutes Margherita had transformed Dix into a man twenty years older who really resembled Peter Morgenstein.

While Margherita was working on Dix, the others focused on events to come. Steve set up the laptop on the table and reviewed their notes. He went over each name that was associated with Pegasus, hoping to find one that was familiar, but no one recognized any of the names listed. The time was drawing close to the start of events, and they still had no more to go on than before they arrived in Munich.

Mariano had made himself known to the chief of security and found out from him all he could. Getting Dix and Maria through security was Mariano's biggest challenge. The others would not be a problem—they weren't wanted by the police and they had the invitations Francesca had secured. Matching their names with the guest list and showing identification wouldn't be a problem. Although Francesca had given the name Jacquelyn Walerian as Maria's name—and Dix was attending as Peter Morgenstein—Francesca had no identification for either of them. Mariano had devised a plan that depended on timing. It was risky, but it was all he had.

He described an orchestrated sequence of events for them to follow, warning them that anything could go wrong and probably would. If it did, Mariano would try to keep Dix from being shot but would have to let Dix and Maria sit in jail until he could find the assassin. Mariano knew that the execution of his plan would be iffy at best. They would probably all be in jail before the evening was over.

Dix, Maria, Steve, Francesca, Mariano and the sergeant had to mingle separately with other guests at the reception and party to try to discover the assassin. At the same time they needed to be aware of each other and to offer help if needed. Dix had to avoid being recognized by any of the guests. Mariano had made a list of everyone attending the reception, dinner, party and meeting. He would fax that list to his headquarters at Land South to be checked out. They planned to stagger their arrivals at the reception—starting with Steve five minutes before seven and ending with Dix and Maria at fifteen minutes after seven.

Maria was supposed to be Dix's niece and assistant. Not the best of plans, but with limited resources and time they had few alternatives. Francesca made a few final touches to Maria's makeup and camouflaged her bruise that lingered from the punch of the old man. Armed with their invitations and strategy for the evening, members of the group departed the room in intervals.

"Dix," Mariano warned as he stood to leave, "be careful and don't get caught. Maria, you too."

"That's not in the plan. You too." Dix smiled at his old friend, who nodded in return.

34

The evening functions and general meeting were held at the world famous Bayerischer Hof Hotel located on Promenadeplatz in the museum district of Munich. Looking after the needs of guests in the three hundred ninety-six rooms and suites of this grand hotel were seven hundred employees providing impeccable service. With three restaurants, seven bars (including a nightclub and piano bar) and thirty-three conference and reception suites, the Bayersicher Hof was the perfect place to hold an important gala.

Dazzling light from the crystal chandeliers in the ballroom greeted arriving guests. A short line began to form as they waited to be cleared by security. Waiters carried trays of drinks and hors d'oeuvres at a hurried pace. As the mass of people grew, lines formed at the mini bars. Mariano had finished talking with the chief of security and was starting to mingle when he observed Francesca enter. They remained separated but close to the entrance. Mariano took a drink from a passing waiter; Francesca, standing on the other side of the entrance, did the same. She was as charming and bubbly as ever. *I hope she doesn't forget what she's supposed to do,* he thought as he lifted the glass to his lips. *Francesca, don't miss your cue.* Slowly turning his head to scan the crowd again, he caught the wave of an acquaintance and responded with a smile and wave. *Not now,* he thought, hoping not to be engaged in a conversation. *Dix and Maria will be here any minute.* As he turned his head around, he saw the acquaintance making his way toward him. He watched a man approach Francesca and engage her in an animated conversation. *Shit!* His thoughts raced. *This is falling apart before we ever get going.*

The din of the swelling crowd was soon drowning out the music. Around the room, everyone seemed to be enjoying themselves—shaking hands, smiling and making small talk. The waiters served drinks and hors d'oeuvres at an incredible pace and never spilled a drop or single canapé. A string trio began to play a Beethoven piece across the room from the piano. It seemed as if the music were trying to regain dominance over the noisy crowd. No elegant touch was spared for this reception.

Dix appeared in the entry about four people behind the security checkpoint with Maria staged to his side. Mariano made his way quickly to the side of the man making the security check. Along the way, he spotted the chief of security standing between him and Francesca, looking in his direction. Unsure of what the chief was doing, Mariano had a dilemma—he needed to act now, otherwise Dix would be caught. But if the chief already suspected something, Mariano's actions might call more attention to Dix and be just the warning signal that the chief was looking for. If that were the case, Mariano would be in serious trouble as well. At a minimum it would cost him time in answering the German's questions. Mariano had a split second to decide whether to sacrifice Dix and continue with his operation or to risk it all in getting Dix past security.

Francesca acted on cue, animated in her actions. "Jacquelyn! Jacquelyn Walerian!" she blurted out, stepping quickly to the dwindling line in front of Maria.

Mariano continued his approach, hoping for the best but expecting the worst. "Peter Morgenstein! It's so good to see you."

Dix reacted as he imagined an older man would, a little slow in movements and speech. "Colonel Simione!" he responded in a raspy voice. He smiled and extended his hand, the elastic resisting his natural instinct to stand erect.

The loud greetings from both sides of the entrance caught the security man off guard. He didn't know on whom to concentrate. Francesca hugged Maria as if they were long lost friends and kept the chatter up. At the same time, Mariano grasped Dix's hand and pulled him closer, hugged him as old friends do. Dix made a half effort to hand his invitation to the security. Maria, as Francesca hugged her, made a sincere gesture of handing her invitation to the man. They had created confusion exactly as intended.

"I'll vouch for this distinguished gentleman," Mariano said to the security man as he pulled Dix from the line. "This is Peter Morgenstein, the celebrated author." Mariano continued without waiting for a reply.

"Colonel, you remember my niece and assistant?" Dix was a little slow on introducing Maria. He saw a flash of concern in Mariano's eyes. "Jacquelyn Walerian."

"It is a pleasure to see you again, Jacquelyn."

"Colonel, do you know my friend Francesca Martin?"

"I do indeed."

So far so good. Mariano corralled the four of them to the side of the security man. Their conversations were in themselves a slight distraction. The names were repeated for the benefit of security, although the show was for cordialities.

"I vouch for Mr. Morgenstein and his niece, Jacquelyn," Mariano repeated as he shot a look to the security man. He then led them away from the entrance—all four engaging in conversation. Mariano saw the security man look to the chief of security who had not budged. He gave a slight nod of approval. The security man continued to check others as they advanced in line. That slight exchange of looks and nod of approval concerned Mariano.

The six had successfully infiltrated the reception as planned. They mingled and milled about the crowd. Francesca's job was to point out each of the senior executives from the G-7 countries and the Russian delegation. She graciously maneuvered to and from her teammates, identifying the executives with a slight tilt of her glass. She was circumspect in her actions and no one noticed. Mariano had the double duty of scouting for the likely suspect at the same time keeping Dix away from the chief of security and the rest of the security detail.

Yeltsin was due to arrive in about five minutes when Maria noticed two men slip out of the main room into a hall. *That's odd*, she thought. She looked around to catch Dix's attention, but he was in a group of people ten to fifteen feet away, with his back toward her. She turned to locate Steve, but he, too, had turned around. She quickly scanned the room for the others but they were out of sight.

Seeing the two men leave the main room just prior to Yeltsin's scheduled arrival had piqued her curiosity. *Why would they leave just before Yeltsin's grand entrance?* Unable to get the attention of any of the others, Maria decided to investigate. Going alone or not telling one of the others violated one of Steve's rules. *Shit!* Maria thought. *I don't have any choice. Besides, I'm just going to stay back and see what they are up to.* She looked around the room once again but was still unable to get the attention of the others. She weaved across the room casually so as not to arouse anyone's suspicion. A waiter passed her, carrying a tray to replenish the hors d'oeuvres. She altered her course slightly and felt someone touch her arm. She stopped with a fright.

"Maria, isn't it?" came the woman's voice.

Maria turned to face a brown-haired woman with plain features. She was in her late forties and wore a blue sequined dress. She smiled, "Yes, that's right." Her blank expression revealed that she didn't recognize the woman.

"We met at the reception in Budapest. I'm Betty, Betty Davidson," she said, expecting Maria's recognition.

"Oh, yes! I'm sorry. It is nice to see you." Maria still couldn't recognize the woman and couldn't be sidetracked by her. "Would you please excuse me? I was on my way to the powder room. I'll be right back."

Maria continued with her advance, barely waiting for the woman's response. *Was I rude to her?* Maria thought as she wove through the crowd. *Well, Betty Davidson, I'm certainly sorry if I was but I have no time for talk now.* Maneuvering through the sea of guests required agility and determination. Maria persevered until she finally reached the door the two men had disappeared through. She grasped the door handle and gradually opened it onto a vacant hall.

Her eyes searched the hall and her ears strained for any sound. The door closed behind her, muffling the din of the crowd in the ballroom. She took three steps and the door on her left, ten feet to the front, began to open. Her heart pounded. *Be calm! Keep going,* she thought, *powder room.* She saw the brass plate on the door ahead on the right indicating the ladies' powder room. *Thank god!* she thought. A waiter entered the hall from behind the door carrying a tray with six glasses. Her eyes locked onto one glass with lipstick on the rim. He smiled as he passed. He had left the door ajar. Maria moved forward, then looked behind to see the waiter exit the hall.

She crept up to the crack in the door and looked around the hall once again to make sure that it was still vacant. She peeked through the opening and saw five men seated at a table. She was unable to distinguish what they were saying. One man stood as he talked to the others. When she saw his face, she recognized him. Francesca had identified him only a few minutes before in the ballroom as an American named Al Blakemore. Then Maria remembered, she had seen him in Budapest as well. She had not met him, but Francesca had pointed him out across the room as the American desk officer for the G-7. That evening in Budapest he was talking to the blond-headed man—the man she shot in Hamilton's house.

Only five men, Maria thought, *but six glasses, one with lipstick, came out. Where's the woman?* She identified one man as Italian. Another she guessed to be French because of his hand gestures. The other two with their backs to her remained silent and Maria was unable to guess their nationality. *What is this meeting all about?* Maria thought. Suddenly, the American stood. It was obvious that the meeting was over. Not wanting to be seen by them, she turned and walked calmly into the powder room.

A uniformed attendant sat unobtrusively in one corner and looked up as Maria entered. She had a vacant expression. A lone, attractive woman sat at the first dressing table with her back to the door. Through the reflection in the mirror, Maria saw the woman raise her eyes as she entered. The woman, wearing a black, low-cut dress, was in her mid-thirties and about Maria's size. Her brown hair was cut to the bottom of her jaw. She was refreshing her lipstick when Maria entered. The woman supported a compact in her left palm. The open lid was resting against her fingers. She held the cap to the lipstick between the first two fingers of the same hand. On the side of the woman's thumb, Maria saw a two-inch scar, then her eyes caught the gold tube with a raised Pegasus on the end. The woman made final touches to her lips as Maria approached the table. *That's an unusual shade*, Maria thought as she passed behind the woman. *The tube is custom. Maybe the lip stick is, too. It looks good on her though.* A delicate inlaid amber carving surrounded the powder in the center of the compact. The woman gently closed the lid and replaced the cap, then slipped them into her small purse. Maria sat down, refreshed her face and sneaked glances as the woman stood and walked to the attendant. The woman spoke to the attendant in French then tipped her and left the room. *French,* Maria thought. *There's something about her. I'm sure she's the one that left the lipstick on the rim of the glass. Maybe Francesca will know of her.*

A large crowd had assembled around Yeltsin and the other leaders who made up the Group of Seven Industrialized Nations. Yeltsin pushed at every opportunity for Russia to be formally admitted into the group and this meeting was no exception. Exchanging the imprisoned spies and turning over the secret files was another sign of good faith by the Russians in an effort to gain acceptance by the West. Yeltsin was shaking hands and talking as cameras flashed.

Maria circled the back of the crowd looking for Francesca and the woman from the powder room. She saw Steve with a plate of shrimp and made her way to him. Casually she stopped next to him.

"Where the hell have you been?" Steve whispered then put a shrimp into his mouth. "We've been looking for you."

"I need to find out something first. Where's Francesca?"

"Over there." Steve nodded to his right front.

Maria walked away from Steve and headed toward Francesca. She stopped beside her and pretended to watch the leaders. She glanced around to see who was nearby and if she was being watched. As she turned her head to the right, she saw the woman wearing the low-cut black dress in the crowd, about ten feet away watching the spectacle.

"Where have you been?" Francesca whispered without looking at Maria. "We were worried about you, and poor Dix was having a fit."

"Later. Who's that woman over there in the black dress?" Maria looked and nodded slightly to the right.

"Short brown hair?"

"That's her. Do you know anything about her?"

"No, I've never seen her before, but the committee officers must know her. I saw her talking with a Russian and a German a few minutes ago. I think I saw her talking to Blakemore too. Why?"

"I'll tell you later. Keep an eye on her. Where's Dix?"

"Over there." Francesca nodded slightly to the left.

Maria sipped her champagne and started to move toward him, then froze in position. She went numb at what she saw. She looked back at Steve. As he turned his head toward her, she nodded toward Dix. She saw Steve shift his eyes to Dix. Two men were escorting Dix to the door. Maria looked back at Steve with frightened eyes. She saw the Carabiniere sergeant nudge Steve and motion with his head toward Mariano. Maria turned to see two more men escorting Mariano out of the room. She looked back at Steve. He indicated for her to remain still, then he whispered to the sergeant. She watched him start moving through the crowd toward the door. Maria felt someone touch her back. Startled, she turned.

"Steve said for us to go to the room he found for us," the sergeant whispered. "Come with me now and look calm."

Maria followed the sergeant as they began their slow, winding journey out of the crowd. He proceeded cautiously. Both scrutinized the room for anyone who might be looking for them.

Several staff members opened the doors to the dining room. Large round tables were arranged at the front of the room for the dignitaries and rows of rectangular tables were for the others. Each was set with fine linen, china and fresh flowers. Bottles of red and white wine were on every table. Place cards designated the seating. Large posters with a diagram of the seating arrangement were on easels at each entrance.

"Francesca, stay alert," Steve whispered as he leaned next to her ear, "They've just escorted Dix and Mariano out. The fuckers must have known they were here. I'm going to check it out now and see if I can find out what else they know. I'll look for you after the dinner."

Francesca took a last look at Maria, then at Steve before continuing her slow advance. Gradually enveloped in the mass of people entering the dining room, she disappeared into the crowd.

Surveying the dwindling crowd once more, Steve turned and saw the sergeant escorting Maria. He tightened his left arm against his side to check his pistol. Steve inched along, watching the men with Dix and Mariano as they disappeared into the hall. Steve quickly moved to the door, then slipped out to follow. They walked along the hall, then turned right and continued. Steve rushed to the corner and saw them continue down the hall, then stop and open a door. When the door closed Steve dashed to the stairwell. He cautiously opened the door and heard footsteps on the landing above. He checked below, then gently closed the door without a sound. Flattening himself against the wall, he crept up the stairs. The door opened and the footsteps fell silent as they landed on carpeting. Hearing the door latch, Steve studied the stairwell, leaned forward and looked up. Satisfied he was alone, he bolted to the door.

Once inside, he gingerly closed the door before he continued. The hall formed a T intersection. He moved to the junction and looked left around the corner only to see a vacant hall. He turned and darted a few steps to the opposite corner. Peering around the corner, he heard the click of a door latch. Inching down the hall, he scanned the space to his front and rear, as he continued to the approximate location of where the sound came from. His eyes darted to the bottom of the door only to see that the lights were out. He checked the room on the opposite side but it, too, was dark. He moved to the next—the lights were on. He listened for voices. Then he heard one of the men say "Connor," but then someone turned up the volume on the TV, and he could no longer hear voices.

Figuring he needed help to get Dix and Mariano out, Steve backed away from the door. He dashed back through the hall to the stairwell and quietly closed the door behind him.

35

Dix and Mariano had been taken to one of the hotel suites. They sat in chairs with their hands taped behind them, facing two of their captors. The other two stood behind Dix and Mariano. One of the men picked up the phone and dialed a number. When the line was answered, the man said, "We have Connor and Simione.... No.... Okay." Then he replaced the receiver and faced Dix and Mariano.

While he was on the phone, the other man peeled the prosthetics and latex from Dix's face. "Good job on the makeup, Connor. The teeth, too." He gestured for Dix to spit out the false teeth, then pulled off his wig and skullcap.

"Connor, you have some computer disks that belong to us. We want them back," said the other man as he hung up the phone and stepped closer to Dix.

"What disks?" Dix said, glaring at him.

Dix knew what to expect but he had to stall for time. *Focus on the man not the pain,* Dix thought as he braced himself for what was coming. He heard a thud as the other man hit Mariano. The large man in front of Dix then drew back his hand and slugged Dix. His head jerked as the hand connected across his face. He heard the sound. The sting of the impact brought tears to his eyes. He blinked and stretched his face as best he could. His lip felt numb and his nose ran. He glared back at the man.

"I thought you'd say that. The two disks from Klaus Müller. Don't fuck around with me! Where are the disks?"

"I don't have any disks from Klaus Müller."

The man in front of Mariano drew back his fist and slammed it into Mariano's midsection. Dix heard the dull thud as the man's clenched fist connected. Mariano moaned in pain. Dix tightened again when the fist of the man in front of him drew back, stopped, then sped toward his midsection. Dix clenched his teeth. The chair slid back. His taut muscles absorbed the impact. He heard himself moan, then felt the deep ache. He gasped and struggled, anticipating and dreading the next punch that was sure to come.

"The disks, Connor! Where are they?"

Dix looked up at the man. "No disks," he moaned.

Dix breathed faster and the pain began to ease. He glared at the man as he ran his hand through his hair to put it back in place. Beads of sweat had formed on the man's forehead. Dix watched him blot the water from his brow with a towel, then pitch the towel onto the bed. Dix looked at Mariano, whose red face was streaked with sweat. Mariano shook his head as a signal for Dix to remain silent about the disks.

The man nodded to one of the others. Dix couldn't see what was happening. Then he saw one of the men behind him hand something to the man in front of him.

"Do you know what this is, Connor?" He held a black, oblong, plastic box that was curved at the end.

Dix looked at the instrument, then stared defiantly into the man's eyes.

"It's a stun gun. A very effective little tool," the man said.

Dix remained silent.

"A five-second shock of 400,000 volts does wonders," the man taunted. He smiled and twisted his hand as if he was inspecting the gun.

Dix looked at Mariano and saw fear in his eyes.

"This little thing kind of short-circuits the nervous system," he continued. "It interrupts the tiny neurological impulses that travel through the body to control and direct muscle movement. Your body will cease to function properly. You will be dazed, your muscles will go into spasms and you will be instantly disoriented. Nasty little thing, don't you think?"

Dix remained silent and mentally prepared for the inevitable. He tried once more to free his hands but the tape was too strong.

"Oh! I forgot to mention, you'll feel like you fell out of a two-story window. You may even pass out. But don't worry. The effects aren't permanent. You'll only be incapacitated for about fifteen or twenty minutes. Then we can do it again if necessary. Once again, where are the disks?"

"I don't have any fucking disks!"

Without another word, the man reached over and touched Mariano with the stun gun. He groaned and jerked, then he grunted and moaned again as his body convulsed. Saliva ran from his grimacing mouth. His body slumped in the chair.

"The disks?"

Dix took a deep breath. "Fuck you!" he said, but he didn't hear a response. Pain filled his body. His head spun and somewhere in all the confusion he knew he was convulsing and thrashing. His eyes wouldn't focus. He couldn't tell if he was conscious, dazed or dead—and he lost all concept of time.

36

With a bundle under his arm, Steve entered the room where Maria and the sergeant were waiting. He closed the door and locked it behind him, then pitched the bundle onto the couch. The two stood, their expressions apprehensive.

"They took Mariano and Dix to a room. I couldn't hear what they were saying, but I suspect they were questioning them about the disks. They're okay so far, but we've got to get them out of there soon."

Steve didn't mention what else he suspected might be happening in the room. He picked up the bundle and unwrapped two staff uniforms—one for a man and one for a woman.

"Put these on," Steve said. He pitched a uniform to Maria and one to the sergeant.

He didn't slow down in laying out exactly what he wanted them to do. Their most important mission at the moment was to rescue Dix and Mariano. He told them that the men Maria had seen in the meeting room with Blakemore were the key players in Pegasus. He described how they were going to take the Italian and Frenchman. If they had enough time before the dinner was over, they would go after the German and then the Russian. Once Dix and Mariano were rescued, they could concentrate on the assassin and Blakemore.

"Are you ready?" Steve asked as he inspected the two counterfeit staff members. "Remember, once you enter the dining room, go straight to the man as we discussed. Don't look around. Move with confidence, whisper in his ear, then…."

The two nodded they were ready.

Maria approached the two German guards at the dining room entrance, sensing their scrutinizing eyes upon her as she drew near. Her heart pounded in her chest. *Relax!* she thought. *Stay calm.* She smiled at the guards and bowed her head slightly when she was within a few feet of them. Out of the corner of her eye, she saw the guard on the right look to the other one. He smiled and raised his eyebrows in acknowledgment of her good looks. She pretended to check the seating chart on the easel by the door, then cracked open the door and peeked in to locate the Italian. She quietly entered so as not to interrupt the speaker at the podium.

Maria walked into the dimly lit room to the second round table and approached the Italian man from the side. She leaned over and whispered into his ear. The man looked at her and wiped his mouth. Maria backed up to wait for him. The Italian excused himself from the table, and followed Maria as she escorted him out of the room. They turned a corner out of sight of the guards. She took him to a seating area next to the wall, away from the main flow of traffic. As she advanced, the sergeant came forward with a telephone in his hand and acted as though he was going to plug it in for the call. He sat the phone on the table as the two arrived. The sergeant handed him the receiver and he lifted it to his ear. But the voice he heard didn't come from the phone.

"Don't move or make a sound." Steve pushed the Heckler

and Koch into the man's lower abdomen. "Slowly put down the phone and come with us or I'll take out your kidney with the rest of your guts."

The man gently replaced the receiver and moved with Steve toward the stairs. Once inside the stairwell, Steve pushed the man faster and faster up the stairs. Maria cracked open the door when they reached the landing and checked the hall before they entered. Seeing that it was vacant, she opened it for the others. Steve rushed the man down the hall to the room they had previously used and forced him into a chair. The Italian protested and demanded to know what was going on. Steve thumped him on the head with the silencer and said, "Shut up, asshole!"

The man did as he was told. The sergeant taped his legs to the chair. No one spoke. The only sound in the room was the tape as it came off the roll and was torn. They taped his hands behind the chair and then taped his mouth closed.

Satisfied he was secured, Steve looked at the other two. "Are you ready?"

They nodded, then watched Steve thump the Italian on the head again.

"Just sit right there and be still. We'll be right back!"

The Italian, with his eyes open wide, nodded he understood. Steve turned and led them from the room.

The sergeant approached the guards just as Maria had done. He walked with confidence and avoided eye contact with either guard. He didn't have Maria's good looks to use, but he had the discipline and self-confidence to pass for one of the staff. He checked the seating chart, opened the door, then entered. Within a few moments he emerged with the Frenchman and escorted him to the seating area. Maria went through the motions of plugging in the telephone then handing the man the receiver—just as the sergeant had done with the Italian. No sooner had he lifted the receiver to his ear than Steve pushed the Heckler and Koch into his kidney.

"Don't make a sound," Steve said. "Slowly put the phone down and come with us or they'll be mopping your guts up from the floor."

The man complied with Steve's command and followed his nudging. They led him up the stairs. Maria again checked the hall when they reached the landing. The sergeant unlocked the door and Steve shoved the man inside. The Italian, still taped to the chair, recognized the Frenchman. He looked at Steve with fright.

Steve told the two captives that he was taking them to the room where they held Dix and Mariano. The Sergeant cut the Italian free. The Italian pulled the tape from his mouth, then rubbed his wrists. Steve confronted them with Pegasus and the plot to assassinate Yeltsin, but the captives denied knowledge of either. They demanded to be released.

"Shut up!" Steve ordered, gesturing with the pistol. "Do exactly as you're told if you want to live."

Maria and the sergeant checked their pistols, then nodded at Steve. Steve motioned for the two captives to follow, and they all left the room and moved into the hall.

Steve knocked on the door where Dix and Mariano were held. Then he stepped aside so that only the Frenchman and Italian could be seen through the peephole. A voice came from behind the door.

"Tell him to open the door and let you in," Steve whispered to the Italian as he brought the Heckler and Koch to the ready.

The Italian complied. The man inside recognized the Italian and opened the door to admit the two men. The man held the door as the Italian and Frenchman entered. Steve, followed by the sergeant and Maria, crashed in, pushing and shoving. Two of the four men in the room jumped to their feet and reached for their weapons. Steve caught sight of the first. He pivoted and fired. The man dropped but the other fired. The Frenchman fell. Maria fired and the second man flipped backwards. The third man fired and hit the Italian in the arm. The sergeant and Steve fired. The third man went down and the fourth one dropped his pistol and held up his right hand. A bullet had struck his left shoulder and he could not raise his arm.

"Cut 'em loose," Steve said to the sergeant, motioning to Dix and Mariano. Keeping his .45 pointed at the fourth man's midsection, he checked the others who were hit and pitched their pistols aside. Then he checked the Frenchman. "Shit! He's dead."

Dix and Mariano, still somewhat dazed and aching from their ordeal, struggled to stand. They made their way into the bathroom to wash their faces and clean up. Steve seated the wounded man in the chair and taped his hands and legs to the chair.

"We don't have much time," Steve said to the others as Dix and Mariano came back into the room. "The police and security are going to be thicker than flies on shit in a few minutes. Let's get ready to get the hell out of here."

Mariano stretched his muscles and shook his arms to rid himself of the remaining effects of the stun gun. He straightened himself and said he was going to head off the police. Unsure how long it would take him to convince them it was Blakemore they wanted, he headed for the door and said, "Dix, I'll do what I can to keep them off you until you have him."

He stopped in front of the door and lifted the Italian by his jacket, "He's coming with me. He'll have a lot to tell the police. Andiamo! Avanti!"

"Go! Go!" Dix shouted and he waved him on.

"Dix, you and Maria go after Blakemore," Steve said as he moved to the side of the wounded man. "I've got to find out how they are going to take out Yeltsin."

Dix picked up a pistol and checked it. Maria kept watch at the door for anyone approaching in the hall. As the stun gun's effects slowly wore off, Dix began to remember a little of what happened. "Steve, I think Blakemore was in here after they zapped us. There was a woman in a black dress too—at least I think there was. It seems like Blakemore said something about dusting. Dusting with ricin, that was it. At least I think he did. Damn, I don't know if I heard it or dreamed it."

Steve turned to the wounded man, "Asshole, listen to me," Steve said sternly. "I don't have time to play games. Who's going to hit Yeltsin and how?"

"Fuck you! I don't know!" the man moaned.

Steve laid the towel over the oozing bullet hole. Then he drew back and punched the man in his wounded shoulder. The man winced and cried out in agony. Tears filled his eyes and saliva dripped from his mouth. His skin began to turn pale and clammy.

"You're not passing out on me yet, you son-of-a-bitch!" Steve growled through gritted teeth. He shook him and slapped his face. "Tell me, or I'll drive the bullet through the back of your arm." Steve drew his arm back again. "Who is it?"

"Okay! Okay!" he groaned. "The woman."

"A French woman in a black dress?" Maria asked.

"Yes! Yes! She's the one." The man passed out.

Steve stood looking at the man, then backed up. "Dix, get the pass key from him." Steve pointed to the body on the floor. "You'll probably need it." At the same time Steve taped the unconscious man to the chair. He figured it would be some time before he regained consciousness but thought it better to be safe than sorry.

Dix rolled the body over and took the key from his jacket pocket. Then Dix removed the restrictive elastic that had been pulling his shoulders forward. He also took out the insole from his right shoe, then stood upright and stretched. Looking at Steve, then Maria, to signal he was ready, Dix sprang out the door with Steve and Maria right behind.

37

Somewhere along the route Steve disappeared, going his own way to find the French woman. Dix and Maria ducked into the room where they originally gathered so that Maria could change back into her evening dress. Otherwise, she feared being exposed as a non-staff member if any of the regular staff were to spot her. As Maria changed, Dix removed as much of the makeup and remnants of the latex as he could. He combed his matted and messed hair and washed his face and hands.

Dix unfolded the list of suites and meeting rooms Francesca had provided and examined it once again. Leaning against the door, he listened for signs of trouble in the hall. He heard two people running. The footsteps grew closer. Maria was ready. He held up a hand for her to be silent as the stomping feet passed. He then cracked open the door and looked out.

"It's clear. Let's go."

They made their way down the hall in the opposite direction of the footsteps. They needed to return to the ballroom area since the dinner was due to be over at any minute. Dix opted not to take the elevator—he believed security would be posted there to check anyone getting out. They were halfway to the next hall when the elevator bell signaled a stop at that floor. His heart pounded. He checked several of the doors but they would not open. *Shit!* he thought. *Nowhere to go. Let's hope this works like the movies.* He embraced Maria and turned his back to the elevator. He kissed her with all his passion as the elevator doors opened. He felt Maria's pounding heart, racing to each beat of his. They pretended not to notice the occupants leaving the elevator. Dix turned slightly when the footsteps passed and saw the legs of one of the staff. Dix raised his head and looked around. "Good thing you're my wife!" Dix whispered. The employee continued down the hall. The doors of the empty elevator closed. They resumed their risky trip through the halls and stairwells. Turning right, then left. Going up, then down. Finally, they passed through a door on the same level as the dining room and ballroom but more towards the rear of the hotel.

They slowed to a casual pace so they would not attract attention. As they passed a ladies' room, Maria tugged on Dix's arm.

"Be right back. I need to make sure I'm presentable."

While waiting for her, Dix started to sweat. He wiped his brow with his handkerchief and sipped some water from the fountain. He looked up to see several people passing in the hallway and more coming toward him. *The dinner is over,* he thought as he wiped his face again. *Now to blend into the crowd.* Maria stepped out, looking composed. She took his arm and smiled. They continued toward the tide of people who were leaving the dinner. Dix maneuvered them through, searching for Francesca.

Through all the bobbing heads Francesca emerged. She smiled as they approached.

"What's all the commotion?" she said as she saw two more policemen rush into the building and get into the elevator.

"Some people got shot." Dix replied as he observed the

crowd. "Where's Blakemore?"

"He and the Russian liaison left the dinner just before it was over. I don't know where they went."

"Maria, you and Francesca stay with the crowd. Keep your eyes open for Blakemore, the Russian or the French woman. If you see them, just watch and find me or Steve."

"Dix, I—"

"Maria, listen!" Dix cut her off, looking deep into her eyes. "If I get caught, you'll have to let Steve know. If they arrest both of us, Blakemore wins. If you see any of them, stay clear—especially the woman. I'll be going down the list of suites they have reserved for their work groups."

Maria decided not to argue. "Be careful."

Dix smiled and nodded. She looked at Francesca and the two women turned and navigated deeper into the throng. Dix watched them step away, then he began steering through the crowd. As he was about to emerge, he saw two policemen talking to a man in a suit at the entrance to the hall where he was headed. He altered course and headed down another hall. He stopped and checked the list of suites again. He picked the closest one, then continued. As he placed his hand on the door to the stairwell, he heard a man's voice come from the far end of the hall.

"Connor! Dix Connor!"

"Shit!" Dix said as he quickly looked back. Ignoring whoever had called out to him, he opened the door and entered. He quickly scrutinized the vacant stairwell, then pulled the door shut. Dix had no time to talk to acquaintances and even less time for the police.

Dix figured that their arrival in Munich caused Blakemore to be nervous and possibly cause him to make mistakes. He suspected that Blakemore would move up the timing of his planned hit on Yeltsin and try to get custody of the files prior to the meeting. Upsetting Blakemore's timetable and tripping him up was what Dix had counted on.

He removed the fire ax from its case by the door and wedged it through the handle and doorframe. *It'll slow them down,* he thought as he adjusted the handle. *Every second counts.* Confident his handiwork would function as anticipated, he withdrew the fire hose, uncoiled it and spread it in front of the door. It was one more obstacle for anyone who might be following to contend with. Dix wiped the sweat from his brow, then bolted up the stairs.

At the landing he took a deep breath and straightened his hair and clothes. Carefully opening the door and looking into the hall, Dix saw two couples walking in opposite directions on either side of the door. He took out his handkerchief and held it to his nose as he stepped out. He gently closed the door behind him and started walking. The door to the room on his right opened. A man emerged. Dix pretended to sneeze into his handkerchief. He sneezed again. The man stepped into the hall behind Dix and walked in the opposite direction. Dix stopped in front of the first suite on his list. Opening the door he stepped in. No one was in the room. Finding nothing, Dix headed for the next room on the list, two doors down.

The corridor was still vacant. Reaching the next door, he entered. The scent of a woman's cologne lingered. *Someone has been here very recently,* he thought, seeing two glasses on the coffee table. He closed the door behind him. He walked into the bedroom, then back to the living room. He sat on the couch and took out his list of rooms again. Looking at the glasses on the table, he saw one had lipstick on the rim. *A man and woman. Did I pass them in the hall?* he thought as he unfolded the paper. The next suite was in an adjacent hall. Returning the list to his pocket, he stepped to the door. Pretending again to be on the verge of a sneeze, Dix stepped out.

A couple approached him just as he turned the corner. He sneezed. Then sneezed again as they passed. *So far so good,* he thought. Stopping in front of the next door on the list, he checked right and left, then gently opened the door. The smell of cigarette smoke greeted him. He pushed the door open cautiously.

"Come in," said a German-accented voice. "Dix Connor, isn't it?"

Dix was stunned. A man sat in an overstuffed chair near the window. A cigarette was in his right hand and a half-filled glass sat on the table next to his left hand. A small envelope lay next to the glass. Unsure what to do, Dix contemplated bolting or even going for his Beretta. Finally, he decided to play out the hand. *He must be the German representative, Blakemore's counterpart,* Dix thought as he closed the door behind him.

"I told Blakemore it was over when we received the message that Hamilton was compromised. I knew what I had to do when you showed up."

Dix watched the man and listened carefully. The man's reference to a message instantly brought him back to the night at Hamilton's. He remembered how Hamilton had finally relented and given him the computer's password. As soon as he entered it, the computer generated an e-mail message on its own. That message must have alerted Blakemore that Hamilton was compromised. The man's relaxed, almost casual demeanor confused Dix. *No gun,* he thought. *No weapon of any type.*

"Sit down, Mr. Connor," the man said.

"Where's Blakemore?"

The man didn't answer. Instead he began to ramble and the more he rambled, the less sense he made. He talked about the organization, then reminisced about Müller, Ingel and the others. He abruptly switched and talked about the treasures. Tears welled in his eyes as he stopped to sip his drink. He took a drag on the cigarette, unconcerned with the large ash that landed on his shirt.

"I am a German," he said. "Not a Nazi. Hamilton lured us in just like Hitler."

Dix occasionally asked the man a question, which went ignored. The German confessed his shame at doing what the Nazis had done—the killing and the profiting from the Fourth Reich's treasure.

"We Germans tried to bury the past. We were so ashamed at what Hitler had done to the world that for a time no one talked of the past. Now I will die a slow, painful death in prison, but my family will also suffer for the rest of their lives because of the shame I have brought to them. We will be labeled as Nazis—profiting from the death of others and, worst of all, what happened to the Jews."

As the man talked, Dix tried to imagine the Nazi past and the theft of the world's art treasures. The man confessed his remorse at having been taken in by a man in the same way his countrymen before him had—brainwashed into believing they were superior to the rest of the world, convinced that they had the right to the treasures.

"The killings had to stop," the German said. "I voted not to assassinate Yeltsin but they wouldn't listen."

"How are they going to kill him?" Dix said. "You can still stop it."

"I told them there were other ways to get to the Russian treasures. Blakemore is mad with greed. He's like a drug addict who can't stop."

He took another drink, then a drag of his cigarette. He lifted the envelope to his mouth, tilted his head back and emptied the envelope's contents into his mouth. "Blakemore," he said before taking another sip, "he's shredding—"

Suddenly the man's body jerked and he gasped for air, then

slumped in the chair. His mouth foamed as he paid the price for his crimes.

Dix sat staring at the body. At that instant the door behind him opened. He sprang to his feet, startled, twisting as he rose.

"Dix, it's okay, I'm alone," Steve said as he stepped into the room and saw Dix's surprised move. "Whoa! What happened?"

"I guess the German took what he thought was his only option. Did you find the woman?"

"Not yet. I've been all over this place. She's managed to stay under the radar. I've got Maria and Francesca posted in the ballroom watching for her."

"He didn't provide any new information," Dix said, indicating the dead German. "The last thing he said was that Blakemore was shredding. He died before he finished the sentence."

"Probably the Stasi files."

"That's what I was thinking."

Steve immediately turned to the door and said, "You find Blakemore. I'll get the woman!"

The staff was clearing the few remaining dishes from the dining room on trays and carts. A band was tuning their instruments in one corner of the ballroom. The party was to be held in the combined area of the ballroom and dining room, which allowed plenty of space for dancing. The staff had opened the panels dividing the two rooms and furiously went about getting everything ready.

Steve maneuvered next to Francesca and scanned the crowd again as the guests began to flow back in to take their seats for the party. The band started to play, their music permeating the space and adjacent areas. Yeltsin, red faced from the Vodka, was in the middle of the dance floor. He grabbed one of the women who passed and stumbled around in an attempt to dance with her, making a spectacle of himself.

Steve and Francesca merged in with the flood of people entering the room. The staff streamed in with bottles of wine, champagne, water and trays of drinks.

"Francesca, keep moving around and if you see the woman, stay away from her. Just signal or come find me."

Steve turned and headed across the floor to Maria. He casually stood next to her.

"Look for anything suspicious," he said in a low voice. "Stay focused on the area around Yeltsin. Dix said they're going to use poison."

"How? He's already eaten."

"He doesn't necessarily have to eat it. I don't know how she's going to do it."

He lied so as not to alarm her and inadvertently warn the assassin. He didn't want to tell her that the toxin, derived from castor beans, was six thousand times stronger than cyanide. If the white powder touched the skin or was inhaled, it was fatal and there was no antidote. Hamilton had selected ricin because it was almost impossible to detect during an autopsy and depending on the dose, death might be within seconds or could take several days.

Steve looked across the room to see Mariano enter with two security men; then the sergeant moved behind him to occupy another vantage point. Mariano nodded at Steve. Then Steve looked toward Francesca. Everyone was in position. The security around Yeltsin was tight but not foolproof.

"I'm going to get closer to the front. Maria, if you see her, keep your distance and just point her out to me. Look natural as you move around."

Steve walked over to Mariano who stood talking to the two security men. He stopped several feet short of Mariano and motioned that he wanted to talk to him alone. Mariano excused himself and walked over to Steve.

"They're going to use ricin," Steve said.

"Damn!" Mariano looked at him in surprise. "That's some lethal shit!"

"Call the HazMat people and tell them to get over here but keep a low profile until we find it."

"Yeltsin's been in the vodka. I think he's well on his way. His security people are going nuts!" Mariano shook his head in frustration. "If she uses ricin, a lot of people besides Yeltsin will die. I'll get their security to get him out of here as well as the other dignitaries."

"Do it quietly so we don't cause a panic in here," Steve advised as he scanned the crowd again. "We don't want to spook her. Do what you can with security; I'm going to find that bitch! But there're so many goddamn people!" Steve growled, scanning the mass of moving bodies. "She could be right here in front of us and we'd never see her," he said as he walked away.

"She'll probably act any minute now," Mariano cautioned, "Keep on your toes."

After checking two more rooms on the list, Dix still hadn't located Blakemore. He stopped in front of the next one and put his ear against the door to listen. He heard a shredding machine, then a voice. *This has got to be Blakemore,* he thought. *He's not alone.* The machine buzzed again. Dix took a deep breath and took out his pistol. With his left hand he tried the door handle. It was locked. He inserted the key and listened once again for the shredder. When the buzzing started, Dix unlocked the door and shoved it open in one continuous move. He bolted in and crouched, keeping the Beretta leveled. "Freeze!"

Two men were in the room. One stood in front of a large shredder, feeding several pieces of paper into the machine. The other sat in a chair behind the table, going through a file of papers inside a box. Another box full of files sat next to it. A pistol was on the corner of the same table and two drinks were on the other corner. A cigarette burned in the ashtray. Startled, the two men looked up. The door swung closed and latched behind Dix. Seeing the face of the man standing, he thought back to when he was dazed by the stun gun. It was Blakemore that he had seen—it was no dream. It was Blakemore who had issued the order to kill him and Mariano after he gave them the disks.

"It's over, Blakemore!"

Blakemore studied him. The other man was the Russian liaison to the G-7 and a member of Pegasus. He shot a look to Blakemore and back to Dix. He was the key inside man to Hamilton's deranged goal of upsetting the delicate democratic process emerging in Russia. He had paved the way for Hamilton to acquire, by whatever means necessary, the treasures the Russian government had buried in their vast array of secret storage facilities. The goal of Pegasus was not to control Russia. It was to access the tremendous amount of treasure stored within Russia since the end of the war.

The files Dix was looking at were the ones from General Kaltenbrunner's office—the infamous Stasi files. The same files Hamilton had tried to destroy. The files he knew would expose him if they were released to the West. This was Hamilton's worst nightmare. Blakemore, now holding the reins of Pegasus, was crazed with fear. The organization was about to fall and Blakemore was no longer rational.

"Connor," Blakemore said in a cold voice, "I can make you rich—$15 million dollars to join us."

"It's not yours," Dix said. "You're finished. Shredding those files won't save your ass. I have Müller's disks."

"You're a fool, Connor! They were all fools! You're throwing away $15 million."

"Not fools, Blakemore. Ethical! Now back up."

The Russian, making his move, grabbed for the pistol on the table and dove to the floor. Dix swung the Beretta and fired at the same time the Russian fired. Dix felt the slug rip into his flesh.

38

Two waiters passed in front of Maria and Francesca, one bringing in a tray of drinks and another carrying out a tray of empty glasses. Couples were coming and going, various groups sat or stood around the room, some people danced while others just watched. The event was in full swing. Maria and Francesca watched Yeltsin leave his seat again to talk with someone. Sweat streaked his red cheeks.

As a waitress entered the room carrying a tray, Maria handed the woman her empty glass. Taking it in her left hand as she walked by, she moved to the first round table and started to collect the empty glasses. Maria watched the woman for a moment. She was about Maria's size with coal black hair, a thick nose and puffy cheeks. *Too much makeup, honey,* Maria thought. *And that uniform definitely isn't flattering. Maybe if you did something with that hair it would help.* The waitress went about her duties. Her tray full, she left the room.

Maria casually looked around. Everything seemed normal. She saw Steve, then the sergeant—their steadfast expressions broken by an occasional smile or comment to someone. Maria watched Francesca approach Steve, almost fifty feet away. She scanned the room once again. Yeltsin returned to his seat, nodding to someone as he sat, then smiled.

Maria watched as the waitress returned and went to the second round table to collect the glasses. When Maria realized she was staring at the waitress, she immediately turned away. She saw Steve walking toward her.

"Nothing."

"Stay alert," Steve said as he observed the people dancing.

Maria watched Steve turn to the left. At first she didn't see what he was focusing on. Seated by herself was an attractive redheaded woman with breasts spilling out of her low-cut dress. Her dress was split high on the side, exposing her crossed, shapely legs.

"Easy, boy," Maria teased, nudging him and breaking his trance. "You were about to step on your tongue, Steve."

Steve blushed. "Just checking out the people." He smiled and scanned the room once again.

Maria glanced back at the waitress. The tray almost full, she made the final touches to the table. *Damn! What is it about her?* Maria thought. Maria began to scrutinize everything about the woman. Nothing registered. As the waitress left the room, Maria turned toward Steve. He was once again captivated by the well-endowed redhead. Maria watched the buxom woman remove a compact from her purse. She gently opened it and checked her lipstick. *The scar!* Maria thought.

"Steve," she whispered.

"Just observing a suspect," he grinned, thinking Maria was teasing him again.

"No, I think it's her. The waitress."

"The waitress? Why her?"

"She's the one. I know it. She has a scar on the side of her left thumb. I saw it just a few minutes ago when I handed her my empty glass."

Maria explained to Steve that she saw a woman in the

ladies' room earlier who had an identical scar on the side of her left thumb. The woman was refreshing her makeup when Maria saw her scar. Her lipstick was encased in a gold tube with an emblem of a raised Pegasus on the end. She also carried a compact that had an inlaid amber carving surrounding the powder. She told him that when she left to follow the two men she saw the waiter bring out a tray of glasses and one had lipstick on the rim. She said that when she peeked into the room only men were in there. When she ducked into the ladies' room, she saw the woman applying her lipstick.

"But the waitress's features are different," she whispered as she looked toward the door for the woman. "Her nose is too thick, her cheeks are too puffy and she has black hair. The other woman had brown hair. Plus this waitress should be arrested for her makeup."

"Makeup… Hmmm." He began to analyze what she had said. "You could be right. And a clever way to be in a room and not be seen—as one of the staff. Where is she?"

"She just left with a tray full of glasses."

"Point her out to me when she comes back in. I'll check her out."

Steve noted the position of Mariano, the sergeant, Francesca and Maria as they waited for the waitress' return. His goal was to check out the waitress outside the ballroom, as far away from Yeltsin as possible.

"Steve, here she comes," Maria whispered as she looked around to Steve.

At that same moment, deep in the room and behind Steve, Yeltsin's security began to usher him out. Mariano had succeeded but the timing was unfortunate. If the waitress continued, Yeltsin would be whisked right past her. The security detail was about to unwittingly deliver Yeltsin to the assassin.

Steve looked at the waitress following a waiter, identified his target, then signaled Mariano. Steve picked up a drink and started out, walking with the air of a man who was enjoying the party and slightly suffering the effects of alcohol. He timed his approach so he would reach her before he came to the men's room. Steve watched her from the corner of his eye. She walked with resolve, carrying a tray with six drinks and a bottle of mineral water. A red ballpoint pen was beside the water bottle. Steve pretended to look around as the woman got closer. He waited until the last second to lift his glass and finish his drink. She took another step.

"Excuse me, where's the men's room?" Steve asked.

"Just ahead of you on the left, sir." She nodded slightly behind her.

Steve followed her nod, holding the glass and pointing with the same hand. The unsuspecting woman started to resume her course, but Steve's hand crashed into the tray, flipping it over. The red pen spiraled upward and forward. Water spewed from the top of the bottle as it tipped over and banged against the glasses. It crashed to the floor followed by the glasses, the liquid splashing in all directions. The red pen bounced on the floor, then slid beneath a chair. In one motion Steve grabbed the woman.

She instinctively tossed Steve back. As he went down he reached for her leg. He pulled and flipped her off her feet. She kicked as she went down and grazed his chin. Steve sprang around and kicked her in the chest. She groaned and came across attempting to connect with his groin. Steve blocked her blow, then punched her in the face. She was tough but not tough enough to withstand the power of his fist.

The security detail, seeing the commotion, sped Yeltsin away along a different route. A constant stream of the other dignitaries followed him.

Mariano, leading the others, rushed out. By the time they reached Steve, he was holding the woman with her hands behind her back. He reached up and yanked off the black wig she was wearing. Mariano motioned for one of the plainclothes police officers to handcuff the woman. Steve reached for the woman's face, grabbing and peeling away the latex that covered her nose. He felt her cheeks then gently pressed. He held the glass to her mouth. She glared at him, then spit cotton rolls from her mouth.

They checked the pockets of her uniform for any weapon and the poison. Her pockets were empty. The sergeant checked her clothing but found nothing. Steve watched the sergeant, then looked on the floor amid all the glass and water. Nothing. Looking at the woman again, he thought back, detail by detail, to what had happened. Then he remembered.

"There was a red pen," he said and held out his arms as he started searching the floor. "It may have slid under something. Don't touch it if you see it."

"Here it is!" Francesca shouted, pointing to the pen under the chair.

"Okay! Everybody get back," Steve warned. "Mariano, the HazMat guys!"

The HazMat team entered wearing yellow suits and respirators. The few people that had gathered nearby after the dignitaries had left were quickly pushed back into the ballroom. The team opened their kits and immediately began to secure the pen, first covering it, then wrapping it for movement. With everything apparently under control, Steve led the sergeant, Maria and Francesca out of the room to search for Dix.

The shock of the bullet penetrating Dix's body had caused

him to temporarily black out. The door to the room opened and an older man stepped in clutching a sleek Mauser automatic in his hand. "Don't move, just relax," came the man's voice. "Who's this on the floor?" He asked, nodding toward the two bodies.

"Who the hell are you?" Blakemore demanded.

"Ulrich Fabian—but you will know me as Schmidt." His voice was cold.

Blakemore relaxed, sensing he had been rescued. "I didn't know you were here. Connor and the Russian liaison shot each other. I'm shredding the files."

"Good. Keep going," he said. He lowered his pistol, as if to reassure Blakemore that he was not a threat.

Schmidt looked around the room and moved closer to the box of files that Blakemore was shredding. He rummaged through the files that were not yet shredded and finally withdrew a file folder full of documents.

"Shred this now," the old man said. He handed the folder to Blakemore.

Blakemore took the folder and opened the file. He grasped several pages, all yellow with age and bearing Nazi letterhead and stuffed them into the shredder. Next, he lifted out a photograph of an SS Nazi major and paused.

"Shred it," the old man said.

Blakemore shredded the photograph. Then continued to shred the remaining contents of the folder.

"It's over, Blakemore! Pegasus is gone," Schmidt said when the final sheet went through the machine.

Blakemore's face was red and his eyes flashed terror as he stared at the pistol trained on him. He looked up at Schmidt, then he slouched and rested his right hand on the shredder. Tears dripped from his eyes. He began to babble incoherently. His nose ran.

"You're a loose end and I don't leave loose ends," Schmidt said in an icy voice. "You're pathetic."

The Mauser snapped. The bullet entered Blakemore's head through his right eye. His lifeless body fell back and crumpled to the floor. Schmidt looked toward the Russian's body and saw the lifeless eyes of the Russian. At that moment, he heard an approaching siren. Not wanting to be seen, Schmidt glanced at Dix and saw the pool of blood that had formed beneath the left side of Dix's face-down body. Believing Dix was dead, he gently released the hammer and pocketed the pistol. Searching the floor, his eyes fell on the 7.65mm casing. He picked it up, then quickly looked around the room before stepping out and closing the door behind him.

Smoke and the odor of burnt propellant from gunshots were heavy in the room. Steve knelt beside Dix and rolled him over. He groaned as Steve inspected his wound.

"How're you doing, buddy?" Steve grinned when he saw Dix coming around.

He placed a towel on the wound in Dix's upper left shoulder to stop the bleeding and propped him up against the bed.

"Shit! Not so good," Dix moaned. He looked over to Blakemore. "You got him. Good."

"I didn't. I thought you did," Steve said.

"Last thing I remember is the Russian diving for his pistol."

"Don't worry about it now." Steve was already looking over Blakemore's handiwork with the shredder.

"They were trying to destroy the files before Yeltsin could turn them over tomorrow. That's the Russian." Dix pointed to the body on the floor. "They were no better than the Nazis who took the treasures in the first place."

Mariano stepped in and inspected Dix, then the two bodies. He told the sergeant to call the paramedics for Dix. Then he stepped to the box of files to inspect the contents. Maria followed him in and knelt beside Dix. Her eyes filled with tears. She kissed him and held his head in her lap.

"It's over now. Pegasus is dead." Dix said as he looked at the others.

"I guess you got the woman and Yeltsin is okay?" he asked looking at Steve.

"We got the little scorpion and Yeltsin is okay."

As the police filled the room, Mariano began to direct their activities. The paramedics wheeled Dix out, followed by Maria, Steve and Francesca. Maria stopped at the door and kissed Steve's cheek. He looked at her and smiled, then withdrew his pouch of tobacco and placed a wad in his mouth.

When Dix was released from the hospital three days later, Francesca and Steve met the Connors at the Vier Jahreszeiten Hotel. Dix ordered room service. Within an hour Mariano and the sergeant arrived. Mariano clarified a few points with them and made a few notes. As promised, Dix told the entire story to Francesca. Mariano gave her the unclassified background and explained when his investigation had started. Maria told of her ordeal in Udine. Francesca was thrilled. She could hardly wait to get with Dix and start to write the story. They both wanted the world to know as much about Pegasus as possible.

"Where are the disks, Dix?" Mariano asked.

Dix smiled. "Steve, go to the wall over there." He pointed to the wall perpendicular to the bathroom on the right side. "Take out your pocketknife and unfold the blade." He instructed Steve to gently insert the blade into the paper and pry open the seam. "Now, gently peel back the wallpaper."

The others looked on curiously. With the skill of a surgeon, Steve gradually exposed the disks embedded in the wall, wrapped tightly in a plastic bag. He lifted the disks out, turned and handed them to Mariano.

"Here they are," he said with a big grin.

"When did you do that?" Maria asked.

"When you were in the shower, just after we checked in."

Dix told them how he came up with the idea. Knowing he could not keep them or leave them in the room where they could be discovered, he noticed a place in the wallpaper seam that was starting to separate. He thought that if he could pull the paper back enough, it would be the perfect hiding place. The paper released with the help of his knife. He dug out enough of the plaster so that the disks would fit flush in the wall. He then wrapped the disks in a plastic bag and placed them in the hole. Using Maria's clear fingernail polish, he resealed the wallpaper. He had placed the wastebasket under the area he worked on to catch most of the dust. You had to know exactly where to look to find the disks behind the wallpaper.

Francesca clapped her hands. "Dix, you're so clever."

Epilogue

Bressanvido, Italy
Five weeks later

Church bells accented the serenity of the new day. A gentle Adriatic breeze carried the scent of blooming flowers. The morning sky was clear and the sun high, like a ball of fire suspended in a sea of blue. At home, Dix and Maria relaxed at the patio table, enjoying the morning. Maria read the paper while Dix made notes on the latest article he planned to submit for publication. In the meantime, he waited to hear back about the story he and Francesca had written about Pegasus. The sound of a car entering the neighborhood disrupted their quiet. Maria looked up to see the postman's Fiat putter to a stop at their mailbox.

"I'll get the mail," Maria said as she folded the paper, "if you'll call the electrician to see if he's coming today to fix the gate."

"All right." Dix laid his pencil on the table and stood. "I've told him a dozen times to replace the switch. He just says, 'All it needs is a little adjustment.' I can hear him now, 'Strange, very strange.'"

Dix watched her walk down the steps to the mailbox before going inside to call the electrician. When he answered and Dix identified himself, the electrician apologized for not coming the day before and promised to be there that day. When Dix returned to the patio, Maria was opening a manila envelope. She took out a letter with tear sheets from a magazine attached.

"Dix, it's from Francesca," Maria said. "The story you and Francesca wrote about Pegasus is coming out next month."

Maria and Dix were excited about the story for the magazine. An inset photo of Dix and Francesca was on the first page. Several photos Steve had taken appeared in the story. Their story injected new life into attempts by those seeking the restitution and return of Nazi treasures. The governments of Switzerland, Paraguay, Argentina, Sweden, Spain and Portugal were under renewed pressure over Nazi bank accounts and money laundering in their countries. The evidence in Dix's and Francesca's piece made it almost impossible to hide or deny the existence of the accounts. It was an embarrassment these governments and banks had hoped would never surface. The article rallied support in the international community for a complete investigation and restitution.

Another letter was from Boris Yeltsin. It was an invitation for them to go to an awards presentation and reception in their honor in Moscow in six weeks. Yeltsin was giving them a presidential award for their actions in thwarting an attack on him and exposing the Pegasus operation. They had already received word from the American Embassy of the award ceremony as the G-7 was also presenting them an award.

As Dix read the letter from President Yeltsin, Maria opened a letter postmarked Antwerp. The letter was from Sonja Abramovych telling Maria that she had been notified that her painting had been discovered and was to be returned. She thanked Maria for her help and invited Maria to visit her the next time she was in Belgium.

Dix looked up just as Mariano's car rolled to a stop in

front of the house. He stepped out, immaculately attired, and waved. Julia was with him, her bangle bracelets sparkling in the sunlight. Dix stepped inside to buzz open the electronic lock of the gate. Maria prepared the mocha pot for more coffee.

"Maria, Colonel Pasquali sends his regards and thanks you again. However, he insists that in the future you notify him immediately if you have any suspicions about a piece of art."

"Don't worry, I will."

"Colonel and Mrs. Marston were very upset about having the painting they purchased confiscated. Don't worry. They don't know you identified the painting."

"I bet Colonel Marston was mad!" Dix said.

"I have the report on the pen the French woman had," Mariano said, closing the magazine. "The pen was actually a unique weapon."

Although it appeared to be an ordinary ballpoint pen on the outside, the inside was quite different. A small amount of ricin was in a glass vial. On top of the vial was a pressure cylinder. When the top of the pen was pressed, the pressure cylinder was pushed into the vial, breaking the glass. When the pressure cylinder made contact, the cylinder released the pressure and forced the toxin through the tube leading out of the pen. A slight puff of air carried the ricin to the target. It would not contaminate the woman as long as she didn't touch the lower end of the pen and was stationary or upwind when it functioned.

Mariano took out a ballpoint pen from his coat and demonstrated how the woman was going to administer the poison. Holding the pen cupped in his hand with his thumb on the top, she could pass by Yeltsin and spray it into his face or on his clothes.

"Almost impossible to see what she did, especially if she

was carrying a tray," Mariano said. He clicked the pen when he passed his hand in front of Dix. "Another scenario, and the most likely method, was that the woman would spray the area on the table where Yeltsin sat. One milligram of the white powder would kill an adult. Ricin looks like cornstarch, and one milligram is about equal to a couple of grains of salt."

Mariano placed about one-eighth of a teaspoon of salt in his hand, then bent over and gently blew the salt onto the table to demonstrate how the pressurized pen would distribute the contents of the vial onto the table where Yeltsin sat. Mariano picked up the pen and cupped it in his hand as before, then continued.

"When Yeltsin sat, he, like most of us, would rest his arms on the table," Mariano said. "Feeling the powder, what would he do next?"

"Brush it to the floor," Maria said.

"Exactly!" Mariano lifted his arms to show the numerous grains of salt stuck to his skin. "More than enough ricin to kill him."

Mariano stood and brushed the salt from his lap and his arms. "Arrests are ongoing in connection with the Pegasus operation in Europe and the United States, thanks to the information on the disks."

"What about the old Austrian man in Udine and the panel from the Amber Room?" Maria asked, brushing the hair from her face.

Mariano just shrugged his shoulders and shook his head. "Disappeared along with the journal. His operation may take a while longer to discover. For the time being Colonel Pasquali has his hands full working with the various Art Theft Investigative units in Europe and the United States. They discovered one odd thing in the hotel room where Dix was shot."

"What was that?" Dix asked.

"Blakemore was killed by a 7.65mm bullet. No casing was found in the room and no one had a 7.65mm."

"All I remember was that Blakemore was by the shredder and the Russian was at the table. Then the Russian went for his pistol and I fired. The next thing I remembered was Steve kneeling beside me."

"Someone else entered the room and shot Blakemore while you were blacked out. That's who we need to find."

"Any ideas who it might be?" Dix asked.

"No, all we have is the 7.65mm bullet."

"Could it have been Schmidt?"

"Possibly. As far as we know, he's the only one who isn't accounted for."

Maria sat back in her chair and contemplated the art she had seen. She knew all along that several treasure caches had not been recovered by the Allies at the end of the war. She gazed in Dix's eyes and smiled.

He returned her smile, knowing exactly what she was thinking.

Author's Note

Hundreds of thousands of innocent civilians were not as lucky as Sonja Abramovych. Aside from losing all their possessions, they lost their lives. Of the survivors, not many of them that were old enough to remember or knew of their families' wealth are still alive. Those that were too young may never know that they or their families may be heirs to fortunes. In vaults and government warehouses vast amounts of treasures sit collecting dust as no one knows who the treasures belong to. Perhaps there were other Hamiltons and Fabians. Or maybe much of the treasures reported lost or destroyed are still waiting to be discovered.

The famous Amber Room is one such treasure that has long been sought after. It has been reported destroyed by fire during the war, another report says it was on the Nazi ocean liner Wilhelm Gustloff that was sunk by a Russian submarine in the Baltic Sea, another report lists it as being put in a salt mine near Gottingen, Germany, and yet another story is that it is in a private German collection. However, over the years several pieces from the Amber Room have turned up. No one knows its true fate, at least no one has come forward with proof.

Stories of hidden Nazi treasures have circulated since the end of the war. Some, in fact, have turned out to be true while others have not. The search for the missing treasures continues.